Ridgeline

THE LONG JOURNEY HOME SERIES

BOOK ONE

BY
PAMELA FOSTER

P
Pen-L Publishing
Fayetteville, Arkansas
Pen-L.com

First Edition
Printed and bound in USA
ISBN: 978-1-940222-33-2
Cover design by Andrea Hansen
Formatting by Kimberly Pennell

To the men of the Fayetteville, Arkansas, Veteran's Administration Friday Morning Focus Group, with my sincere respect and deep gratitude.

Other books by Pamela Foster:

Fiction

Bigfoot Blues

Redneck Goddess

Non-fiction

My Life with a Wounded Warrior

Clueless Gringos in Paradise

He who learns must suffer;
And even in our sleep
Pain that cannot forget
Falls drop by drop upon the heart,
And in our own despair,
Against our will,
Comes wisdom
By the awful grace of God.
　　　　　– Aeschylus

ಬಿ

The past is never dead. It's not even past.
　　　　– William Faulkner

ಬಿ

It don't mean nothin'.
　　　　– Jack Jones

RIDGELINE

Chapter One

Arkansas Boston Mountains

1869

At the ridgeline, Jeremiah reined in the mare, bent low over the sweating neck of the horse. Winter branches of hickory and pin oak framed the small form silhouetted in the open door of the cabin in the hollow below. Maggie. His Maggie. His prize and salvation. Twice now he'd ridden away, abandoned her, first in a young man's quest for honor and then, that second, shameful time, out of anger at betrayal and fear of who he had become when honor proved no more than bloody, awful killing. The woman, the gentle swell of one hip resting against the doorframe, seemed to gaze up the hill just as if she'd been right there waiting patiently for him through all these endless months.

The mare blew and side-stepped, her hooves making sharp, skittering sounds on the rocky ground. His cheek almost touching the horse's dark mane, Jeremiah breathed the animal's tang deep into his lungs and, in his mind, saw two perfect pearls of sweat flow slowly from the woman's collar bone, braid themselves into one languid trickle between high breasts. He sat the horse and tasted again the salty joy of his mouth on warm, firm flesh, saw again the obscenity of that purple boot-shaped bruise like a dark sacrilege on the pale, tender skin along her right side.

Prayer had failed him at that moment.

His silent call to God had gone unanswered as the desire to inflict pain and death upon the man who had stolen her in his absence, marked her body and injured her spirit, rose in him like a beast. Even as he plunged into the warm welcome of her body, his mind a steamy cauldron of confusion and desire, the battle-honed animal within had laughed softy, bided its time. Her voice was a soft pleading, her eyes dark and shimmering in a slant of moonlight between the wash-worn bedroom curtains. She did her best to call him back to grace, moved slowly beneath him.

In the lilac hours just before dawn he had crept, in stocking feet, to the barn, leaned against a lopsided rail and pulled on his boots. He closed his mind, caged his desire to kill and rip and tear and ride off with soft, warm plunder pressed to his back. Instead he made ready to flee once more into his calling. The boy of eighteen who'd slipped the bible and the essays of Ralph Waldo Emerson into his saddlebags beside a new leather-covered journal and joined Arkansas's 3rd to ride off in pride and ignorance seeking glory and proof of manhood—that boy was dead and gone. The boy who had loved Maggie Sullivan since the Sunday morning light through a church window made a halo of her dark hair while his pa preached of Jesus's return on a pale, fire-snorting horse—that boy's soul was mangled beyond repair. Not even God All Mighty could heal that which bloody war had torn asunder.

The woman whose memory had kept him clinging to the edge of sanity from the first shot at Cheat's Mountain, all the way to Petersburg and the shame of Appomattox, that woman slept now in another man's bed a few yards away. A shaking, like a mighty hand at the scruff of his neck, took him, dropped him to his knees with the effort to suppress the red desire to annihilate the man who had laid his hand, his filthy boot, to his Maggie. He had craved then, like a hunger long denied, to strike and cut and strike again until the killing beast within was satiated. Jeremiah knew, with the conviction of the damned, that once released into civilian life, the beast would never again be contained. In that moment, on his knees in the barn's dirty straw, Jeremiah ached for the killing path above all others.

Maggie was better off without him.

On that morning so many long months ago, Jeremiah had listened to the husband's red roan nicker for his sturdy stall mates—the mules—which were, in all probability, even then trudging their way back to that untidy barn from Fort Smith. He imagined the buckboard bouncing over rough ground, making its slow way to this barn, saw the reins held by the poor excuse for a man, the interloper who had claimed Maggie as his own. The preacher pictured the woman as he'd left her, asleep on her left side, legs drawn up like a child's, a purple-black brand of ownership almost invisible in the gray light of dawn.

The desire to kill had very nearly consumed him in that moment.

His voice low and ragged, a lost child calling in the wilderness, bone dry and with no hope but to inflict no further damage upon the world, the psalm had poured through him like water on hard stone.

"Hear my prayer, O Lord, and let my cry come unto thee. Hide not thy face from me."

Jeremiah had saddled the mare, the creaking of leather and the soft rustle of the bridle the only sound in a cold so brittle the air seemed to shatter in his throat with each prayerful word.

He had ridden hard and fast then, in the hopes of outrunning the animal within that roared for bloody release. Even as he whipped the mare into a froth, war-born rage reared its ugly snout, demanded the killing of the woman's worthless husband. He clenched his teeth until pain focused his mind, pressed on. His heart cold in his chest, the sway and heat of the mare carried him further and further from what was either his salvation or his destruction, he could not have said which.

But he had not abandoned the woman completely.

Under the lumpy pillow on which he'd slept, rested a defense and penance, a tidier path to deliverance than a smoking gun or a bloody knife. Jeremiah had left a blue bottle no bigger than the thumb that had, just hours before, stroked hard, brown nipples as she threw back her head in the moon-streaked bedroom, her hair a dark, flowing river of desire falling over slender shoulders and carrying him to a momentary peace he had not known since before the first cannon roared smoke and confusion.

The cloudy contents of the bottle had splashed against the inside of the blue glass as he secreted the poison under the rough cotton, placed the bottle deep into the heady scent of their love-making, the primal smell of his seed and her spent desire. A gem-like offering of repentance—a tidy, near tasteless addition to a steaming bowl of beans, a few drops in the jar of liquor her husband secreted behind the hay loft, and Maggie would be cleansed of her betrayal, free to join with him upon his return.

The preacher had slunk away like a beaten dog, an animal one strike away from madness, the beast caged and the woman left to settle her own destiny.

From mid-March to late October, he had hidden the ache and inner rage under the mask of a saddle-preacher. The Lord allowed this deception. Again and again, God poured His spirit through Jeremiah.

He had stood under the fluttering leaves of an ancient oak and joined a young couple in matrimony, the husband awkward in a borrowed suit, the belly of the bride already swollen under her mama's wedding gown. He slept that night on a bed of sweet hay and when the bride's sister came to him, opened her dress and lay beside him, he did not turn away from that fine and good substitute for the release he craved.

He had spoken God's love and consolation over a baby buried months earlier in the cold, rocky soil of an Ozark winter. Left the wife on her knees in the dappled afternoon light praying over the tiny grave while he joined her husband for whiskey that sparkled in the glass as clear as the promise of a spring day and hit his belly like the solid kick of a Missouri mule. Later, with shadows stealing the color from the locust trees that rimmed their homestead, he sat with the grieving couple and partook of hull peas and ham hocks, washed the meal down with cold spring water that sent pain like a knife point racing from a bad molar up into his brain.

He had paced and strutted along the length of a makeshift stage as the spirit moved over a tent revival while folks leaped in joy, hands raised to the heavens, glorying in the Holy Ghost as, one after another, sinners were knocked flat to the ground with the devil plumb defeated by the abundant power of God. He raised one hand in fervent prayer, placed the other on the cool forehead of a twelve-year-old boy who hadn't walked since the crippling fever the winter before burned him hollow. The boy, blue eyes wide in a pale, narrow face, lifted himself from the chair on which he'd been carried forward by his mother and aunt, stood for a long moment like a colt on shaky legs and then leapt into the air, God's praise on his lips. The mother and her sister came to the preacher that same night, offering their own thanks and joy in the grace of God.

On the ridgeline, Jeremiah shifted in the saddle and breathed deep the smell of wood smoke floating up from the chimney of the cabin below, drank in the sight of Maggie, his woman, leaning in the open door of the cabin from which he had ridden away seven months earlier. He indulged his vanity and fed his hope by believing this woman had stood right there through all the long days he'd been gone serving the Lord, through every star-filled night while he curled, dog-like, around an open fire and watched the stars turn in the sky and imagined her just like this, watching the horizon for his return, patient even as he tarried.

As if, in his absence, she'd not gone about her daily life, tended her ragged garden, tolerated the touch of her brutish husband as he ran a rough hand up and over the birthmark that stained the inside of her left thigh, the reddish mark the near exact size and shape of a mouse, the curlicue of the tail disappearing into her dark warmth. As if, in place of what had become of her life, through all these days and nights, the woman had simply waited, her longing quietly drawing him to her as a ripe moon calls the rising tide.

The bay tossed her head, a quiver running from withers to nose. Jeremiah gathered the reins and spoke low, his words a silvery fog that hung in the motionless air for a moment before floating wraith-like to join a cloud of cooling sweat rising from the horse. Winter-robbed of all but palest gold, dawn's fingers crept over the eastern rise and glinted cold light from the woman's hand—a deep, lethal-blue flash the preacher knew all too well as the gemlike color of a tiny, killing bottle, no bigger surely than the seed of sin born in David's heart when first he looked upon Bathsheba.

The snarling voice of the woman's husband split the morning air, destroyed all hope. The sound floated up the hill, ominous as the first

5

notes of a bugle on a misty morn with men lined on either side of some godforsaken hill or bloodthirsty meadowland. Jeremiah spurred his horse down into the hollow even as Maggie raised the blue bottle to her mouth, her head thrown back, her tender, white throat exposed as she swallowed his dreams drop by drop, condemned him to hell for all eternity.

"Nooooo!" His plea pierced the heavens.

The rest took but a few moments in the great wheel of time that flows and relentlessly devours until a man's life is no more than a shadow in the mind of strangers.

She sank to the cabin's front porch as though slipping into dark water in the same moment the preacher dug his heels into the sides of the bay. The mare stumbled and slid on the steep hillside. The husband's voice echoed from the darkened house, spurred the preacher forward. At the cabin, the mare struggled to stop her forward movement, brought powerful front legs up tight under her heavy chest. Her neighing scream seemed to fling Jeremiah from her steaming back as he slid from the saddle.

The preacher covered the three canting steps of the cabin with no thought but one. He lifted the woman's head and pressed her bruised and swollen cheek against his chest, stroked dark hair from her wide forehead even though he knew she could not feel the gentle touch of his hand, had, in fact, escaped this life of tears using the only trail she could see her way clear to follow.

The metallic click of a cocking rifle lifted Jeremiah's head. The sound elicited in him, not fear, but joy, the certain knowledge that the red mist of killing was loosed. Words of some indeterminate meaning came from the husband's mouth. The preacher did not stop to decipher their import. He laid the woman's head gently on the rough boards of the porch, stood to accept the risen power of the beast.

Chapter Two

Stepping over Maggie's warm body, his hand rose to grip the barrel of the husband's Henry rifle. With an anguished scream, Jeremiah wrenched the heavy gun from the brute's hands and brought it back around in a mighty arc. The walnut buttstock slammed into the side of the man's face, knocked him to his knees as the gun fired loud in the confines of the cabin, the deafening echo of the shot drowning the preacher's last hold on sanity. The misspent bullet grazed Jeremiah's shoulder, completed his transformation from man to beast.

Jeremiah grinned, tossed the rifle aside. The husband turned his head and watched the long barrel turn and spin end-over-end, his defense gone as the gun came to rest, stock down, against the cabin's chinked wall, as though the weapon waited there for whoever would claim it.

Jeremiah lifted the man who reeked of rotgut whiskey and bitter fear, hit him with a punch to the mouth that knocked the enemy backward, butt-flat onto the swept dirt floor.

The man raised his head, spat blood. "You the sonofabitch that whore's been pinin' for?"

The world closed around the preacher in a welcome fog. God banished, Jeremiah smiled, lifted his bone-handled knife from its sheath and went to work on the woman's husband.

A tow-headed young soldier, his eyes huge, blood blooming on the chest of his tattered blue uniform, stood with his back resting against the cabin's wall. A bearded sergeant leaned against the cabin's only window.

Half his jaw blown away by a minie ball at Sharpsburg, Sarge flicked his bluish tongue and smiled obscenely. Jeremiah, used to their company, ignored the phantoms, continued his mission with the knife.

It was the warmth of the morning sun on his blood-wet skin that returned him to himself. The husband, or what was left of him, lay where he'd fallen. Jeremiah walked casually to the room's rough counter. He lifted a dented tin cup beside the water bucket, helped himself three times to cool water the woman . . . his Maggie . . . had undoubtedly drawn earlier that morning.

Slowly, like a stream coming to life as snow melts in the sun of mountain ravines high above it, he came back to himself. He carefully returned the tin cup to its spot beside the bucket, stepped to this last in a long line of women he had loved and failed.

His mother, dead of some pox or plague, or of starvation or neglect, what did it matter the cause. He had shaken her off as she clung to his arm, begged him not to join the Arkansas 3rd. In his arrogance, he'd marched away cradling close some misbegotten image of what it meant to be a man. At his return five years later, she was cold in an unmarked grave dug by strangers while he'd been busy ruining himself on one bloody battlefield or another.

He cradled Maggie's cold, stiffening body to his chest, watched low clouds the color of an old bruise leach warmth from the day.

"I'm sorry." His words as dead as the woman whose long hair he loosed and stroked, his thoughts twirling in a dull miasma of pain and remembrance of past failings.

His sister, sweet Grace, had simply disappeared into the confusion of war. Gone upon his return. One neighbor said she'd left with a man headed for Oregon, another that she'd been taken by the Yankees and never seen again, a third man swore she'd cut her flame-red hair, put on trousers, joined up and fought at Pea Ridge.

He pressed his mouth to Maggie's forehead, the skin as cold as marble under his lips.

Rage roared up from his core and a scream tore loose from a shallow grave.

His pain ripped at the sky. "No! Not Maggie. Please God, not Maggie too."

Not this woman whose locket he'd carried from Cheat Mountain to Sharpsburg to Chickamauga. Three years ago, when he rode away from Beulah, the small plantation to which his father, disgraced at his pulpit in Virginia, had dragged his family, he rode directly to this farmhouse. He expected to find his love waiting, just as she had in his dreams throughout the long years of war.

But Maggie had not waited for his return, for his love.

He found her married to a bully of a man, found her battered and, yes, even as rage at her husband rose in him, some part of him rejoiced in the pain those bruises told. She had betrayed him, went on with her life while he fought and killed and became someone different from who he'd been when he rode away. He had thrown away every good in him, destroyed himself as surely as if he'd swallowed the barrel of his Colt, and she had abandoned him, forsaken him to marry the first man to offer her succor.

For a week he'd hidden, watched from the ridgeline as the couple went about their lives, waited until the husband hitched the mules to the buckboard and rode away. Then Jeremiah had ridden into the clearing of the cabin, dismounted the bay and claimed what was rightfully his. Afterward, when dust floated lazily in a narrow slant of light at the bedroom's small window, she begged him to take her with him. But his anger at her treachery had overlayered his love, buried his need of her under a black mountain of rage.

He had punished her then, refused her love and rode away into a warm spring, suffocating summer and a cool fall as a saddle-preacher.

It was late autumn when he returned, hid in the woods and, once again, waited. The leaves of oak and maple were already bleeding in air so crisp and sharp each full breath filled his lungs with icy needles, the nights overwhelmed with a mighty display of stars. The second day, he watched the husband ready the buckboard once more and ride toward town.

He had claimed her as his own then. Forgiven her sin of desperation. Yet some hard kernel in his center demanded Maggie prove her loyalty. He had left her the tiny blue bottle of poison. Given her the means to redeem herself of her betrayal. Promised he would return and the two of them would begin a life together. A new life, with the field cleared, the bloodied land holding a promise of healing.

Jeremiah lifted the rigid body, carried her inside and wrapped her in a pieced quilt.

Late afternoon light slanted low through the gray, moss-dappled trunks of the pin oak and buckeye to the west of the glade when he laid her to rest. The preacher bowed his head, folded hands tight with the dried blood of her husband and the black dirt of her grave, and commended her spirit to God. The first star appeared in the dark, jagged ribbon of night that rimmed the Boston Mountains. The beauty of this whirling ball of light, this eternal demonstration of false promise drove Jeremiah to his knees in the dirt of the new grave.

His heart cold and hard in his chest, his mind dead and gray as ash, still he murmured to a God he cursed. Even as the dual burden of shame and guilt pressed his soul to powder, released the devil's own chortling laughter, still Jeremiah clung to a last remnant of faith, his voice weak and dry as dust.

"My days are consumed like smoke, and my bones are burned as on a hearth."

In the cold light of a fingernail moon the psalm hung like mist, refused to rise to the heavens.

Face down in the cold blanket of dirt that covered his last hope, he lay for dark hours while images consumed him. The tips of bayonets flashed in row upon row in a twenty acre cornfield at a bloody mess the Yankees called Antietam. He felt again the smooth, silver locket in his palm, while terror took him, and bluecoats rose in wave after wave. Then the command to fire, and he was running, racing forward into the smoke and stench of battle. All thoughts gone but one. Kill. Kill. Kill again. Men and horses fell, cried and screamed in panic and terror. Jeremiah, cold and still inside, forced his mind away from the headless man beside him, stepped over the gut shot, crying soldier with whom, just the night before, he'd shared the last of the camp's chicory coffee.

There in the dark of a quiet Arkansas night, battle consumed him again, spit his lifeless soul from its gaping mouth. He screamed God's name into the night, lifted himself to his knees, arms extended toward the stars.

"Kill me, you coward. I'm ruined. A worthless, empty shell. Take my life and condemn me to hell. The devil holds no fear for me. *His* power, I know well. Where is *your* strength, God? Where were you at Harpers Ferry and Shiloh and Gettysburg? Where were you at Petersburg when, starving, we ate the leather from the shoes of the dead?"

The stars moved on their inevitable course. Jeremiah cursed God and begged for death until his voice was gone, his spirit dead and his body exhausted. Face down in the fresh dirt, his voice scratched the night like fingernails on a coffin lid.

Void of all hope, still the psalm rose from the depth of his despair.

"My heart is smitten, and withered like grass. My bones cleave to my skin."

Maggie, his Maggie, came to him then, from out of the mists of war. Dark hair swirled about her face and shoulders, pleading eyes found his and pierced his soul.

"My love." Her voice so soft it wounded him beyond redemption.

"Why?" He reached for her and found only starlit night. "Why did you leave me?"

Her words floated in the still air, closed over him in sadness and swallowed him whole.

"The same could be asked of you, Jeremiah, my love."

Insanity took him then, carried him to an eternal killing field, the screams of the dying mixing indistinguishable from those of the living. A dead, gray world where God turned away his face and the devil romped in power and joy.

When it was he passed from waking nightmare to bloody dreams he could not have said, but he opened his eyes to a view from a fresh mound of earth, a locket digging deep into his palm. Dawn, weak and streaked with a promise of rain, but dawn nonetheless, lined the mountain's jagged tree line. Jeremiah rose from the grave, shook the dirt and blood from his clothes, gently returned the silver talisman and scourge to his inside pocket. He placed one boot in front of the other and got on with the day.

He led the husband's mules from the barn, released them into the rustle of brown cornstalks in the field beside the house. The preacher eased the dead man's stallion from his stall, looped the roan's halter to the low limb of an oak.

In the day's dawning, he entered the cabin once more, lifted his long legs and stepped over the beast's bloody handiwork. Jeremiah retrieved the Henry rifle from where it stood, propped against the cabin's wall, as though waiting for his claim. At the porch, he searched on hands and knees until his palm felt the cool curve of a thumb-sized transgression. The sun's ascent a mere glow along the tops of the Boston Mountains, the glass was robbed of color. He held it up to the rising light nonetheless, angled it to the day's meager warmth, the bottle no bigger in his hand than a good intention.

His voice was weak and rough, his recitation of the ancient words rote and dead.

"For I have eaten ashes like bread, and mingled my drink with weeping."

Words were dust in his mouth.

"My days are like a shadow that declineth, and I am withered like grass."

He bowed his head in defeat, had not the strength to protest God's cruel love. The bottle joined the silver disk in the pocket of his jacket, hidden and close.

He found the mare standing, reins dragging in the dirt, under the gnarled oak beside the roan. Whispering low, Jeremiah unfastened the cinch and slid the saddle from her back, ran his hands over her shoulders, down her legs, removed the bit and bridle, and lifted each foot and turned it gently in his palm. Satisfied she was not harmed, he laid his mouth against the warmth of her ear and murmured apology for his neglect of such a fine animal.

In the barn he found and lit a lantern, retrieved a halter from a nail beside the roan's stall. Back outside, the sun had risen from the backside of the mountain, the jagged ridgeline now marked by a thin, shimmering thread of red as bright as the fresh blood on the coat of the young soldier who trailed beside Jeremiah.

The sergeant propped a booted foot against the oak, picked at his teeth with a piece of straw.

"Now Preacher, all that praying ain't gonna help you one mite. You ain't never gonna be done spilling blood. You got no more chance than me of going home."

Jeremiah tucked the ears of the mare through the stiff halter, fastened the rusted buckles.

"Not the first time you've been wrong, Yankee-boy. In '62 you predicted you'd be eating your mama's fried chicken come spring, after you strolled on down and taught us rebel boys a quick lesson."

The private picked his teeth, smiled at the man who had sighted down the barrel of an Enfield and stolen his life at Harpers Ferry.

Jeremiah lifted the saddle onto the back of the roan, took the time to open the bags and run his palm over the soft leather of the books inside. He kneed the dead man's horse and tightened the cinch, slid the bit, still slick from the mare's mouth, between the teeth of the red stallion. The roan tossed his head, skittered side-wise and tongued the metal. The preacher soothed the horse with promises of long days through new country, adjusted the bridle and looped the reins to a bare oak branch.

He made one last visit to the cabin.

On his return to the horses, he swung quickly up onto the roan's back, heat already leaping behind him, flames loosed into the morning sky. The fleeing of the mules pounding through dead cornstalks came from his right. The mare lifted her head, neighed once, the sound comforting in the day's fiery dawn. The horse allowed Jeremiah to lead her into a wood where battle smoke hung in the low branches and flames reflected from the bayonets of the soldiers who stood like sentinels, marking the path through haunted woods.

Chapter Three

Freshwater, Arkansas

Adeline parted the yellowed lace of the boarding house curtains, peered down through the second-story window onto the dust of Main Street.

He'd be coming for her right soon. Only so many times a sixteen-year-old farm girl can say no to a relative of Jesse and Frank. Even a distant relative like Brett. The nephew of some cousin from up in Hannibal, Brett James was hanging onto the coattails of his outlaw cousins like a bulldog to a juicy bone.

He'd found her at church. Came in like one of the consecrated and squeezed in next to her on the fourth pew from the front. The seat her family had claimed since Pa hawed a six mule team through the red mud of the town's only road on a late October day of 1860—the mountains on fire with autumn's warning of winter and the river running like a rumpled sheet of silver.

That was six months before Lincoln tormented General Beauregard into firing on federal troops at Fort Sumter. Young men and old alike already conversing of little else but war and the glory of battle. Adeline was but nine years old then, still in calico, her hair in a straw-colored braid that brushed her backside at each step, and even she knew there was nothing glorious about Pa leaving Mama with six young'uns to feed while he traipsed off to fight a war against other men who'd left their own daughters and sons defenseless.

'Course, as it turned out, Pa never made it any further than up near Springfield, was killed at the Battle of Oak Hills. It was a drummer boy who found Mama and them and told how it happened. She still saw it all in her mind just as though she'd watched it from the top of a fence, her feet tucked under the second rail, eyes wide as the scene unfurled. The boy told how Pa was trampled and crushed under the sharp hooves and mighty weight of his own mule team as the animals panicked at the first sound of cannon fire. The boy recollected how the mules reared and fled and fell, their lines twisting and braiding like black snakes while Pa struggled fruitlessly with all his considerable strength and knowledge to gain control of his team.

It fell to Adeline to watch over Mama while her two brothers and three older sisters did their best to keep the family fed. 'Course, Robert and John joined up right soon after news of Pa's death reached 'em. Ain't heard from either of them boys since. Which don't necessary mean they're dead. Could be they just wandered off in '65 and never made it back to Freshwater. Emily and Martha May got themselves hitched right soon after the war ended and all them boys came staggering on home.

All that leaving left Mama with only Adeline and the child born at the beginning of '62 when the snow laid thick, and ice was hard as a cold shroud over the hills, and the deer died in droves. Mama had named her winter baby after her favorite flowers. Lily Rose came into the world a full month earlier than expected, wrapped tight in the cord that tied her to Mama. Her older sisters both at a church social, ten-year-old Adeline delivered the baby. She still woke from dreams with the feel of that hard, pulsing rope in her slippery fingers, tight at the neck of her unborn sister, Mama's screams lifting the hair from the back of Adeline's neck.

The child lived only two summers. She died suddenly of the fever, in her own quiet, gentle world. It took Mama another year, but she followed along into the peace of death on a morning in November as cold and gray as ashes. Mama had looked past Adeline, stretched out a grief-wasted arm, whispered the name of Lilly Rose, closed her eyes and forgot to draw the next breath.

So, when Brett James slid his warm thigh against hers on that worn church pew and flashed a smile of only slightly-crooked teeth, the sixteen-year-old smoothed the hem of her skirt, but she took her time about moving her long leg from the warmth of his. She stared straight ahead throughout the service, never once glanced sidewise to meet his eye or offer any encouragement save the heat that built between them as the preacher talked of the four horsemen and the coming days of judgment. When she attempted to stand for final prayer, her knees wobbled beneath her and sweat collected under her breasts and trickled down the straight hollow of her spine.

For a short time, she allowed her mind to imagine Brett James as her salvation. Until the sharp twist of her arm to force a tongue deep into her mouth after a church picnic left dark bruises like dirty sin on her upper arm and Adeline redrew her image of just what marriage to Mr. James would hold.

A sharp knock at the door of her tiny boarding house room startled Adeline, reminded that her contemplation was ended. She let the curtain fall from her fingers, drew a deep breath. Time to make a decision, choose a path and follow where it led.

"You fixin' to stand there all day, starin' out that window, or you got time to converse?" The woman who stepped into the tiny rectangle of a room had red hair near about the exact color of fire that leaps from the untended pit and sweeps through the house of the careless, consuming their hard work and daft dreams.

"Morning, Miss Kate."

Adeline indicated that the owner of Big Kate's should lower her wide backside with its covering of pinkish silk into the room's one worn chair. The girl perched on the edge of the narrow bed, straightened the rough cotton of her dress over her thighs and watched the dance of light on the soft folds of the older woman's skirt, thought how the silk's shimmering beauty made the deep wrinkles and wide pores of the whore's face all the more noticeable.

"I spoke with Mr. Clayton last evening." Kate flicked a soft finger along the necklace at her throat, as though to reassure herself the luminous pearls hadn't been lost in the folds of her neck. "He'll give a ten-dollar gold piece for your first time. I don't generally do this, but, I like you, Adeline. Instead of the usual split, I'll pass into your hands two full dollars."

Adeline attended church with the Claytons. Samuel was coming up on forty probably, but a gentle soul who seemed to have no purpose in life but to stay out of the way of his heavy-drinking, hard-fisted daddy.

"Where would Samuel get that kind of cash?" she asked.

Kate's red mouth opened in a dark hole that revealed the gaps in her tooth line. Her laughter filled the room, bounced and echoed against the thin walls.

"Lord have mercy, Adeline, you are a delight." Her eyes sparkled in their slits. "It's Clem who'll be payin' for the privilege of spreadin' your legs."

Adeline's heart seethed up in her chest. She could not remember how to draw air into her body.

"Now don't carry on so. Clem Clayton's been a customer a mine since afore the war. It's no more'n five minutes of your time. He ain't generally rough with the new girls, but if he marks your face bad, I'll give you an extra buck and you'll not work the parlor till you've healed up some."

Adeline's mind turned in tight circles, slammed hard up against her situation. She had no cash, no seed, and no way to run a farm on her own. Just last week Monday, Mr. Jopson at the bank had adjusted the polished brass buttons of his gray vest and assured her that, while the farm and its fifty acres might be of value at some time in the future, right now, she'd be lucky to find a sharecropper to take over its running.

She had left the bank, stopped in each shop and establishment in Freshwater and first inquired of—then begged for—a job. Any job. With the opening of the Butterfield stage line four years earlier, buildings had sprung up like mushrooms after the first hard rain. Now folks talked of the golden spike being driven into the ground at the base of some desert mountain out west. A shiny new railroad track was just over an hour's ride to the north of Freshwater, and brick and clapboard buildings along Main could be bought for a song.

No one was hiring inexperienced shop girls.

As if her situation weren't bad enough, Mrs. Collins had followed her from the general store out onto the elevated planks above the street to place her lips against Adeline's ear and whisper wetly, "Ain't none will dare hire you, dear. Not with Brett James puttin' out word that you'll soon be his wife."

Adeline rose from the hard bed of the boarding house too quickly, her head going all funny and light. The walls of the room whirled darkly. She staggered to the window and stared down onto the street below. A Cheyenne squaw trudged toward the general store, a stack of woven blankets in a rickety wheelbarrow, the silver at her neck and ears reflecting a soft glow in the morning's meager light.

A man in a ragged butternut jacket, a broad-brimmed hat pulled low, rode toward Adeline on a red stallion, leading a pretty bay mare who pranced, tossed her head, rolled her eyes at the sights and smells of the town. Orange dust rose in a cloud, swallowed the feet and fetlocks, tickled at the bellies of the horses. The preacher turned the roan to the hitching post outside the saloon across from the boarding house, swung a long leg over the stallion's back and dropped stiffly to the ground.

Adeline took in the dark hair, the wide shoulders and tapered waist of the man, but it was the bay mare that focused her attention. The horse seemed to feel Adeline's gaze. The mare's ears alert and forward on her pretty head, she lifted her blazed face and stared directly into the eyes of the young woman looking down at her through the dusty boarding house window. The horse nickered. Adeline smiled.

Chapter Four

H **e sipped bad whiskey** in a dank establishment not much bigger than a horse stall. Jack's Saloon the sign outside claimed, though the room was naught more than a table and four chairs with a narrow bar hand-hewn of locust wood by somebody who'd have done better to stick to rougher work. Through the open door, Jeremiah watched a girl with hair the near exact color of ripe corn stroll from the boarding house across the street and sidle up to his mare.

The horse pushed the flat of her face against the girl's front. The girl's skirt was outgrown and brushed the tops of worn boots, a too-tight dress strained at full breasts and the swell of hips. One moment, she stroked the horse's blaze, the next she swung up onto the mare's back in a move so quick Jeremiah didn't even have time to finish choking on his first taste of whiskey before there was nothing left at the hitching post but a cloud of dust and the stallion, bobbing his head in agitation at the loss of the mare.

There wasn't any point in interrupting his evening to give chase. The sun had already dropped below the mountain. The girl wouldn't get far in the dark and, when Jeremiah was ready, the stallion would find the mare. Besides, at that moment, likely the girl needed a horse more than he needed two. He craved a hot bath and a meal of something besides the hardtack, beans and salt pork that were, even now, bouncing away into the mountains in the saddle bags of his horse.

A soft voice whispered, reminded that the last time he tarried, it cost him everything. An image arrived in his mind full-blown—Maggie, sinking to the worn boards of a plank porch, a flash of blue he meant as salvation still clutched in her hand. He shook off a shiver that tickled his spine, raised the hairs on the back of his neck.

He needed a bath and a good meal. A horse thief wasn't all that hard to catch. The chase could wait.

An hour later he was sitting bent-kneed in a tub of steaming water, deep into Gibbon's *Decline and Fall of the Roman Empire,* when a key was inserted into the lock of the door to his room. A fat whore in a dress of mauve silk waddled in like she owned the place and offered to scrub his back with a boar bristle brush. She folded a towel carefully, knelt beside him.

"I'm only paying for the bath." He laid his head back against the tub's rim, looked up at the underside of the woman's breasts and the rolls of fat at her chin.

"That's all I'm offerin'." Her voice was raw and raspy, her breath smelled of whiskey, and the gold of a front tooth winked at him.

The feel of the hard brush on his back was better than most sex.

"What you fixin' to do when you catch the little gal what stole your horse?"

"Nobody stole nothing belongs to me."

"I'll pay you ten dollars, you fetch her back here to me."

She scooped bath water into a tin bucket, poured it over his head so it ran down his face and exposed shoulders and chest in warm rivulets.

"That why she was running? You got some old man willing to pay for the evil of drooling sin on that child, ruining her for the life God promised his children?"

"You a preacher?"

He caught her wide wrist, pressed until flesh yielded to bone under his fingers. "I am but a sinner scratching at the gates of heaven and begging God's blessing. Will you pray with me, sister?"

She twisted her wrist from his grip, leaned so heavy against the tub to lift herself up off her knees that, for a moment, it seemed she would tip him dripping to the floor, steaming water spilling in a baptism of waste.

"I will not pray with you, preacher." She wiped her hands on the folds

20

of her skirt. "But, you bring that gal to me and I'll pay you in gold and give you a free ride besides."

"I do not lie with whores, nor trade with the devil." His arm hung over the side of the tub, rested on the butt of his Colt. "I will, however, pray to God that you receive what you deserve in this life and the next."

Lace peeked from the bottom of her skirt, her boot heels drummed hard with each step across the smooth wood of the floor. At the door she turned and faced him.

"Suit yourself, preacher. I know things that can make a man forget God and his mama and the bloody flag of battle."

"Of that," Jeremiah said, "I have no doubt. Now go. Make haste, before God, or some other powerful being, stirs me to remove your loathsome soul from the burdens of this world."

She swept from the room, slammed the door with a bang that rattled the panes of the window. Jeremiah smiled, stared at the filigreed darkness through the lace curtain. He'd start after the girl at first light. It wouldn't do to leave her in the wilderness alone for long. Warriors of several shades, desperate for a life already stolen and gone, still roamed the Boston Mountains. He knew well the notion that, when everything you once cherished has been taken, courage rides easy on a horse called vengeance.

An hour later he stood naked, dripping cold water onto the boarding house floor, his face lathered for the first good shave he'd enjoyed since, well he had to stop and think on that. An image came to him then, of cool hands and long thin fingers, hair like a raven's wing. Uh, huh, his last fine shave had been after a tent revival in Auburn Springs when he'd spent the evening with the town's school teacher.

His mind lingered on that spinster lady, the feel of her breasts and the heat of her welcome, when the door at his back burst open with the slam of a booted foot against a cheap lock. He drew the razor down his left cheek. In the mirror, he studied the narrow strip of exposed skin visible through the white lather, like the first strike of a waking beast.

The man standing in the open door behind him wore the clothes of a dandy. Or a scoundrel. His striped vest displayed the gold of a watch chain, his boots were polished to a high gleam and his derby sat his narrow head cocked at an angle he probably mistook for rakish.

Jeremiah drew a second path in the lather. He laid the straight-razor gently to the far right of the dresser, out of the path of the Bowie he'd carried since Seven Pines, the weight and heft of the knife's bone handle a comfort and a joy in his palm.

The beast smiled. "This isn't your room, son."

The man slipped his hand under his jacket front, rested his palm there on what Jeremiah assumed was a weapon of one kind or another. Given as how the dandy hadn't already pulled a gun and shot him in the back, the preacher figured it wasn't his time to die just yet. Leastwise, not by the hand of this coward.

"My fiancée, Adeline Mitchell, done run off on your horse." The man opened his legs a mite wider. Likely he'd seen some gun slinger do that once. Some now-dead gun slinger. "When you fixin' to carry her back here?"

"Folks call me Jeremiah Jones. What might they call you?"

The man's stance widened still further. "Brett James. You might'a heard a me and my kin."

Jeremiah did not turn around. In the mirror, he studied the intruder.

"Well, now, in fact I have heard of Jesse and Frank James. They rode with Quantrill and his bunch, called themselves home guard and employed war as an excuse for murder and mayhem among the poor and defenseless."

The man drew his hand from his waist. The long black barrel of a pistol had not cleared his coat flap when Jeremiah turned to face his assailant. The flashing of a knife distracted Mr. James and his shot blew out a pane of glass in the window a good two feet to the left of Jeremiah.

The preacher's aim was better. The bone hilt of the knife quivered in the man's wrist, secured his gun hand to the open door behind him. The door swung wildly as Brett James struggled to pull free.

His bare feet cold on the plank floor, Jeremiah crossed the room to the screaming man. He kicked the pistol to the side, smiled at the blood running into the sleeve of the fancy suit. The man's wails and general carrying-on were about to get on his nerves.

The red-haired whore appeared in the hall, raked Jeremiah's naked body with the fatted slits of her gaze. "You got yourself quite a weapon there."

"Hold still," Jeremiah ordered the ranting man, "or I'm just liable to take off the hand retrieving my blade."

The beast leaped in Jeremiah's chest, roared free, his grin wide and awful. The preacher withdrew the knife with the smooth familiarity of long use in close quarters.

"I'm gonna kill you!" Brett James held his bleeding wrist up to his face, as though needing additional proof that he had, in fact, just allowed a man to pin his arm to an open door with a knife.

Jeremiah snatched James's bleeding wrist, slammed the captive's hand hard against the top of the entry table beside the door. One fast swipe of the blade, a quick and casual downward pressure, and the first joint of a cleanly severed trigger finger twitched on the table's yellowed, cotton-lace doily.

The preacher's nose touched the side of his victim's cheek. "Next time you see me," he whispered in the man's ear, "kill me quick, or you will beg to go to the devil."

Brett James staggered backward at Jeremiah's push, cradled his bleeding hand to his chest, and leaned heavily on the fat madam. The two reprobates walked backwards down the hall, disappeared at the turn of the stairs. Jeremiah sat on the edge of the bed, quickly pulled on his trousers and adjusted the Colt and Bowie at his waist. Shirt and jacket, he tucked under his arm. Footsteps, hard and fast, informed him a window might provide him a more prudent exit than the front door.

Two nights later, flames licked the edge of the cold. Jeremiah sprawled back against his saddle, stretched out his legs until heat threatened to set fire to his boot soles. An hour ago, a wisp of gray smoke spiraling pale against twilight's sky told him the girl had settled in for the night just over the next rise. He sipped warm water from a dented canteen, his stomach growling at the insult. Behind him, the stallion whinnied, pawed the rocky ground and lifted his nose into the wind.

Jeremiah stared at the fire. A length of oak burned through, shifted in the embers and sent orange sparks dancing into the black sky. He'd trailed the girl all day. First light tomorrow he'd ride into her camp, begin the business of gentling the child toward trusting him.

From the pure darkness of the woods just outside the fire's rim the private appeared. He hitched his trousers, swatted at the flapping of his blue jacket over the hole in his chest.

"You look a mite hungry." He grinned at Jeremiah, squatted beside the fire and lit a cheroot with the glowing tip of a smoking branch.

Jeremiah stared into the dark eyes of the boy. "You ever going to tell me where you hail from?"

The soldier's teeth flashed white in the firelight, tobacco smoke rising to form a halo around his hatless head. "Don't matter where I'm from," the boy said, "matters where you're going to end up."

"I am not partial to philosophical discussions with ghosts."

"That's a shame," said the sergeant stepping into the light, his jawless mouth a gaping wound from which words fell as though spit from the barrel of a .58 caliber Springfield, "'cause me and Gil here, we got us all the time in the world. And you? Far as I can see, you got not one living soul in your wasted life what you ain't runned off, abandoned, or killed outright."

Jeremiah fished under the flap of his knapsack, withdrew a bottle from its folds, pulled the cork and tipped the whiskey to his mouth. He kept his own counsel until the soles of his boots smoked in the cool night air and a pine-scented wind tore the phantoms to wisps and tendrils that blew through him and melted into the dark woods at his back. He lay on his side, rolled in a ball, pulled his blanket over him and dreamt of horses that screamed with the high-pitched terror of violated women, young men who exploded into bloody chunks of meat with voices that begged and shrieked for their mamas, the air reeking of gunpowder and the bitter taint of blood and burning flesh.

When dawn etched a thin, ragged outline to the east, mountains rolling in darker and still darker waves toward his cold campfire, Jeremiah staggered to his feet, raised his arms to the gray sky and addressed God.

"It suits you to keep me alive another day," he said, "though whether you do so out of mercy or punishment I cannot say."

The stallion tossed his head and nickered, side-stepped and fought his hobbles. The smell of the mare was apparent now, even to Jeremiah. Her snorts and neighing calls carried easily across the short distance that separated the two camps. That the girl hadn't taken note of the entreaties of the stallion was testimony enough that the child should not be alone in these mountains.

Jeremiah drank his canteen nearly dry, arranged his straight razor and shaving kit along the scaly bark of a low oak branch and commenced to finish what he'd begun two nights ago. He shaved carefully in the near-dark, pulled the razor tenderly over the jagged white scar that ran from the bottom of his ear to the underside of his chin, prodded with gentle fingers to assure that dirt or pebbles or a shard of battlefield metal was not, once more, working its way to the surface of his face. Satisfied he had done his best to make himself as presentable, as non-threatening as possible, he saddled the stallion, removed the night-hobble, swung up and gave the horse his head.

Halfway up the first rise, the roan reared, taking Jeremiah by surprise and nearly unseating him. With air between the seat of his pants and saddle leather, the preacher heard a shriek of terror. His mind reeled and he was back on the battlefield, mules screaming into the smoke and blood and exposed bowels. He gathered the reins, spurred the horse and rode hard toward the sound.

Chapter Five

S he woke to the dawn call of a whippoorwill, rubbed morning grit from her eyes, lay still to preserve body heat under the horsey smell of the saddle blanket that was her only cover. The whippoorwill called again, this time from behind her, the lonesome melody followed almost immediately by the screeching of ravens that lifted themselves from a nearby tree with loud squawks and the urgent beating of dusky wings.

Adeline's breath caught, heart beat hard in her thin chest. She sat straight up, let the rough blanket fall to her waist. The child struggled to untangle panic-numbed legs when the dark shapes that had disturbed the ravens emerged from behind the gnarled trunks of the oak trees all around her. Three warriors rushed the camp, hair so black in the early morning light it seemed to shimmer in blue waves around their white-streaked faces.

It was then she screamed. One long piercing wail of terror before a hand that tasted of meat and smelled of dirt and rancid grease closed over her mouth as she bucked and kicked and struggled. One of the braves mounted the mare. A second Indian stood just at the edge of the small clearing, knees slightly bent, a knife passing from hand to hand in front of his buckskin-covered chest, staring toward the wood. The third savage lifted Adeline by the waist, slung her onto the bay in front of the mounted brave with no more regard or effort than shucking a sack of potatoes onto the back of a buckboard.

A tight band of raw terror squeezed breath from her chest. She fought to form thoughts in a mind that failed to make sense of what was happening, that sought to shut down and sink into the murk of disbelief.

Astraddle the mare, Adeline threw back her head, hoping to collide with the nose of the man pulling her roughly against him. The Indian made a sound like a chuckle. Something hit the side of her head, and pushed her hard toward night.

Knowledge, like an open-mouthed animal appearing from out of a warm fog, descended on her, growled that she was about to pay the price for daring to want more than life with a man who used her like a slave and kicked her like a dog when the spirit took him, or the long, laudanum-dulled nights of a small-town whore. In some wood between worlds, she dreamed of Pa tucking her in each night, his warm whisper in her ear, "Dream big, my girl. Dream big." She lived again the moments when Mama struck her hard for lollygagging and instructed, "A woman is born into this world to obey God and her husband, Adeline. Don't go gettin' notions."

Her last thought as darkness swallowed her once more was that being kidnapped by Indians might well prove even worse than opening her legs to Clem Clayton.

She woke to the sway of a horse, the smell of sweat, the dust of oak and locust thick in her nose and throat.

Dear God. Where was she? A vision flashed like lightning across the dark of her mind. Wild, black eyes. Painted faces. Rough hands. The smell of bear grease. A hard blow to the back of her head. Kidnapped! Taken by Indians!

Bile rose in her throat. Terror froze her muscles so that she had not the strength even to lean forward while bringing back up the hardtack and jerky she'd eaten last night as that day's only meal. Vomit warmed her chest. Her body shivered and twitched, then went still.

A dark calm claimed her. No more shivering. No more fear. She hung limp against the Indian whose arm circled her waist, one hand resting on her breast as though he owned her, as though she had no more right to her life than a horse or a mule, some animal that could be mauled and prodded at will. Secreted in some dead place without fear, without thought, she played possum, retreated. Her head bounced on her neck. From the quiet center of her soul she studied, as though from afar, the smooth, calming movement of muscles under the shoulder of the mare. She let the rhythmic beat of hooves on stone and dry leaves take her to a safer time, a better place.

In the long nights of winter, the fire popped with new sap and warmed the cabin. Mama worked with needle and thread, and Adeline nearly always won the game of memorizing the scriptures that were Pa's favorites. One of these long ago verses floated into her mind.

The righteous cry out, and the Lord hears, and delivers them out of all their troubles.

She claimed the promise.

Behind her came soft chanting that sounded like the language the Egg Woman spoke. Mama used to buy handmade baskets and fresh duck eggs from shy, reclusive Mary Owen who was rescued two summers past after being taken prisoner as a child and raised by the Osage. The woman had a half-breed son the whites called Walter and who called himself Running Water. Walter disappeared into the woods two winters ago. The following spring Mary abandoned her cabin and white society, or what passed for it in tiny Freshwater, Arkansas. To a thin stack of neatly folded, worn cotton dresses, she pinned a scrawled note saying simply *Leev me be*.

For a long, endless time astride the horse, Adeline pretended sleep while her mind flowed freely between dead calm and blinding terror. In the grip of panic, her body shook and trembled. Teeth rattled in her mouth and her heart was a trapped bird in her chest. Then, each time, just as she accepted that she would die right there with her body pressed roughly against a savage, warm calm settled over her and she escaped, her mind floating away to freedom.

God is our refuge and strength, a very present help in trouble. Therefore we will not fear.

The day passed in a series of trances broken by panic-driven violent shaking.

Thin light speckled the leafy ground. Tree shadows shrunk, between her shaking fits and dead calm, until the sun rose overhead and long, crooked fingers of shade dissolved into the trunks of the oaks and hickory and maple. Wind from out of the south shifted slowly toward the east. When the Indian reined the bay to a halt in an oblong clearing with the dead leaves of sleeping trees so thick the mare's hooves crunched with each step, the air had turned bitter cold and blew from almost due west.

A warrior appeared at the horse's side. The arms that had held Adeline roughly all morning loosed and she slid from the horse and up against the chest of a tall brave in a deerskin vest. Adeline recoiled at this new man's touch. He stood her on the ground, squeezed her cheeks almost gently, and turned her face to his. His grin was white and wide, his voice soft.

His words had no more meaning than the cold wind that bent the tops of trees.

A tremor passed through her. She twisted away from him, gagged at the thick smell of earth and bear grease that wrinkled her nose and filled her mouth with vomit. He led her by the leather thong that tied her hands at her waist, pushed her into a sit on a flat rock littered with brown leaves. In a desperate attempt to stop her body's violent shaking, Adeline pressed a palm against the stone, dug fingers into the pale green moss and lichen that pocked the rock's surface.

The Indian leaned close enough she could see the cracks in the white paint that streaked his face, a jagged scar that ran across the curve of his left eyebrow, through a puckered eyelid, down his high cheekbone and ended at the corner of his mouth. He pressed his warm mouth to her ear, his tone like that of a man murmuring nonsense to an inexperienced horse.

"Do not move. I need you alive."

How had she understood his words? Was she so far gone into terror and confusion that she imagined his language to be English?

The tremors took her again, along with the sure knowledge that she had fled a bad situation to fall into worse. Much worse.

She knew what savages did to white women. Mama had tried to shield her from details of the raid on the Samuels' family cabin up in Bear Holler, but rumors had shifted through the chinks of the cabin walls like sand in a wind storm. Within hours of the Butterfield stage driver making the announcement, every soul in Freshwater knew Jethroe Samuels had been tortured and killed, his scalp taken. His wife, Elizabeth Lynn, had been raped, her scalp now hanging beside that of her husband, decorating a brave's belt. The twelve-year-old son, William, had been taken, and his ten-year-old sister Annie was found huddled in a dry well behind the cabin, her mind shattered so that she'd never yet, after all these months, spoken a single word.

The stone on which Adeline sat was cold through the thin cotton of her dress. She wrapped her arms around herself, forced air deep down into her belly the way Pa had taught her to seek calm. She concentrated her mind on the smell of wet stones and moss, the sharp tang of the mare's fear. The horse showed the whites of her eyes and twitched, blew hard as if to rid herself of the strong smell of these new men who'd taken possession of her.

The Indian who'd gripped Adeline's breast roughly all morning stared from the tree line. Adeline guessed him to be no more than fourteen. The brave with the scar on his face, the Indian whose words she had somehow understood, swirled his hands in movements that reminded of bird's flight and fluttering leaves. The boy and a third Indian, whose long hair hung greasy and shiny as the belly of a black snake, spoke in low grunts. The boy looked her way, then shuffled through the deep leaf cover, lifted her roughly by the elbow and pushed her toward the heavy shadows of the woods. She kicked out at his groin, brought her bound hands up to collide with the underside of his chin. His head snapped back. Blood trickled red from the edges of his mouth.

Adeline ran.

Someone caught her before she'd made three strides. Arms lifted her from the ground by her waist, and, her legs kicking, body bucking backwards, carried her against one hip, dropped her beside the flat rock. She looked up, watched the scar-face Indian turn and walk away as though from a chastised dog.

Terror of her situation came down upon her like a hawk on a young rabbit, sank talons deep. She scrambled on hands and knees, panic erasing all thoughts but escape. A dark shape appeared, towered over her. She forced herself to look up. The Indian with the long, shining hair stood in her path, legs spread slightly, a hatchet raised high above his head. Adeline cringed, tried to bury herself in the year's dead leaves, curled in a ball.

The whistle of the stick sang in the air, fear climbed to terror and then, in the same instant, became, again, calm acceptance.

The woods exploded. The savage poised above her twisted to meet the sound and Adeline kicked hard at his bare ankles. Explosions, one directly after the other, seemed to come from inside her pounding heart.

Chapter Six

Three against one was not a contest he sought, nor did he seek a fight against men who found themselves in a position similar to his own. Their land and way of life stolen by strangers, alone and struggling to make a new beginning in a world that changed faster than a man could possibly adjust.

He'd tethered the stallion a half-mile back. Enfield in hand, Jeremiah had worked his way from oak to hickory to fallen locust until he gained a tree-slatted view of the clearing. The girl sat straight-backed on a rock. The braves flashed sign language at each other and postured in disagreement. The boy and an Indian with the flowing hair of a Cheyenne or Kiowa appeared to be arguing with the tallest Indian, an Osage.

Jeremiah had befriended the Osage scout who guided his unit through Indian country on the Confederate's futile and bloody attempt to drive back their own invaders. Why these three warriors would be traveling together, the preacher could not fathom. The Cheyenne and Kiowa were allied, but the Osage had spent fifty years raiding the camps of both tribes, pushing and fighting over the land's natural boundaries.

As best Jeremiah could decipher, the Osage in the deerskin vest wanted the captive as his own. The long-haired brave, probably a Cheyenne, appeared to want simply to use the girl, rob her of her white hair and move on. Jeremiah had to admit, in their situation, alone in occupied territory, this was the solution that made the most sense. The boy, who cut his eyes toward the girl at every opportunity, no doubt wanted what all young men of that age seek—a taste of sex and glory.

Peeking through the trees and brush, Jeremiah caught only bits and pieces of the sign language flying through dark fingers. The Cheyenne instructed the boy to lead the prisoner through the woods to a small creek where she might drink. The boy nodded and started toward the girl, his smile turning up the corners of his mouth the instant his back was to the older men. By the time the young Indian crossed the clearing, bent over the girl, his hand already reaching for the captive, the look on his face was unmistakable. The girl kicked out, struck hard with her bound hands, and bloodied his face. The Osage rescued her from humiliation-fueled retaliation from the younger man by simply lifting her like a squirming sack of shoats and dumping her back in the clearing.

The girl, in an act that could only have been fueled by desperation, struck out at her rescuer. On her hands and knees, she scrambled toward the woods. In seconds, the older Cheyenne towered over her, a tomahawk raised above his head. A serrated feather, where the blade met the handle, swept straight back, the cutting edge poised to sweep toward the child's head.

Jeremiah rose from the ground, leaf litter falling around him like a cloud. He raised the musket to his shoulder, called upon the Lord with the desperate voice of an abandoned prophet, and pressed his finger to the Enfield's trigger. The weapon exploded into the quiet of the woods. The tomahawk fell to the ground beside the body of its owner.

A blue-coated private formed in the smoke around the preacher's head. Jeremiah dropped the rifle, the muzzle-loader useless now in this fight. The garbled screams of a ghostly sergeant came from just behind Jeremiah. The Colt pistol held in front of him like a talisman, Jeremiah roared into the clearing between his phantoms, gave loud voice to battle lust.

The Indian boy appeared in his path, long knife raised, mouth wide in a twin of Jeremiah's killing cry.

The preacher pulled the trigger.

The boy fell, sprawled face up in the dead leaves.

The Osage stood at the edge of the clearing, the girl held against the buckskin of his vest, an antler-handled knife bloodying the hollow of her throat.

Jeremiah's pistol pointed at the scarred face of the last Indian standing in those autumn woods. It was not lost on the preacher that, positioned thus, face to face, the two men and their battle scars were near mirror images, one of the other.

"Leave her," Jeremiah said in what he hoped was understandable Osage. "I do not want to kill you."

"Liar," said the Indian in perfect English. "Your kind knows only killing."

Gurgled chuckles came from the sergeant on Jeremiah's right.

"The redskin's got you there," spoke the private on his left.

In the woods behind came the sound of a large animal moving fast through low branches and breaking brush. Jeremiah did not need to turn to know the stallion had broken his tether and made his way to the mare.

The dark eyes of the Indian met Jeremiah's pale blue gaze.

"Take the stallion," the preacher said in English and then in Osage. "The girl stays with me."

Jeremiah lowered his pistol.

The Indian released his captive who dropped to her knees.

The preacher turned with the Indian's movement, prayed he wouldn't have to raise the Colt's barrel from the muted reds, golds and browns of the leafy ground, throw fire and lead into flesh once more.

The Osage was at the stallion's side before the girl could bring her hands to the blood trickling from her throat, staining the torn cotton of her dress.

Satisfied the child would stay put for the moment, Jeremiah raised the pistol toward the brave. "Leave the saddle and bags."

The Indian turned his head, met Jeremiah's stare, released the cinch and removed the saddle. He opened the bags, tossed a leather-bound journal and a ragged copy of James Fennimore Cooper's *The Last of the Mohicans* into the leaves. A faded cotton sack of jerky and a half-bottle of amber whiskey he tucked into the waist of his leather breeches.

Jeremiah took aim at the Indian. "I'll need the blanket as well. I'll not ruin a horse just to keep from killing one more Indian. Leave the whiskey and what's left of the venison."

The Indian deliberately tucked a handful of jerky into a pouch at his waist. He dropped the bottle into the leaves and swept the blanket from the horse's back, momentarily blocking Jeremiah's view. The preacher's finger caressed the curve of Colt's trigger, every muscle taut with readiness. He did not draw breath until the stallion reared when the Indian leapt to the horse's back. The roan bowed and did his best to unseat the man who now claimed him. The Indian dug his heels into the animal's sides and they disappeared into the muted light of early afternoon.

One foot propped on the flat top of the boulder, the private watched Jeremiah walk to the girl and squat beside her.

Jeremiah touched a finger lightly to the young woman's chin, lifted her face.

"It's over."

She shook her head, touched her throat and brought a bloody hand to her face.

"You're not hurt. It's nothing more than a scratch."

Her eyes were gray, wide, and so pale as to be almost translucent. Wild and speckled with broken leaves and twigs and dirt, her hair was a nimbus of gold around a pale face.

"Whoa, now, Preacher." The garbled voice of the sergeant came from behind Jeremiah. "You rescuing that young'un or getting set to bed her?"

The preacher took the girl's hand in his, pulled the child to her feet. She leaned against him and he was reminded of cupping a wind-blown fledgling in his hand, its tender fate fallen to him.

"I'm Jeremiah Jones."

Her gaze held neither recognition nor understanding.

"I'd as soon have some other moniker for you than horse thief," he said. "You got a name?"

Her wide mouth turned up just slightly, a stray cat who's just picked up the scent of cream, knows the treat isn't for the likes of her, but can't help hoping for a lap or two.

"Adeline," she said in a voice that was scarcely more than a whisper. "Adeline Mitchell from Freshwater, Arkansas."

Like a child reciting in a Sunday school competition.

"I'm right proud and pleased to meet you, Adeline" he said. "Now let's get out of here before that brave changes his mind about the bargain we struck."

She blinked once before she fainted, her slight weight falling full against him. Jeremiah lowered the child to the ground, strode quickly to the strewn contents of his saddlebags. He gathered the splayed books to him, brushed dirt and crushed leaves from the pages of his journal, closed each volume gently and tucked the books back in with his other essentials.

He ran his hands over the mare. The horse tossed her head. Foam speckled the animal's mouth. He spoke softly of better days, slipped the blanket and saddle onto her back.

Behind him, a boy's moan leached into the air. The single cry settled a dark mist over Jeremiah's mind, an oily memory of gun smoke and terror-filled men and animals that seeped from his core, coated his very skin. He turned, filled his vision with the Indian boy writhing in the detritus of another year's passing in an old woods. The blue-coated private stood quiet beside the sergeant. Both looked down at the Indian, shook their heads.

Jeremiah strode to the boy, aimed his pistol. With the toe of his boot, he turned the wounded young brave, looked deep into eyes already dark with approaching death.

"May God bless you and the spirits guide you home."

The boy turned his face from Jeremiah's words.

The shot was loud. The bullet entered in a hole no bigger than his little finger where blue-black hair touched the young man's right ear. On the left side of the head a silver-dollar-sized gap opened, blew brains and life and suffering and joy onto the russet ground.

The figures in blue vanished into afternoon's cold light, rude laughter fluttering what few leaves remained on the oak and hickory. The preacher stripped the boy's body of breeches and vest before stepping to the girl.

Her dress was easier torn away than unbuttoned. The bluish softness of her skin, the swell of young breasts and hips against plain underwear— these were powerful temptations. He dressed the girl quickly.

Jeremiah stood, swept his eyes along the edges of the clearing, listened for the whisper of leaf against buckskin or the startled cry of a bird. He saw only an ancient woods, disturbed but briefly by man's folly. Heard naught but the breeze in the leafless tree tops—cold and warning of winter. From a leather pouch at his waist he poured the last two lead balls into his palm, rubbed them between his fingers. It had been foolish to waste a shot to put the Indian boy out of his misery. Yet, even as he understood this, he was back at the Battle of the Wilderness, wounded men crying for mercy as night fires swept toward them and he lay helpless and listened to their pleas die with the crackling of the flames.

He reloaded the pistol, stepped around the bodies, and retrieved his Enfield. Standing in his original position at the edge of the clearing, he measured and poured black powder, tamped and loaded the musket. His hands performed these tasks without thought, the familiar movements reminiscent of battle, when every nerve and muscle sang with God-like power.

Jeremiah stood for a moment in a world gone gray and lifeless, then strode to the horse and slipped the rifle into its sheath. His boots crunching in dead leaves, he returned to the child, carried her to the mare and slung her limp body, as gently as possible, across the animal's shoulders. Once astride the horse, he positioned Adeline tight against his chest. He'd seen men survive a cannon's blast, live through battlefield amputations. Others took but a flesh wound and died quietly at the first opportunity. He could provide this child with warmth. The rest was up to her.

The girl trembled against him. He sat the horse and searched the shadows. The woods were quiet. No movement. No squirrel chattered over the last of the year's acorns. No raven cawed. He contemplated on just how much time he had before the brave returned for his revenge, or the James gang organized their own retribution for his mutilation of their kin. Either way, best to hurry along.

Chapter Seven

Adeline shivered, struggled to make sense of the world into which she had awakened. Her thoughts floated, fuzzy as the yellow fluff of a new-hatched chick. A flat-bottomed circle of coppery light about twenty feet from where she lay drew her gaze. She squeezed her eyes shut and then snapped them wide, fought to make sense of a dark crucifix shape silhouetted against the pale light. There was the tang of pine and the crisp taste of cold mountain air. Surely heaven was warmer than this and hell nowhere near as familiar.

She squinted and the cross became an angel standing in a halo of light, his wings extended, feathered tips fluttering in a weak breeze. Michael or Lucifer, she knew not which.

From behind came the neighing of a horse, the unmistakable sound of hooves pawing hard rock. She swam from dreams, struggled toward reality. She ground tight fists into her eyes and the smell of bear grease and old wood-smoke hit like a fist to her stomach. There was more than one kind of hell. A small cry escaped. She fought her way out of a wrapping that bound tight as a shroud.

The angel turned, lowered his wings, became larger with his approach.

The shape became a man. He squatted beside her. Touched his hand to her arm.

"You're safe now. I'm Jeremiah Jones, remember? Saddle preacher from out Fayetteville way. You stole my horse."

Memories flooded. The desperate flight from Freshwater astride the stolen mare. Waking with Indians rushing into the clearing. The smell of black powder. Vivid strokes of blood red brushed with wisps of gun smoke. The whistle of a tomahawk sweeping the air.

The preacher's breath warmed her face.

"We're in a cave I stumbled upon a few years back. There's a narrow, rocky ledge at the front door and a long drop to the river. Don't stray."

Her hands found leather and buckskin where the soft cotton of her dress should have been. She shrank away from the man squatted at her side.

"What's this? Who dressed me?"

"Your clothes were torn and didn't provide any warmth to begin with."

Her head throbbed. In the near darkness of the cave, this strange man so close the knee of his britches touched her blanketed hip, Adeline was in a shadow world. Somewhere between what was real and the land of dreams, or nightmares.

His voice came soft out of the murky darkness.

"The Cheyenne that raided your camp donated those items."

The lilting melody of his words calmed her, lulled her into a sense of safety she did not understand, but nonetheless sank into gratefully.

"You kilt 'em," she said and did not know if this knowledge caused fear or gratitude or awe.

"Not all of them," he said, "and you were in shock, needed warmth. Which is why I changed your clothes and why we've sought shelter in this cave instead of being halfway to Texas by now."

"Will they come for us?" Her voice seemed not to belong to her at all.

The man chuckled and the sound was like a scraping of two rusted hinges that had not moved freely, one against the other, for many long, dead years. He stood and his knees popped in the darkness.

"With luck," he said from above her. "They'll *all* come after us. That fat whore from Freshwater? She'll not come herself, but she'll prompt that low-life home guard James boy to do her bidding. And the Osage brave? He doesn't have a thing to lose. Like me, he seeks death."

She pulled the blanket tight around her shoulders, shivered. "Why'd anyone go looking for death?"

"It's a long story and one not for children." He walked away from her, melted into the darkness at the back of the cave.

"I ain't no child. I'll be seventeen come May."

"Can you eat? We've naught but deer jerky and hardtack, but it'll take the edge off."

Her stomach growled at the mention of food, her mouth instantly filling with saliva and then with the rising contents of her stomach. She disentangled herself from the blanket and ran toward the light at the mouth of the cave.

From behind came boot heels on stone and the man's calm voice. "It's only the fear finding its way out. Don't fight against its escape."

Adeline bent double and released long strings of vomit. The man stood behind her, quiet, so close she could feel his presence shimmer the air in the few inches between them. He did not touch her. When she straightened, gasping, her breath coming slowly back to normal, he turned her to him, wiped her mouth with rough palms. The heat of his touch frightened her beyond understanding. She leaned into it.

"We can't risk a fire." He turned her sharply to the left, to a rough alcove farther, deeper into the cave. "But we're out of the wind. You'd do well to chew slow-like on a piece of jerky, give your stomach something to gnaw on besides fear. I'll mix a little whiskey in water. That'll settle your nerves."

She hesitated, torn between fear and a need for comfort she thought she'd outgrown about the time Mama died. Her mind chewed on this conflict. Her body followed him into the dark of the cave.

"You ain't like no preacher I ever met. Pa taught that whiskey was the instrument of the devil."

He handed her a chunk of meat no bigger than her thumb, guided her toward a folded length of oil cloth only just visible in the near darkness. She sat, brought the jerky to her mouth. The first salty taste awoke a ravenous hunger.

"Go slow there," he said, "else you'll bring it all back up again. As for the devil, well, I spent almost five years working right alongside ole Scratch, employed every trick he invented and they tell me that was in the service of good, though what good I cannot tell you."

"You was in the war?"

"Third Arkansas Regiment. Joined up when I was not yet seventeen. Right about the age you are now. Marched away from everything I loved as if I were Ulysses."

She stared at him. "Ulysses? Is he in the Old Book? Pa was mostly a New Testament man."

"Chew slow on that jerky." His smile touched his words. "Ulysses comes from a very old book. I mean to say only that I joined the war to test my manhood, be a hero."

"Pa was a muleteer. Killed at the Battle of Oak Hills. Jerome Mitchell. Did you maybe . . . did you maybe run into him?"

The preacher poured water from a canteen into a tin cup, mixed it with a goodly portion of the contents of a flat-sided bottle. He offered the cup to Adeline.

"Sip it slow."

She shook her head.

"It's medicinal," he said. "Your pa didn't have nothing against medicine, did he?"

She wrinkled her nose at the smell, but accepted the cup.

He lowered himself onto the cloth beside her. Behind them the mare nickered, shod hooves clacked on the cave floor.

The whiskey warmed from throat to belly and then spread outward. Adeline had a moment of panic that something which felt this good had to be of the devil. The moment passed with the next few sips. She chewed at the dried meat, sneaked looks at the man whose horse she'd stolen. Her thoughts drifted to how Pa always said that God had made Lucifer to share in His glory, and about how the angel had fallen, broken God's heart with his pride.

The preacher drew from his saddle bag the nub of a tallow candle and a leather-bound book. A match flared and sulfur tainted the air. He lit the candle and secured it to a ledge in the cave wall, lowered himself a few feet from her. Waves of flickering light flowed over the pages in his lap.

Adeline fell then into a comfort and security she had not known since Pa marched off to war. She felt as a child.

"So, did you know my pa? In the war. Did you maybe meet him?" Her voice was small in the darkness.

His chest rose and fell as though, with each breath, he swallowed the world whole and then released it again at the exhale.

"Your pa fought bravely and did his best." His flat words brought an end to the conversation.

Adeline listed to the side, focused on the candle flame's dance across the white and black of the open book. A sense of well-being overtook her. Her bones seemed to melt like the yellow wax of the candle and she curled in a ball beside the man. The wool of the horse blanket scratched when he tucked it around her face.

"Mr. Jones? I'm right sorry I stole your horse."

"Extremis malis extrema remedia."

"What?"

"Latin, child. Desperate times call for desperate measures."

The only sound then was the soft chuckling neigh of the mare and the pages of the preacher's book turning like leaves on a warm summer day. Her eyes already closed and sleep lapping at the edges of her mind, she rolled to her back, turned her face toward the man.

"You think Pa thought about me and Ma when he died? You think he wished he'd never left?"

His sigh fluttered the light. His hand pressed a firm weight on her shoulder.

"Your pa wished with all his might he'd stayed home and his last thought before he died was of you and your brothers and sisters and of your mother."

The world swam in a teary fog.

"You cain't really know that." Though she wished with all her soul to believe it true.

"Oh, but I can," he said. "If I know nothing else, I know this. Every man, be he butternut or blue, thought of naught else but home at the moment of death."

She swiped her face, fought to tame the peculiar swirling of the cave walls, studied on the odd way the whiskey made her feel sad and yet comforted all at the same time.

"How'd you come to be a saddle-preacher? Don't seem like a natural path from soldiering."

He closed the book on his finger, turned and gave her a full view of his pale face. Eyes like dead ash. Like he'd seen a haint. Or lived with them. A scar marked him from eyebrow to chin. She thought of the thin squiggly lines worms make just below the surface of the earth after a soaking rain. She thought to trace that jagged stripe with the tip of her finger.

He stared at her so long, she squirmed under the blanket, figured he wasn't going to answer her question. When he finally spoke, he seemed to be speaking not to her at all. She took a notion that he had forgotten she lay beside him, that he addressed some inner demon he meant to calm, or maybe to challenge.

"Father took his degree in theology from William and Mary. The first ten years of my life were spent in Virginia where he pastored a large, prosperous congregation."

"So, how'd ya end up in Arkansas?"

"Father had principles which required him to instigate confrontation with evil, even if evil was no more than differing from him in one's opinion."

His eyes were flat, lifeless stones.

"He preached once too often on the sin of slavery." He blinked, seemed to come to himself once more. "We were forced to vacate the parsonage. Looking back, it's possible Father lost his mind at that junction. He felt it best to take my city-bred mother, my eight-year-old sister and myself into the wilds of Indian country where he attempted, badly, to eke out a living on a rocky homestead he named, as though it were a grand plantation, Beulah."

The mare neighed softly, the sound echoing against the rock walls.

"When war came, I joined the Confederacy for the duration. That was the strongest slap I could summon to aim at the cheek of my father."

"Is your pa still in Arkansas?"

43

The question twisted his face. He blinked, turned from her.

"They're all gone." His voice so dead it gave her the shivers.

He lowered his head to his book.

"Which part of the Good Book are you studyin' on there?" Still on her back, hands under her head with elbows stuck out to the sides in what Mama used to call chicken wings, she concentrated on making the cave ceiling stay put.

"The Lord and I are not currently on speaking terms. Tonight I read the poet Henry Wadsworth Longfellow."

She sat up. The blanket slipped, bunched at her waist.

"I thought you was a preacher. Pa always did say that no good came of reading, 'cept of the Bible. Words not of scripture are of the devil himself."

A wave of panic, suppressed for days now, rose up and presented her situation in bold relief. Running from Indians and outlaws, alone in a cave with a murderer, and her drunk on the devil's own brew. This man, this preacher whom she'd seen kill with no more effort than it took to squeeze a trigger—his moods seemed to swing from dark to darker-still. Yet, something about him drew her.

Ma had taught her to read from the Bible. Pa told that man's intellect was best concentrated on God's word, that the avoidance of temptation was the best defense against a heartless and vigilant devil. A conviction took her that she was not safe with this man. Not safe at all.

"Your pa," he said in that dead voice of his, "sounds a man well-acquainted with the works of the Great Tempter."

She meant to stand, but her body was uncooperative. She staggered, fell against the preacher and found herself flat on her butt, legs tangled like those of a foal still wet from his mama.

The man laughed. Not the creaky-hinged laugh of his earlier chuckle. This was laughter enough to rile the horse to stamping, send sparks into the night as metal shoes met the hard rock floor of the cave. Laughter bounced off the walls and surely roused every Indian in the territory.

"You, sir, are cruel and cold!"

Her words slurred and merged and filled her mouth with saliva.

Shamed, she straightened her legs the best she could, fell sideways and settled on dragging herself to the blanket and turning her back on the man's ill-bred outburst.

He gained slow and sporadic control until his laughter became more like sobs and tears, though she refused to roll over and pay him any mind.

"Every man has his secret sorrows which the world knows not." His voice came from the darkness. "And often times we call a man cold when he is only sad."

The words drew her, calmed somehow, so that she forgot her fear.

"I don't know that there Psalm."

"That sentiment," he said, "is from a fellow who, like me, leans hard toward the devil."

She should be frightened. She knew this. But a warm, soft blanket of contentment had settled over her. She saw Grandma Murphy's nine-patch quilt ripple faded color and re-stitched hope. She imagined Mama, spring breeze ruffling her hair, standing wide-legged, shaking out the dust of another year. She felt the soft tuck of that pieced blanket, familiar and solid, pressing her toward sleep.

The preacher moved behind her, lay down and stretched himself so close the heat of his long body warmed her back. His breath on her neck like the building of joy, the lifting of hands to God at the tent revival last spring. She feared his touch, wanted that touch more than she'd ever wanted anything in her life.

He rolled away and cold rushed in to fill the space between them. Abandoned and aching with a need that clotted shame in her throat, she curled tighter under the rough blanket, pressed her eyes shut to stop the darkness from swirling. Exhaustion took her then, sleep rose up and claimed her.

She woke from a dream of drowning in a river that ran warm and red as a cardinal's wing. From the darkness behind her came a voice raised in anger, moans and hard flesh struggling against itself. The clear whoop whoop of large wings disturbed the air, the soft flutter of feathers ruffling and struggling against one another returned her to an uneasy sleep where she fought to determine if she were being sanctified or devoured, wondered if there was any difference.

Chapter Eight

T he last two inches of whiskey burned his throat, settled like brimstone in his belly. Jeremiah fingered the smooth glass of the thumb-sized bottle in his pocket, studied the girl. He had tainted her sweet breath with the liquor, yet she slept as a child, on her side, one hand tucked under a downy cheek. Earlier she had awakened from shock and exhaustion to discover him at the cave's mouth, his hands extended fully from his shoulders, beseeching a God he did not trust and yet sought in the same way a laudanum addict seeks his own sweet poison. He had hurried to her then and she stared at him with gray eyes wide, mouth parted in what seemed to him nothing less than awe and wonder.

That look, that one look, had reached into his chest, touched some need in him to nurture and protect. His desire to touch her skin, run his hand up her thigh and find her center had shivered his arms, turned his legs to water. He ached to press her against himself, save her and, in doing so, heal himself as well. That one look from those dove-gray eyes had produced a reaction in his loins that forced him to rise from her side with an audible pop of his knees and walk away from the girl as quickly as he could manage.

The candle flickered grotesque shadows on the cave walls, guttered, and was no more. He sat in the dark, cursed himself for a fool. He had failed to save his mother from death. Could not even locate his sister, Grace. And Maggie. His Maggie. He had left her for the false promise of glory and manhood. Compounded his neglect by condemning her betrayal of marrying during his five year absence. Rode away and left her what he, in his idiocy, perceived as a solution to the problem of marriage to her brute of a husband.

Darkness pressed in on him, the air itself heavy and cold as death. He had killed them all. In one way or another, his selfishness and ineptitude killed every person he ever loved.

From behind him came the giggles of the private. The sergeant strolled into view and squatted over the sleeping girl, raised his eyebrows and turned his ruined face to Jeremiah.

"Ever miss our war, Preacher? We was Gods with them rifles, wan't we?" The sergeant's blue tongue flapped and struck air, yet his words were clear and cutting. "Only God has the power to take a life. Ain't that what the Good Book teaches, Preacher? But we damn sure shared that gift with The Almighty and was prayed over and blessed in our mission before each one a them battles."

Jeremiah threw the empty bottle over his shoulder, glared at the apparition. "You go to hell."

"You been lusting for that child since you saw her busting out a that dress a hers way back in Freshwater. 'Bout ten seconds a'fore she stole your mare."

The sergeant's hand hovered just over the girl's face, like that of a faith healer, or a succubus. He looked up at Jeremiah, stared into his eyes until the preacher turned away.

"Truth be told, Preacher. You could a put that savage's clothes on this child without removing that soft cotton dress a hers. This here need a yours to rescue, it ain't nothing more than that old wartime need to play God. With a mighty fine twist. Between you and me and Gil, here? We know what you been up to with this young'un from the get go. Like them giants of old that lie with the human womens, this here interfering, playing God, this here has a mighty mix a lust."

Gil appeared just behind the sergeant. His image was as clear as that of the girl yet formed no silhouette against the cave's mouth and the stars that shone and sparkled in the moonless night.

"She's a right pretty thing." Gil's grin flashed white in the dark. "Though

I think you might would have done better not to have collapsed yourself into that laughing fit over her drunken fall, 'special since it was you give her the whiskey. I ain't real good with the fair sex, but I know they don't like being made the butt of a joke."

Jeremiah's fingers closed over the sharp edges of a stone. His throw sent the rock through the body of the private and out the cave's entrance. Both soldiers dissolved into the night, their laughter reverberating like the echo of a gunshot in the cave.

Those two knew nothing of his mind or intentions. Still, he was shamed that laughter over her fall had stolen him earlier, wounded the girl and revealed his black soul. He could find only two reactions for the ridiculousness of a child abandoned by a loving father and mother, hunted by a man who would use her first to prove his manhood and then as a brood mare while working her slowly to death on some farm on the backside of beyond. Sought by a whore, that advocate of the devil who meant to feed from her sweet flesh until the young thing was no more than a rotting corpse awaiting death. Kidnapped by Indians who meant even more harm than the James boy. Yet, in all this, the child held true. What panicked the girl, this Adeline, were written words not sanctified by a long-dead council of meddlers.

He could only laugh or kill them both to escape the absurdity of this life.

Adeline rolled to her back, threw one arm over her head. Eyes long adjusted to darkness, he watched the coarse blanket outline the rise and fall of her breasts, the open V where long legs joined at her womanhood. Jeremiah groaned deep in his throat, rose and crept like a thief to the deepest reaches of the cave. He dropped to his knees, the stone floor hard and unrelenting, and raised his eyes in the blackness. He craved union with the sweetness, the innocence of this child like a promise of redemption, knew beyond any remnant of doubt that to fall upon her would lead them both down a path of destruction.

Palms pressed to the back wall of the cave, he laid his forehead against the cool surface.

"God, you conniving coward."

His words like hot bile.

"You tell me you formed me in my mother's womb. Why? Why did you bother? Why save me when everyone around me dies a bloody, awful death? Do I amuse you in my struggles? Are you naught more than an eternally-bored entity forever entertaining himself with the suffering of those he claims as his children?"

His hands slid down the rough stone, until he lay on his belly, shivering in the dark, pouring pain and anger into the ear of a God gone deaf. He clutched a silver locket, saw again the slow fall of his last dream.

"You claim to be like a hen who gathers her chicks under her wing. Liar! You are no more than a bloodthirsty beast, a wolf who rips and tears his prey into bite-size chunks. Tens of thousands dead in bloody, awful, senseless battle. Maggie. Mother. Sweet sister Grace. These sacrifices aren't enough? Now you lay at my door this innocent child? Tempt me with her need and her warm body."

His voice tore his throat like ground glass, a razor-sharp knife sliced his gut.

"Damn you to hell," he rasped. "Leave me be. Just. Leave me. Be."

A noise like the beating of wings surrounded him then, hot breath on his face as in some forgotten dream. Jeremiah gathered himself from the cold rock floor, turned and stepped into the heat and the moving air and the awesome power of that which might well beat him to death.

Long hours later, he opened his eyes to morning light, saw small bare feet, slim ankles disappearing into buckskin.

"Are you all right?" The girl's voice like the call of that first, hesitant sparrow in the purple light before dawn.

He pushed himself up, his butt numb and cold against the cave floor, his face at the girl's waist.

"You stink of the guts of that Indian," he said. "We have to get you out of those clothes."

Adeline stepped back from him. Her cheeks reddened and her arms came up to cross over soft breasts. He had, once again, hurt her.

"Look, here." His head pounded, his stomach rose up and threatened to pour its contents into the cold morning air. "You and I need to form an understanding."

Adeline nodded, kept her arms over those breasts.

"I behave in ways that are a mystery to myself and to those around me and am fit company for none but the phantoms and devils which pursue me. At the earliest convenience, you and I must part company."

The girl stared at him. Silent. She cupped her elbows, rubbed palms against exposed skin and shivered.

"I got nowhere to go," she said. "Can't run the farm alone. If'n I go back, sure as winter follows fall, Brett James will take me for his wife."

"I know a couple might be happy to have you board with them for a while. The wife's lost four babes now. The husband struggles to make a life with a woman cut off from everyone and everything she loves but him. Might be they'd welcome you into their home."

She dropped her arms, exposed the delicate bones of her clavicle. "I intend to travel to San Francisco by way of the new railroad."

He stood, wiped his mouth with an open hand, clenched his hands to keep from running a finger along the hollow of her throat. Her spirit brought to mind a hungry pup that's caught the scent of fresh meat.

"How do you intend to pay for a ticket on this new transportation wonder?"

Her chin tilted up, she caught his eyes on the swell of her breasts, but did not re-cross her arms to cover herself.

"I'm young and strong. Can earn my keep and put some money away. Might be this young couple would pay for help on their homestead."

"Not likely," he said, "they barely have food enough for themselves."

Adeline met his gaze. "Pa raised me to believe in my dreams and Ma taught me to be a hard-worker. I ain't asking for charity. I'll travel with you to the next town and then we can part company, Mr. Jones."

"To my knowledge," he said, "the next town in the direction in which I'll be riding is somewhere in Texas. That's not country for young girls. You'll stay with these folks if I successfully make the arrangements. You and I will go our separate ways."

The girl turned and shuffled away from him, awkward in moccasins too big for her feet. Before he dressed her in the clothing of the dead Indian boy, while she lay vulnerable and open before him, he'd scrubbed the buckskin, wiped at the evidence of his first shot, did his best to scrub flesh and guts from the leather shirt and pants. Still, the girl trailed the scent of open bowels and rancid blood, a smell which awakened his ghosts, returned him to battle, and stripped him of all civility.

The private tapped his knuckles on the cave wall, garnered Jeremiah's attention, and shook his head.

"'Member you all the time give me a bad time 'bout how I thought our war was gonna be over and done with in time for the spring planting? You a bigger fool than me, you think you're gonna be shed a this young woman 'fore you draw your final breath."

Chapter Nine

"**H**ave yourself another little bit** and some a this here cornbread." The woman ladled beans into a brown bowl. Steam rose up spicy and glorious into Adeline's face, filled the cabin with the smell of home.

"Thank you, ma'am. I've not took nothing but hardtack for a number of days now. This here tastes real fine."

The woman swept her skirt behind her, lowered herself onto the bench across the table from the girl. "You go ahead and call me Maudie. No need for ma'am. 'Sides, you ain't much younger than I am."

"I'll be seventeen come December." The girl bit a small polite corner from the hard-as-nails cornbread, spooned more beans into her mouth. "Where's the preacher?"

The woman cocked her head to the right, stared at Adeline until the girl lifted her head from the steaming bowl and met her gaze.

"Preacher Jones is a mighty conduit for God, nobody in these parts will say different, but a child like you ought not to be traveling with him. It was Jeremiah said words over the grave of my last baby and for that I'll be forever grateful. But that preacher has a seducing spirit, especially for women what ain't fully grounded in . . . well . . . let us say in a satisfying marriage."

Food warm and solid in her belly, Adeline wanted nothing more than to lay her head on the wooden table, close her eyes and sleep warm and full. She shook herself some, roused a few of the manners her mama taught.

"I'm real sorry for the loss of your child." Adeline rubbed her eyes, hoped she didn't fall asleep before her hostess got her a bed prepared.

The woman smoothed stray strands of silver-streaked hair back up into the knot at her neck.

"I'll be twenty-two next month. Married Henry at sixteen, not long after he made it back from up north where the army done discharged him. Left Carolina one month later. Everything we owned on a mule. Nights under stars that was as bright as jewels."

"Where 'bouts are the men?" Adeline hadn't seen the preacher or the woman's husband since a few minutes after she and Jeremiah arrived, the mare slow-footed and both riders walking numb-butted. The two men had greeted each other like brothers, ventured inside the cabin long enough to shovel beans in their mouths and then disappear outside again.

"The preacher's visit makes a fine excuse for testing a new batch of whiskey. Those two'll talk war stories now 'till near daybreak."

"You got a nice place here," Adeline stifled a yawn, spooned the last of the beans into her mouth.

The woman's eyes glazed over, she slumped as though a great weight had settled on her narrow shoulders.

"We done buried four babies. One on the trail and three out yonder under that big locust tree." She looked out a small pane of glass, into the darkness of early evening.

"I'm real sorry, ma'am. Maudie. I don't guess life often works out the way we plan."

"No, it don't. But Henry and me, we still got hopes and trust in the Lord."

Maudie smiled and looked, in that moment, like a young girl instead of the tired old woman she had become.

"I guess we can't never tell what The Good Lord has in mind for us," Adeline said. "Maybe there'll be a child come along?"

The woman flinched at the words, head jerked, gaze dropped to hands that twisted into knots in the folds of her skirt.

"That ain't likely," she said, "I've not had much . . . interest here lately."

Adeline felt the heat of shame on her own face, watched as a splotchy blush spread up the neck of the woman across from her, consumed her sun-browned complexion all the way to the roots of her graying hair.

"Well, now." Maudie rose from the bench seat, rubbed palms roughly together as though grounding herself in courtesy and a brisk manner. "Let's get you settled for the night. Henry and I sleep in the loft."

Adeline followed her gaze to a platform at the back of the cabin, a crude ladder no more than six feet from where the two women stood awkwardly. The girl ached for the comforting touch of the other woman, some small hope that life would not always be as hard, as brutal as these last years since the death of her father and mother and sister. She yearned for reassurance that abandoning the farm, running from the grasping hands of Brett James and the fat madam, the terror of dark shapes in an oak-rimmed clearing, all of this would be but a passing cloud and that life would open before her like the first day of a new spring.

"I don't mind bedding down in the barn." The girl swallowed her need for a gentle touch, did her best to accept the situation the Lord provided. "If you got a extra blanket that'd be real fine."

"That won't do."

A loose strand of hair floated across the woman's cheek when she shook her head. She brushed the offending lock back, secured it into the bun at her neck.

"The preacher'll bed down in the barn. It ain't proper for you to sleep out there along with him."

Adeline had curled on the opposite side of a campfire from Jeremiah for three nights now. But in entering this small farm on the backside of the Boston Mountains, they'd returned to civilization.

Rules was rules.

"'Course not." Adeline bowed her head. "Where you want me to sleep?"

"I got an extra blanket and I'll build up the fire right good. I'll make you a bed right here at the hearth, put a hot stone at your feet like Mama always did for me on cold nights."

Adeline did her best to help Maudie prepare her bed, had barely fallen into sleep when a shuffling sound woke her. A small noise too quiet, too muted, to portent good. She opened her eyes to the embers of a dying fire. The sound came again. Just behind her head. The soft murmur of boots sneak-sliding on a plank floor. She rolled slowly to her other side, pretending sleep, heart slamming in her chest. Small, flickering flames and the glow of orange embers cast a weak light over her view.

The mottled reflection from the long barrel of a Winchester single-shot hung over the front door.

A tall, stealthy shadow reflected in the panes of the window glass beside the rifle.

Adeline had grown up with two older brothers and a whole multitude of their friends. This wasn't the first time she'd awakened to a male at her bedside with an unwelcome proposition. She kept her breath slow and calm, stretched and turned her head toward the sound of shuffling feet.

Her voice whispered in the dark. "You ought to be ashamed a yourself. Your wife sleeping not ten feet from here."

The man squatted at her head, his big toe poking through a hole in a worn boot inches from her face. Adeline wrinkled her nose at the smell, lifted herself off the mat.

He laid his hand under her chin. "Maudie's special medicine from Doc Clarkson'll keep her dreaming of dead babies 'till long after dawn."

The pulse in his squeezing palm seemed to join with the small beating of her heart at the soft indentation of her throat. His voice was young and filled with what sounded like more pain and disappointment than a body could naturally bear.

"You don't want to do this," she said.

His breath smelled of tobacco and whiskey harsh enough to scald a hog. He swayed, swung one leg over so that he straddled her, one hand still at her throat, the other hard on her wrist.

Adeline screamed into his face, now inches above hers. A hand closed over her mouth, his voice harsh in her ear.

"Shut up, goddamit! You been traveling with that preacher. Think I don't know what that means? The man's got a trail of women from here to Kin-tuck watching the road each spring for his return."

He pressed his weight against her hips, pinned her to the hard floor. With one hand he pulled her arm over her head, the other pawed at her breasts, tore the pale yellow cotton of the dress his wife had lent her not two hours earlier.

"Don't act like you don't know what I want."

At that moment, a mist of hatred and terror came together in Adeline's mind, or perhaps in her soul. Pa going off to fight a ridiculous war that weren't about nothing had to do with them. Ma giving up like that and dying. The banker and the whore and Brett James, all with their own ideas about what her life should be. The Osage thinking she was nothing more than property and plunder. This brew of rage took but an instant.

Reality devoured innocence.

The girl smiled into the face of the man whose sour breath wet her cheeks.

"I know exactly what you want," she whispered in a new voice. "I got just what you need. But Maudie just did lend me this here dress. Let me slip it off easy like and I'll give you a night you ain't gonna forget."

The woman's husband stopped his groping at her chest. He raised his head, relaxed his grip on her arm, shifted his weight just enough that Adeline slipped, laughing, from his grasp. The girl stood beside the fire, the man, still on his knees, his back to her, turning, turning slowly to watch her undress.

The stone was still warm from the fire where Maudie had plucked it, wrapped the rounded stone in a baby blanket and placed it at the girl's feet a few hours earlier. Adeline raised the hard comfort high, brought it down on the husband's head, striking him just above his cheekbone, wiping the smile of anticipation from his face. He fell to the side, lay with his knees still bent under him, his neck twisted, blood painting the wood floor.

Adeline raised the rock again.

Chapter Ten

Jeremiah **shifted his weight,** burrowed deeper into the straw of the barn's floor, hoping to find a more comfortable position for sleep.

Henry had drunk far more whiskey than was good, confessed to thoughts of saddling his horse and riding west with no more thought to his future than to escape the tiny cabin and perpetually-sad wife he would leave behind. Henry had begged the preacher to pray over him. Meaning to accomplish no more than force the man to the bed he shared with his wife to sleep off his over-indulgence, Jeremiah had laid hands on his head and formed words filtered through dry hope and bone-white acceptance of the pointlessness of all life.

The preacher listened to mice scurry busily about their nocturnal lives. Tomorrow morning, before daybreak, he'd ride away from this hard-scrabble farm, leave Adeline with this struggling family and get on with whatever existence was left to him. His lust and desire to rescue this young girl were, as the sergeant foretold, no more than his need to play God and to save himself in the process.

Vanity, vanity, all is vanity said the poet and prophet Solomon.

His mare shifted in her stall, nickered softly. Jeremiah widened his eyes to improve his night vision. What had the horse heard?

Footsteps. Running footsteps. Coming this way from the cabin.

He sat up, slipped the Colt from his jacket pocket.

The wide barn door let in the pitch black of the night, a thousand stars and the silhouette of one young girl.

She found him in the dark, ran into his arms like the seeking mouth of a babe finds his mama's breast even in the dead of night.

"There's blood," she said. "Lots a blood. I hit him."

He crushed her to him, her heart like a tiny bird fluttering against his chest. The top of her head smelled sweet, smelled like his last chance at salvation. His arms shook when he gripped her shoulders, held her away from him so he could see her face. He would protect this young woman with his life, felt alive for the first time since a thumb-sized bottle flashed a blue warning on a cold Arkansas morning.

"Slow down," he said. "Who? Who did you hit?"

"Maudie's husband. Henry. He came at me. While I slept."

He remembered the man's desperation, his own dry prayers.

Adeline burrowed into his chest. Her body trembled and he saw a new, unfurling leaf shivering in winter's last storm.

The barn door rattled in the wind. A shape blocked the stars.

A man. The silhouette of a rifle barrel leading him toward Jeremiah and Adeline.

Jeremiah bent to the girl's ear, whispered, "Stay here. Don't move." He guided her to his right, laid his palm briefly, for just a moment, against her warm cheek.

Jeremiah stepped to the left, moved fast at the man with the gun. This was no civilian. He would need to be careful. Control the Beast. Until he removed the Winchester from the hands of his target.

He ran hard at the man. Behind him and from the right came the swish of some large object slicing the air. The rifle swung toward that sound. The solid weight of Jeremiah's shoulder slammed into the man's chest. The rifle clattered onto the straw-littered floor. Jeremiah lifted the man by his shirt front. He cocked his arm and punched his fist to the man's face with all the force of his anger and failed responsibility.

The man twisted away and Jeremiah felt the hard toe of a boot against his shin. Then they were down, rolling in the straw. In the dark it was all flesh on fists and moans and hard breathing until Jeremiah stood straddle-legged, the man held against him like a lover, the barrel of the preacher's Colt tight against the man's throat.

"It ain't like she told it," Henry said. "She was waiting up for me. Begged me to lay with her and then ran when I tried to put it in."

Jeremiah's voice was like the rumble of a mountain on a moonless night.

"You asked me to pray over your hide."

He shook the young man until his arms ached from the shaking, kept the cold steel of the Colt against the man's cheek.

"It was my mistake not to properly accommodate that prayer request."

Jeremiah kicked the man in his scrotum, heard the air and life rush from him, watched silent as the form fell sideways, knees drawn to his chest. The man retched, fought to bring back his breath. The preacher stood silent, waited in the dark until the vomiting was mostly done and he believed the target thought he might someday, if he were very lucky, draw a full breath again.

He squatted beside the man's head.

"Henry? You ready to stand before the Lord an honest man, pray with me now in truth?"

The man rasped out words the preacher took as an indication that Henry was, in fact, not yet quite ready to pray from the heart. Jeremiah lifted the man by his shirt front, brought his knee deep into his gut, dropped him gasping back onto the straw.

A lantern flared yellow light behind him and Adeline's voice came to him.

"There ain't no need to kill him. Maudie won't make it here alone."

Jeremiah watched the man writhe and moan, fight to draw breath. A few feet from his bloody head laid an empty grain bucket.

"Thought I told you to stay still, not take it upon yourself to throw away good feed to create a distraction."

"Ain't but stale oats," she said in the dark to his left. "And I was aiming for his head."

"Ah huh," he said. "You did okay. What'd you hit him with back at the cabin?"

"Warming stone."

Jeremiah squatted once again at the man's head, lifted his face from the pool of vomit in which he lay.

"I feel the power of the Lord moving in me," he said flatly. "Rise up. The time has come to pray the devil from out of your soul. Are you prepared and aching for sanctification, son?"

He lifted the man to his feet, held him far enough away to avoid the strings of saliva and blood running freely from his open mouth. Henry raised his eyes to meet the preachers gaze, nodded his head.

Jeremiah secured the Colt in the waist of his trousers. From his belt, he withdrew another tool. The preacher leaned forward, touched his mouth to the man's ear.

"That's good, son. That's fine. Before we start with the Lord's work though, I got a message of a personal nature to share with you."

One quick slice and the lobe of the man's ear laid white and fleshy on the floor of the barn. Jeremiah's rage smoldered, the knife point seemed, of its own volition, to desire the soft flesh at the base of the man's throat.

The sergeant coughed up phlegm, spat into the dirty straw.

"Hey there, Preacher." The ghost laughed wetly. "That fellow there? He that much different from you? Be right careful what you do now. Could be you take his life and he'll be bunking with Gil and me."

From out of the red mist that shrunk his vision to the point of a steel blade indenting the neck of the scoundrel he held against him, came a voice of such sweetness that the preacher hesitated in his undertaking.

"Jeremiah," Maggie whispered like a cool breeze over deep, fast-running water. "Life ain't all war. There's more than one way to convert a man."

The preacher blew hard, cussed God and all that was fine and good in the world for keeping him from his desire.

"I am feeling generous this evening," he said to the man who had tried to rape and ruin the girl in his care. "The Lord gave us real clear instructions. *'If your right hand causes you to sin, cut it off and cast it from you lest your whole body perish in hell*. You remember that scripture, son?"

The man's breath was ragged. He raised his gaze to meet Jeremiah's and the fear at what he saw there shone like black pinpoints in his wide eyes.

"Listen good now. Every time you look in a mirror, or put your hand to your lopped off ear, I want you to remember this. You ever force yourself on another woman and I will return to you. I will cut your manhood from the exposed, weak sack in which it hangs. You hear me, son? You comprehend clearly what it is I'm sharing with you?"

The man nodded.

Jeremiah held the slumping body away again while bile and vomit leaked from its mouth.

"Now," the preacher said. "I believe the spirit has opened our hearts to God." Jeremiah smiled at the man. "Let us pray."

Chapter Eleven

Adeline could hear Henry fighting for breath the way a horse'll do when he's foundered. The two men, Jeremiah and Henry, stood so close in the shadows of the barn they appeared to be one two-headed beast.

"You ain't gonna kill him, are you?"

"I expect not. Go to the cabin now, Adeline, bed down with Maudie. We'll leave at first light."

She was still awake when dawn turned the lumpy quilt to tiny patchwork squares of worn reds and yellows and browns. The cabin's front door squeaked open.

"Wake her up." Jeremiah's voice carried a power that trembled Adeline's heart. The open door brought bright color into the morning. "Send the woman to the barn. The Lord has stretched out his hand and restored that which was destroyed."

She left Maudie to rise from her laudanum stupor and prepare herself for whatever it was the preacher had in mind. Adeline cooked a breakfast of cornmeal and fatback. She set the thick mush on the back of the stove to keep warm, poured the luxury of a hot cup of coffee and stepped into the morning. A few minutes later, Maudie hurried from the cabin, ran across the bare yard toward the barn without so much as a glance at Adeline.

On the eastern rise the sun caught in the bare branches of the oak and hickory. Sweeping her borrowed skirt under her, Adeline sat on the top step of the cabin's porch. She sipped what was mostly hot chicory, stared at the streaked gray of the barn and pondered if she yet knew the answer to the puzzle of this preacher, this war-damaged man, this Jeremiah. He seemed eaten alive by a power most people rarely touch. Devil, or God, or some peculiar mix of the two known only to those who walk among the dead in battle after bloody battle. She could not cipher it out.

Long shadows shrank as the sun rose up the backside of the mountain. Be he Lucifer or Michael, she was drawn to Jeremiah like she'd never been to anyone before. A line from Job spun in her mind like a stick caught in a whirlpool. *Though he slay me, yet will I hope in him.*

The barn door moaned, the sound a drawn-out wail of old wood thrown open to a fresh day. Maudie and Henry were small against the dark, yawning interior. The couple grew larger as they stumbled toward the house. Maudie's arm was around her husband supporting his weight as he limped beside her. Faces down, the two seemed to carefully place each slow step. Adeline stood, watched the preacher shut the barn's wide doors, turn, and move toward her.

"There's mush," she said when Maudie and Henry reached the porch, "and a little fatback. Made hot coffee too."

Jeremiah caught up, stood quietly behind the couple. At the bottom step, Henry glanced back at the preacher, then lifted his gaze to hers. His chest rose and fell in little panting gasps. His eyes were dark in a pale face. A thin trickle of bright red followed a jagged line of crusted blood from his missing ear lobe down under his chin and disappeared at his shirt collar.

"I'm shamed by what I done. There ain't no way to make it right, but I'm sorry as can be and I hope you'll accept the gift of my mule, Hector, as insuf . . . insufficient resti . . . restitu . . . restitution for my transgression."

A commanded recitation, no doubt of that, but the words seemed heartfelt nonetheless and she couldn't remember a time when a male of any stripe had apologized to her for, well, for anything.

"I can't take your mule." She moved to help Henry and Maudie up the steps.

Jeremiah shook his head.

"Leave 'em be, Adeline. Together, they can manage."

His voice had that deep rumble that brought to mind the growl of a painter or a bear, some large animal, wild and dangerous and on the hunt.

The preacher's dark eyes drew her in, made her notice the square of his shoulders and the scar that split his cheek and jaw. Her hand fluttered with a desire to trace that jagged white line. She pressed her palm hard against her leg, looked away, studied the fingers of light and shadow the swaying treetops painted along the side of the barn. Adeline forced herself to turn her entire body away from Jeremiah and toward the east where the sun cast gold over the mountain.

On the porch's second step, Henry clung to his wife. "You'd be doing me a favor to take the mule," he said to Adeline. "The animal tore something loose in his chest last year. Never healed right. Hector's fine for riding but can't pull a plow." He dropped his gaze. "Plus, truth be told, that mule is downright ornery with other animals."

Adeline studied the man.

"I offered the horse," he said, "but the preacher said the mule would meet your needs."

"Come on inside," she said. "The mush is gettin' cold."

"Adeline?"

Her name in the preacher's mouth stopped her dead still as she turned to go inside.

"Stay with me a moment."

A simple request.

The sun hung at the crest of the mountain, set fire to the tops of the pines. Adeline came down the steps and walked to the man who would be her salvation or destruction, she knew not which.

He smelled of blood and hay and horses and some deeper underlying scent that touched her deep in her belly, made her breath catch in her throat. Close enough to touch, yet his arms hung loosely at his sides. His eyes though, those dark hollows of pain, took her inside himself. He laid a rough palm along the curve of her cheek.

"I'm done running," he said and Adeline thought of a river butting against a child's dam, biding its time, building the energy needed to destroy the stones and mud and find its true path once more.

"I've a mind to make my stand." He stepped into her, his mouth now inches from hers, his words warm on her face. "Child, you need protection and help with the running of your farm until you're grown and can find a suitable husband. I need a place to find God or welcome the devil."

Adeline took a step back, her cheek suddenly cold with the dropping of his hand.

"I'm sixteen." She glared. "No child. And you, sir, spend a mighty amount of time wrestling with spirits to avoid what's right in front of your face."

His smile was horrible in its sadness.

"Go now, child. Eat the food you've prepared. Say goodbye to Maudie and confirm your peace with Henry. We have many miles yet to travel through country riddled with desperate Indians and, unless I've read every sign wrongly, your suitor, Brett James, is even now close enough to heap trouble on our heads."

Chapter Twelve

Bare branches scraped a low sky. Dark, gnarled fingers against clouds the color of dead ash. Jeremiah let the mare pick her way up the rocky embankment. Behind him, on the mule, Adeline sang some hymn of praise he could not place, her voice a murmur that brought to mind the rustle of a single mouse threading through dry leaves.

Deep shadows blanketed a narrow ravine on the left. Jeremiah blinked away the image of blue-coated soldiers lying in wait, the dull shine of bayonets in weak light. The notion took him that danger waited, poised, just out of sight. He drew a slow draft of crisp air, released a warmed cloud. His breath hung expectant in the bones of the woods.

The sharp rattle of leaves and thrashing of bare limbs exploded into the quiet like the crack of a rifle shot. A doe and two yearlings leaped from the hollow. The Colt pistol fit perfectly in Jeremiah's hand, aimed steady at the flash of white tails, reddish-brown rumps disappearing up the mountainside. Heart loud in his ears, jaw clenched on a bad molar, he returned the pistol to his belt.

The sergeant leaned against a dead oak, grinned up at him, saluted as the mare passed. Jeremiah fancied he saw the ghost's words float like icy vapor in the cold morning air.

"Stay alert, Preacher. Winter in these woods means they ain't no cover. Cheat Mountain to Petersburg, we fought in woods thick with new leaves."

The ghost smacked his lips, flicked a cold, slimy tongue.

Sweat trickled down Jeremiah's spine. Shadows of bare branches became bodies, grotesquely bent. A windblown hickory was a fallen private begging for water, pleading for death. The bay tossed her head, and Jeremiah picked up the sound of a creek flowing deep in a narrow ravine. He turned the mare toward the unseen water. The crunch of the mule's heavy hooves was loud on the rocky ground as the hardy animal followed the horse.

"Today's Sunday," Adeline said from behind him. "After service on Sunday, even in winter, 'less the weather was bitter, Pa'd take us young'uns on a woods tramp."

The creek grew louder as it sought its winding way toward destiny. A sense of danger, a lifting of the hairs on the back of his neck and a tightening in his gut, gathered in Jeremiah like a rising tide. He twisted his body on the mare, stared back up the ravine, searched the play of shadow and light on the hillside, found no movement, no breach of the ordinary. Yet his breathing slowed, a tingle ran from belly to hand as he caressed the curved butt of the Colt.

"I 'member there was one time where the whole bunch of us, Robert and John, Emily and Martha May and me, we was all trampin' through woods like this one here, with that beautiful silvery light we get 'round here in the winter months. Pa, he had me ridin' up on his shoulders so I couldn't a been more than four or five."

There!

Just to the left of that maple with the orange leaves still clinging to its bottom branches like a ring of fire. He squinted to the side of the flaming tree, let the corners of his eyes find their target. A shadow crept from tree to a rocky ledge. The snort of a horse raised the hairs on his arms, tipped the corners of his mouth. Jeremiah guided the mare away from the creek. The air suddenly brilliant with promise, he turned the horse and pointed her nose uphill.

"Robert and John was chunkin' hickory nuts at each other. The whole bunch of us was whoopin' and hollerin' like wild Indians. Don't know why that day stands out in my mind so."

He coaxed the horse up the hill, away from the water, until the bay stood side by side, nose to rump, tight against the mule. A fog of warmth rose from both animals, filled his nose with the honest smell of sweat. His view of Adeline shimmered, as though he saw her from a great distance, through some imperfect but glorious pane of glass.

"Stop talking, Adeline. Listen to me."

Her head came up hard, eyes gray pools of hurt, but she nodded, tugged on the reins to keep the teeth of the ornery mule away from the rump of the mare.

"Take the mule to the creek. Seek shelter. Behind a ledge, or a hole under a fallen tree. Find a hiding place. Do not move until I come for you."

If he did not come for her, all innocence would end for Adeline. This child who seemed his last hope would be cast unprotected into a hard world.

She stared at him.

"What is it? Indians?"

The spattering of freckles across her nose and cheeks darkened, stood out from her face in sharp relief as she paled.

"Jeremiah, please, I want a gun. Give me the Henry rifle."

This, the first time she'd spoken his given name.

He looked away from the softness of her cheeks, the sudden rise and fall of her breasts. Now was not the time for distraction.

"Our company is not Indian." He untied the Henry, handed it to her like passing on a hard-won inheritance.

Reaching across the small space between them, he tilted her face to his.

"Hide. That's your best defense. If it comes to it, do not, under any circumstances, fight fair. Shoot the enemy in the back. There is no fair. Aim and pull the trigger until the attacker is dead. Nothing less. Do you understand?"

She nodded. Her hold on the rifle whitened her knuckles, widened her eyes.

He leaned through the wavering light between them, touched his mouth to her warm cheek.

"Do not think, Adeline. Aim and shoot."

She traced the scar along the side of his face, touched her mouth to his so quickly he wondered if it had truly happened.

"Yes," she said. "Aim and shoot. God protect you, Jeremiah."

Her words startled, came to him more curse than blessing.

"God has nothing to do with this." His voice flat and mean even to his own ears. "This is about killing. And dying. Now go. Do as I tell you. Find shelter and wait for me to finish this."

Her face splotched red. Her lips, usually full and soft, became thin and stubborn hard. She pressed her mouth together, sat up straight on the mule's spade back.

"I will not hide like a child while you fight my battles."

The trouble with traveling with a woman instead of fellow soldiers was that the contrary creatures always question orders, appear indeed to misunderstand the entire concept of chain of command. This misconception gets people killed. He had no more time for niceties.

The mule, eager for a cool drink, snorted and lowered his wide head, refused her instruction to turn away from the water. The flat of Jeremiah's hand on the mule's rump was loud and sharp.

"Heyah! Get up, mule."

The mule startled, broke into a trot toward the creek, the girl low over the animal's neck as though whispering threats into the big ears.

The horse responded to the pressure of Jeremiah's knees by slipping sideways. The mare regained her footing and pushed hard up the hill toward what Jeremiah could now see were three distinct shapes positioning themselves behind the dark trunks of maple and oak at the narrow ridgeline. Three to his one and the enemy had the high ground.

Warmth flooded Jeremiah, flowed energy to his very fingertips. His smile hurt his cheeks. The Enfield slipped to his shoulder like a favorite child cradled against a loving parent. A rebel yell burst from him, filled the woods with terrible joy. The mare scrambled on the sharp incline, fought to carry him to his fate.

A bullet sang past his left ear and the preacher laughed that he still rode hard, the bay's nose aimed straight for the enemies' center, her hooves pounding with the beat of his heart. A man with a feather tucked into the band of his porkpie hat leaped into the saddle of a piebald. The spotted horse reared and the enemy pulled strong on the reins to regain control. Jeremiah sighted casually up the barrel of the Enfield. The rifle kicked against his shoulder. The mare skittered sidewise with the jolt.

The arched neck of the piebald disappeared, the rider's chest and face hidden in a spray of blood and gore. The spotted horse fell screaming, slid down the backside of the ridgeline. Jeremiah rode through the smoke, sheathed the Enfield and pulled the Colt. Joined in joy and awe and power by Gil and the sergeant and a multitude of roaring soldiers dead these long four years, he nudged the mare directly at an enemy standing wide-legged on the narrow ridge.

The man extended a wavering pistol. "We don't want trouble with you, sir. We's a part a the James gang. Just give us the girl!"

Jeremiah pressed the trigger of his pistol and the other man staggered. His gun dropped to the ground. The preacher reined the horse beside the enemy who swayed on his feet, looked up at Jeremiah.

"Coming up against a man with a gun is some different from blowing trains or robbing fat bankers, wouldn't you say, son?"

The man opened his mouth. White flashed wide around his eyes.

Jeremiah's shot entered at the bridge of his flared nose. The man fell backward, arms flung wide in the dead leaves of a passing autumn.

The preacher's gaze searched the naked woods for the third man. A woman's scream came from behind. The mare turned sharp at his command. Something hit hard at Jeremiah's shoulder and he toppled from the horse. The sound of a shot rang clear in his ears, caught up to the pain in his chest, as flashing hooves filled his vision.

The girl. Adeline. It was Adeline. A second scream echoed and then darkness swallowed him.

Chapter Thirteen

At the first shot, the stubborn mule quickened his awkward trot toward the creek, refused Adeline's demand to turn back toward the fight. Bare limbs and rough brush tore past, gouged at her chest and arms and face, tore at the rifle clutched in her right hand.

A full-throated rebel-yell that seemed to her filled with joy and terror and awe flooded the woods. Adeline shivered, clung low to the neck of the mule. The animal shied, side-stepped, ran full-speed into a low-hanging oak branch. The limb, thick as a man's forearm, struck her chest like the swing of a club. The rifle flew from her hand. She fell. The rocky ground slammed against her back, stole her breath. Frantic for something to grab, to break her slide, she flailed, slid down the hill's steep side.

From the ridgeline came the explosion of a rifle shot, the scream of a horse. Adeline skidded into a moss-gray boulder, fought to catch her breath. She pressed her hand to a shattering pain at the back of her head, blinked stupidly at the red blood that covered her palm. She struggled to her feet, aimed herself at the shooting on the ridgeline and ran, fell, got up and ran on.

"We don't want trouble with you, sir. Just give us the girl." The words were frightened and mean and pleading, all at the same time.

A pistol shot and she was at the crest of the hill in time to see the preacher's mare run fast toward a man standing wide-legged on the narrow ridge even as the man fell backward, arms out to his sides. From up out of the hollow behind the preacher, appearing as if in a dream of jagged pictures and jumbled thoughts, rose a black gelding, the horse's face split with a lightning-bolt of white. The rider, the brim of a hat pulled low, lifted his face and grinned wide when he saw her.

Adeline's heart pounded in her ears, drowned out all thought, all feeling. Her feet felt buried on the ridgeline, as though movement would require the digging away of layers upon layers of ancient dirt that trapped and imprisoned. Brett James sat the gelding, a rifle balanced in the crook of his left arm. A dirty-brown bandage wrapped his right hand. The gun shifted until the long barrel aimed at the preacher. She watched the preacher's bay mare—a hard, sweaty knot of muscle and courage—turning slowly, as though in a dream, toward the aiming rifle.

Adeline screamed.

James took the time to throw his head back and laugh before squeezing the trigger. She was still staring at the breathy cloud swirling around James's laughing face when the preacher fell from his horse. The ringing of the shot echoed in the naked woods, stole her hearing and her reason.

That same quiet rage she felt bringing the warming stone down onto the head of Maudie's husband now poured like kerosene onto the fire of her hatred for Brett James. In contempt and carelessness he had bruised her arm with his fingers, forced his tongue deep into her gagging mouth and given her a taste of what life would be as his wife. Now, on this cool morning in November, James had shot the preacher. Jeremiah. The rifle blast still ringing in her ears, the cloud of James's breath settling over him like the devil's own blessing, in that moment, Adeline accepted her love for the wounded man lying on the ground beside the bay.

Brett James seemed to study on her, standing there in the woods in a borrowed yellow dress. She stood solid, glared into his face. A few feet away Jeremiah's mare tossed her head, shuffled sideways to put herself between James and her rider. On the ground beside his horse, Jeremiah moaned.

James grinned. "Good to see you, Adeline. It ain't good, you running from your soon-to-be husband."

"You can force me to be your wife," she said to the man astride the dark horse. "But, sooner or later, I will find a way to kill you."

Another groan from the preacher set loose a flood inside her belly. She ran toward where he lay.

"Leave him be!" Brett James dismounted, his voice tight and mean.

Adeline paid him no mind. She was drawn to Jeremiah in some way she did not understand and did not care to sort out now, knew only that she would do whatever needed doing to get to this man. But James was closer, and faster. He stood squarely between her and Jeremiah, held his arms out to Adeline. Winked. She turned away, saw in that instant the life that would be hers if ever those arms closed around her.

She ran, leaves slick under her feet, slipped on the uneven ground, fell and rolled down the backside of the ridge.

"It ain't no use for you to run." His laughter like broken glass and ruined dreams. "I'll find you and have you. After that, we'll see how nice you can be. Decide if I want to marry you or give you to Rose. The old whore offered me a twenty-dollar gold piece. Said she didn't even care how much I'd enjoyed your charms afore delivery."

Adeline shivered, clung to the steep hillside. In the deep shadow of a hollow where the wind had toppled a hickory tree, a man lay pinned under a dead horse.

In that moment, time froze.

Adeline was reminded of Joshua commanding the sun to stop its path across the sky. For the first time since Jeremiah had slapped his open palm to the rump of her mule and disappeared up the hollow, her mind cleared of fear. She felt the cold threat of a storm teasing her face, saw pewter light slanting low through bare woods. A smell like that of butchering done badly mixed with that of rotting leaves and black powder smoke hung in the still air.

Adeline stood in the moment and felt herself branded forever. Knew that for the rest of her life, this exact slant of shimmering light in winter woods, the bite of an approaching storm on her bare face, would set her right back here in these woods staring at this man pinned under this piebald horse. She shivered, forced herself to look upon the scene.

The man's face and chest were naught but blood and what looked like the makings of the sausage ma made from the hog killed early each winter. His porkpie hat perched firm on his head, a hawk's feather set rakish in the band. Just beyond his right hand, which was thrown over his head as though he thought to reach for it, laid a dull-gray pistol.

That feather, stuck nonchalant in a hat band, the man's one vanity maybe, it was the sight of the feather that hit like getting the wind knocked from her body. Adeline gasped, bent double and vomited into the leaves at her feet. Twice in a week now she'd stood spraddle-legged in terror and thrown up the meager contents of her stomach. She was getting a mite disgusted with fear, beginning to think anger a good and fine substitute.

"Get on up here, girl." James's voice was calm. She could tell he was smiling. "I want you to watch me shoot this here preacher. Be nice now and I'll let you decide if'n I should gut shoot the bastard or just end it quick-like with a bullet to his pretty face."

On her hands and knees, Adeline scrambled toward the gun.

"You go to hell, Brett James."

Pa always said the skill of shooting was unsuitable for a young woman. But, over the years, she'd watched Pa and her brothers closely. Though she'd never fired a gun, she knew well enough how to point and pull the trigger. The pistol heavy and cold in her hand, she crawled back up the hill toward Jeremiah and the man she would kill. Sooner or later, whatever happened in the next few minutes, she would kill Brett James. Of that she had no doubt.

James was bent over Jeremiah, reaching for the preacher's Colt when Adeline stepped onto the ridgeline about a barn's length in front of him. *Aim and shoot, Adeline. Do not think. Just aim and shoot.* She brought the heavy pistol up and fired at James's chest.

His eyes widened and then a horrible grin spread across his face.

"Best not to play with that gun, sweet Adeline."

Aim and shoot. She steadied the pistol, pulled the trigger again. A chunk of bark flew from a tree to James's right. The black gelding startled and ran. Jeremiah's mare tossed her head but stood solid.

Brett stood, pointed a pistol at Jeremiah where he lay on his side, one knee bent oddly behind him, blood leaking into the ground at his chest. Adeline exhaled, aimed for James' black heart and squeezed the trigger.

A tiny spot of blood appeared high on his left thigh.

He blinked.

The stain spread.

Brett James staggered and leaned against the scaly bark of an oak.

A strange power flooded her senses, blocked all but the feel of that curved metal under her finger, the line of sight down the barrel of the gun. Adeline adjusted her aim and pulled the trigger again.

A second stain appeared high on the left side of James's chest. The pistol dropped from his fingers.

He fell to his knees.

"Adeline? Help me. I never meant you no harm, girl." He swayed, crumbled and slid a few feet down into the hollow.

He lay silent.

She ran to Jeremiah, knelt and pressed her ear to his chest.

"No. No. No. Please God, no."

Her mind left her then. A howl, insane and wild as that of a wolf, filled the air. Her throat grew raw with grief and rage and terror and still she screamed. From afar she saw a lunatic smear dirt onto her wet face; grind dead, crushed leaves into yellow hair. She watched this insane young woman cover a man's body with her own, heard her screams become whimpers.

There came eventually, into that dark, crazed time, the knowledge that she must either return to herself or disappear forever into a desolate land.

It was then she heard the whisper of movement through heavy brush, looked up to see a bloody scalp adorned with the feather of a hawk hanging from the belt of an Osage brave wearing a porkpie hat and casually cradling Jeremiah's rifle.

Chapter Fourteen

"**We go now.**" The Indian spoke casually, as though exchanging pleasantries with Adeline at a church picnic.

Frozen in place, there in the winter woods, shielding Jeremiah's body with her own, Adeline could not look away from the scalp hanging from the waist of the brave. The rusty smear of the crinkly skin, the matted hair the color of an old hickory nut.

"Leave him." The Indian pointed his chin toward Jeremiah.

From somewhere deep inside, Adeline heard the soft click of a door closing, locking this moment away forever. She blew like a winded horse, forced her gaze away from the scalp and looked into the eyes of the Osage warrior who had, not that long ago, helped to kidnap her in a clearing at daybreak.

"You speak English?"

The Indian nodded. His eyes were as black as stones at the bottom of a winter creek. Low light through bare branches striped him in shadows.

"Blackrobes stole me when I was nine. Grandmother was a white slave."

If the Indian's face held any emotion, Adeline could not identify it. The brave appeared carved of some hard, dark wood, seemed some unknowable part of the forest around them.

He stretched his hand to her. "Come."

The smell of bear grease wafted from the Indian, threatened her stomach. A low moan, barely audible, came from man whose body she protected.

"Jeremiah?"

She laid a hand on Jeremiah's cheek. His eyes fluttered.

"Maggie?"

That one word, like a knife.

"It's Adeline." She smoothed hair from his forehead, looked up at the Indian standing over her. "I will not leave him."

"You can do him no good." The Indian did not move.

The pronouncement sent a shiver along her spine. She shook off the premonition, stared hard at the brave.

"I will not leave him," she said again.

Jeremiah groaned, shifted against her. The Indian smiled, teeth white in a dark face.

"I am called Montega. In your language, New Arrow."

Her heart pounded loud in her ears. The chirping of birds, wind rustling the tree tops, the voice of the Indian, everything came to her dulled and from some far away land that did not matter, did not even maybe exist. She blinked, gathered up her thoughts like rounding hens for the night pen. To save Jeremiah, she would need help.

She looked up into the Indian's dark eyes. "I'm Adeline. You are Osage?"

"Osage, yes." He stared at her, silent, unmoving.

She did not drop her gaze. Jeremiah trembled and then lay still.

"Please. Help me with him."

"We help each other." A statement, solid and unyielding, leaving no room for negotiation. "A baby comes soon, before the first hard frost. My sister and me, we are alone with no woman to help."

Adeline nodded.

The Indian, Montega, extended his hand. She raised up onto her knees, the two of them on that lonely ridgeline, a young woman in a borrowed yellow dress and an Osage brave with a bloody scalp still dripping against the buckskin of his leggings, the two shook hands like fat men concluding the sale of a horse.

"Maggie?" Jeremiah's voice weak as though calling from a dream.

"Hold him steady." Montega knelt beside her, pulled his knife and slit the cloth over the preacher's bent leg. He waited until she pressed her weight against Jeremiah's upper body pinning the wounded man to the ground the best she could.

The Indian's movement was hard and quick. Jeremiah's scream a sharp cry of pain that pierced the quiet of the woods. When Montega rose, the preacher's leg was more or less straight.

"The wound here." He touched Jeremiah's bloody shoulder. "The bullet passed through. If it does not fester, it will heal. Do not let him move."

The Indian rose and stepped behind her to the body of the man she had watched Jeremiah shoot in the face. She twisted around, saw the Indian draw a knife, bend at the waist over the dead man. Adeline turned quickly away. Some things were best left hidden.

"Jeremiah?"

His breath was shallow, but his eyes had cleared.

"Child?" The word so soft she leaned forward and laid her ear just above his mouth, his words warm and soft on her cheek. "Go. Leave. You cannot save me and I will bring you harm."

Night came early this late in the year and clouds were a low, dark ceiling that blocked all view of the sky. She put it at less than two hours before darkness overtook them. She stared deep into Jeremiah's eyes.

The words sprang from her mouth like unexpected mice from a grain sack. "Who's Maggie?"

The preacher sighed, dropped his hand from her cheek.

"A woman I betrayed." He turned his face from her, seemed to gather his thoughts, looked up at her again. "Run, child. You are in grave danger."

"The Indian and I made a pact. He needs me to help birth his sister's baby. He won't do me harm."

He lifted his hand to her forearm, squeezed with more strength than she thought he possessed at the moment. His voice came hard. She thought of an old branch that snaps with the slightest pressure, its core dead and wasted.

"Run, child. It is not the Indian who will betray you."

The hills to the west were crowned with the sinking sun when the Indian led the way, his red stallion threading a path through bare woods.

Jeremiah's bay mare trotted beside the roan, the reins of her bridle held loosely in the hands of Montega. Adeline walked beside the mule, spoke softly to the man on the travois dragged behind.

"Hang on now. The Indian says we ain't got far to go." Her words no more than a hypnotic drone in her ears. "If he don't kill us both, you and me, we'll head on back to the farm. How's that? I don't have to worry none about Brett James. Not no more."

Jeremiah moaned at each jerk and bounce of the travois.

As though looking through a dusty pane of glass into another world, Adeline watched the flash of a cardinal in the underbrush. The bird flitted in the dull leaves of a buffaloberry bush, the fruit, which she knew to be red, robbed of color by the woods' deep shade. She felt as she had as a child, waking fevered in the night, her familiar world somehow changed. Her soul adrift in a dream world where her mind could not follow.

"I killed him." Her voice came from far away, as if some other person spoke with her words. "You said aim and shoot. And that's just what I done. I pointed and pressed the trigger. There was blood. Did you see the blood, Preacher? Red like a rose blooming there on his chest."

"Listen to me, child." Jeremiah's voice found her, drew her back to the bitter cold of the winter woods, the tingling numbness of her hands and feet. "'Sufficient unto the day is the evil thereof.' You did that which was required. Tonight dwell only on living. Sunrise will soon enough bring its own troubles."

They came to the clearing under a vault of stars, the full moon making smoke of the dirt stirred by the rough travois dragging behind the mule.

A lean-to appeared in the shadows of the loblolly pines on the far side. At the opening of the rough shelter, a young Indian woman bent double, her palm pressed against her swollen belly.

Montega turned on the horse's back, spoke to Adeline.

"Go." He pointed with his chin to the travois where Jeremiah lay moaning. "I will care for him."

Adeline looked at Montega and knew four lives were at stake here.

The woman at the flap of the lean-to looked already far gone into childbirth. Her thick hair hung limp, eyes set deep in a face swollen from what Adeline assumed was hours of pain. This young Indian woman was in trouble with birthing this child, of that there was no doubt. If she died, the child would likely die with her and then Montega would surely kill both her and Jeremiah.

Adeline gripped the mule's lead-line in her hand. As a child she'd spent a hot summer day under the porch watching a hound give birth to five wet pups. She'd seen cows and pigs drop their young. And then of course, in the dead of winter, with no help coming, she had birthed her younger sister. She swallowed her panic, felt again the warm pressure, the slippery cord pulsing under her fingers, tight around the neck of the tiny Lily Rose.

The squaw cried out, one sharp exhalation that clenched Adeline's own stomach. She dropped the reins to the ground and ran to the woman at the lean-to.

Chapter Fifteen

Jeremiah's head ached. His leg throbbed as though a rodent, trapped deep in the bone, gnawed, squirmed, chewed. The thought brought battlefield images of rats fleeing in a dark, undulating carpet as flames rose high from the burning bodies of the dead horses. He squinted against the vision, cursed God for returning him to his tormented mind and ragged soul.

Breathing through his mouth, he focused his pain on the small fire throwing shadows onto the face of the Indian across from him.

"How long I been fading in and out?" Jeremiah sucked air deep into his lungs, grounded himself in wood smoke overlaying the sharp, cold bite of piney woods.

"Three nights." The Indian sat still as stone.

The preacher felt again each bump of the travois, heard the girl's steady chatter, the scrape of the mule's hooves on rocky ground, saw, as through river mist on a cold morn, their arrival at this clearing. Three days?

A woman's scream tore the darkness.

"Where is the girl? Adeline?" He lifted himself from the ground where he lay stretched like an invalid. Pain stabbed his head, sliced through his chest. For a moment—a long, black, jagged moment—he believed the Indian had simply shot him, ended his struggles. Then the pain released him just enough to remind that he had still a ways to travel before the escape of death. He slumped back onto the ground.

The Osage squatted beside him, held a shallow chipped bowl to his mouth. "Drink. It eases pain. Your woman is safe. It is my sister, Niabi, whose screams you hear."

"Where are the rest of your tribe?"

The Indian returned to his place on the other side of the fire, lowered himself again into a pose of such stillness that Jeremiah blinked to convince himself he gazed not at cold stone, but at a living being.

"I am Montega. My people are gone. The buffalo killed. The fire that burns the spirit and marks the body with the deep bites of death took many. Bluecoats killed others."

Long, piercing screams sliced the night, sent shivers dancing along Jeremiah's spine. Montega raised his eyes, stared toward the edge of the clearing. Sparks from the fire winked between the men for an instant, then disappeared into the black night.

"Niabi will not live." The Indian's words fell like sharp stones. "She is weak from hiding in these woods, moving always to avoid the soldiers. The child will go with her into the spirit world."

A centuries-old lament rose unbidden from Jeremiah's mouth. "*A voice is heard in Raman, mourning and great weeping, Rachel weeping for her children and refusing to be comforted, because her children are no more.*"

Montega lifted his gaze from the fire, stared directly into Jeremiah's face. "And your people, who also fought the bluecoats? Where are they?"

"Gone. All. Gone." Jeremiah concentrated on the pounding pain in his leg, hoping to drive from his mind the slow-motion fall of Maggie, sinking to the planks of the porch, that twinkle of blue still clutched in her soft hand. He shut that mental door firmly, forced himself to meet the eyes of the Indian.

The screams from the lean-to grew weaker, no longer piercing, but now the soft moans that humans utter when death's light finds them.

"Your sister's name is Niabi?"

"In your language, Fawn. A bad totem for these times."

"And Montega? What does that mean in my tongue?"

"I am New Arrow."

"Perhaps a more fortuitous moniker." Jeremiah adjusted his throbbing leg, rode out the pain the movement brought. "Appointed by Jehovah. That's the meaning of my name. Though for what I've been blessed or chosen, I cannot tell you."

A glowing branch collapsed in the fire's center. Sparks leapt into the blackness. Jeremiah accepted Montega's prediction of what this night would bring. Death for another woman and for a child who would not draw breath. The world is a cold and brutal place and God a jealous and cruel being who delights in punishing equally those he calls his children and those his counselors insist He does not claim.

"Death finds us all." Jeremiah said.

He studied the hard lines of Montega's face, the sharp cheekbones, hatchet nose and the jagged white line down the man's right cheek, a near-twin of Jeremiah's own scar. From the pines behind him came the private's high-pitched giggle and the choking rasp of the sergeant's laughter.

"Death finds us all," Jeremiah said again. "You could have gathered two more scalps. My own flowing locks," he grinned at the Indian. "And the hair of Brett James. Could have taken the girl for your own. Why help us? Why bring us here if you knew your sister, Fawn, and her unborn child were marked for death?"

The sounds coming from the lean-to were so muted now that Jeremiah had to strain to make them out over the low crackling of the fire, the settling of charred wood.

Montega sat perfectly still. A skill Jeremiah had often noticed of Indians in general and one he coveted greatly.

"The spirit led me to you." The Indian's voice pitched low, his words slow. "Your woman, Adeline, she and I are joined somehow. In what way I do not yet know."

Jeremiah leaned forward until heat burned his face. "That child, Adeline, is under my protection."

The dark man raised his eyes, stared across the fire. "You and I, Jeremiah Jones, we are both warriors. Let us not be enemies. I seek an alliance."

Jeremiah spoke softly, fingered the empty knife sheath at his waist. "I'm not so far gone in my injuries that I don't see the way you look at that child. Leave her be. She's been through far too much already and now she's been forced to kill a man. That act will mark her, scar her soul. Do not place obstacles in her path."

"You see not my heart, but the reflection of your own. The blackrobes say that teaching is in your own book. Is it not?"

Montega unfolded himself effortlessly from the squat he had maintained throughout the conversation. "I go now to Niabi, to release her to the spirits."

He stared down at Jeremiah. "Your woman did not kill that man."

Jeremiah's heart slowed, an expectant calm descended upon him, he twisted his neck to look up at Montega. "What do you mean?"

"That fine horse with the fire-bolt blaze? Would I have left that animal if he wandered alone in the woods?"

"You were anxious to return here." Even as Jeremiah spoke the words, he understood their falseness. "Your sister and her child are far more important than any horse."

The Indian's teeth flashed in the night. "You know our ways better than that. Besides, I have long hunted the men who sought your woman. The three came upon Niabi while I hunted." He fingered the scalps at his belt. "Niabi's passage tonight is only the end of a long dying."

Jeremiah did not turn to watch Montega stride toward the death that awaited his ministrations in the lean-to. He adjusted his throbbing leg, stared through dancing sparks out into the moonless depths.

Winter woods are silent, blank and hungry.

Chapter Sixteen

The child slid from between the woman's bloody thighs. Not much bigger than a hound pup, he lay still as death in Adeline's cupped hands. She lifted the infant, sucked gently at the nostrils the way she'd seen Pa do to remove the phlegm and liquid from Bessie's first calf. Adeline spit into the dirt of the lean-to, brought the tiny face toward hers again. The small weight in her hands shifted slightly, the baby's chest rose. Fell. Rose again. A mewling cry brought tears to Adeline's eyes.

Chants filled the coppery air.

Adeline lay beside the dying woman, positioned the child at his mother's breast. Small as he was, the baby sucked greedily, pulling the brown nipple completely into his mouth, gulping, kneading his mother's breast as if he knew this would be his last and only contact with the woman who would die bringing him into the world.

It had taken three days to coax this too-small infant from the womb. Three bloody nights and scream-filled days of pain and a need for strength the mother did not have to give and knowledge sixteen-year-old Adeline did not carry. Lying beside the babe's mother, fatigue washed over Adeline like the settling of a warm blanket. She stretched her legs. Exhaustion swept her into dreamless sleep.

She opened her eyes to bright light around the edges of a blanket hung from bent pine saplings at the opening of the makeshift hut. Adeline struggled to find her place in the world. The smell of blood. She brought her hands to her face and stared blankly at the rusty stain, the caked brown under each nail.

The Indian woman. And the child. Had the mother and the naked, mewling infant died while she slept?

Jeremiah? If the woman and child were dead, had Montega killed a wounded and weakened Jeremiah in retaliation? And what then were the Indian's plans for her?

These thoughts rushed and scattered through her mind as she scrambled from the lean-to and stepped out into a morning that stunned and blinded with stark, clear air.

"Jeremiah!" She ran. "Jeremiah!"

The Indian stepped out of the winter woods and into the clearing. His scalplock glistened in the day's bright light. He wore a loin cloth over deerskin leggings. His ears reflected the blue-green of turquoise and, together with the reflection from the silver at his neck, gave off a soft glow. He seemed a prince of the woods. A terrifying prince.

He extended his hand to her. "Come. We release Niabi and the child."

She froze in place. That the mother would die Adeline had accepted. But the child? The child had died?

Montega must have cleaned up for the ceremony, which made sense. Didn't whites put on their Sunday best to attend a funeral? Still there was something odd about seeing the Indian dressed like this while she stood, smeared with dried blood and reeking of sweat, her hair ratted around her face.

The blood on her hands and arms had tightened and puckered her skin as it dried. She wanted, more than anything right that moment, to wash the horrible stuff off, to cleanse herself of the nightmare of the last three days. More. To cleanse herself of everything, every moment, from the desperate time she'd leaped onto the preacher's mare until that instant, standing in a clearing covered in muck and death looking into the eyes of an Indian who held her life in his hands.

She wanted to run. Every muscle was poised to run.

"Where's Jeremiah?" She made herself stare into the Indian's dark eyes. "Did the child die in the night? While I slept"

Three days and nights of struggle and she had fallen asleep and left the child alone in the end.

"Your man is here. I have given him a potion to help with the pain. Come." Again the Indian extended his hand to her. "The child is not meant to live. He will go with Niabi into the spirit world."

A cry leaked into the clearing. She envisioned a tiny fist kneading at his mother's breast, eyes squeezed shut and mouth searching for comfort and sustenance. Adeline ran toward the sound. Montega stepped between her and the crying.

"We have no way to feed this child."

His words, it seemed to her, held no sadness, just an understanding of the way of the world as though he were instructing her that, winter snow must always follow the sweet days of autumn.

She pushed past the Indian who stood like a statue at the edge of the woods. Adeline followed the sharp cries of the child her hands had cradled, helped with his passage into the world. A hundred yards into the woods, raised on a narrow platform and fitted into the hollow of a pine, laid the Indian woman known as Niabi. She was wrapped in a trading blanket, silver glowed warm at her ears and throat. Under the blanket, at her breast, plaid wool rippled with the struggling of the child.

Adeline unfolded the edge of the blanket, lifted the squirming, naked baby and pressed him to the warmth of her own chest. The child's cries grew louder. Behind her came the voice of Montega.

"You believe you do good. But you rob Niabi of the comfort of the child on her passage. The boy is the seed of great sin and misery. You will bring him only pain."

She swirled around, the thin cloth of her skirt stirring the dust and leaves of the woods, the child squirming in her arms.

"You! You and Jeremiah both! You think yourselves wise with your superior man-wisdom. You pretend that the right path is to surrender to pain and sorrow, to accept that there is no justice, no good in the world, no joy in life."

She stomped and dust rose around her ankles. For the first time since her mad dash from sleep, she realized her feet were bare, the soles cut and painful from her sprint through the rocky path into the woods. The naked child squirmed and fussed in her arms.

"I will not leave this child. You!" She pointed her finger at Montega, pretended she did not notice the way the hand trembled. "You go. Pray to the Great Spirit or whatever it is you call God in your language. Wake Jeremiah. Tell him to pray to Jesus and Jehovah God Himself. We leave now. My family's farm is less than day's ride away."

Montega did not move.

She had no defense against tomahawk or arrow or knife or gun. If the Indian did not allow her passage, she had no power to enforce her plan, no way to save herself or the child.

She filled her lungs with cold air, felt herself swell with resolution.

"I will not leave the child. If life is no more than survival, then you may kill me now and my death be on your soul."

Part II

Freshwater, Arkansas

March 1870

Chapter Seventeen

Bum leg propped on an oak round softened with a folded quilt, Jeremiah adjusted his butt in the narrow chair, studied the new day from the cabin's front porch. Morning sun soothed the night's aches and pains, hot coffee softened with goat's milk warmed him. Whiskey would warm deeper, but Adeline had, early on, banned that particular remedy from her home. Soon as he could straddle a horse, he'd be on his way to his yearly preaching circuit. First stop would be the procurement of a bottle or two of the good stuff to ride along with him, warm those chilly nights when he wasn't bringing truth and grace to some comely congregant.

His need for movement clawed at his nerves. Early March and here he sat. Like a society lady's castrated house cat. Spring was the time of battles. The earth's very smell carried him back to cornfields scythed with cannon balls, terror and panic and rage wrapped tight with the sweet scent of peach blossoms and the tender green of new life rising from ground enriched with men's blood and dreams. He cursed himself for a fool whose need to play God with a young girl had imprisoned him in a trap with teeth no less sharp and tearing for being soft and beautiful.

Brilliant red flashed in the new green of the oak beside the house and a Cardinal's call of *purdy, purdy, purdy* mixed with the morning sounds of domesticity. From the cabin at his back came the cooing, gurgling of the child harmonizing with Adeline's low humming of *Jesus, lover of my soul*. A warm breeze fluttered the tops of the hickories. Wood smoke hung thick in the morning sun and the smell of frying venison wafted from the open door to his right.

Jeremiah massaged the calf of his bad leg, swallowed coffee to push back the bile that rose in his throat, the scent of burning horses, the crackling sound of wounded dying in the rushing fires at the battle survivors called The Wilderness. His right hand dropped to his pocket, caressed the familiar comfort of a silver locket. The sergeant and Gil wavered in the yard's smoke and sunlight, threatened to materialize and stroll over for a morning visit.

"Jeremiah—"

The threat came from behind him, movement from out of his blind spot. He swung his arm in a vicious upward swipe, instinctively cutting off the attack on his right.

Adeline cried out, pressed the baby tight to her breast. The boy's wails joined those in his head. The swish of pale blue cotton around bare ankles and she stepped away, turned her back to him.

"I only wanted to know if you could hold William for a moment."

"Sorry." What else could he say? How to explain himself to this woman-child who had never seen battle?

He did not belong around normal people. Broken, that's what he was. Not fit for good company. A few inches. That's what had separated the woman and child from a ruining blow dealt by a madman. He wiped his palms on his pants, pasted what he hoped was a look of civility, of sanity, on his countenance.

Adeline stood with her back to him, her body curled over the child riding the swell of her hip. She leaned away, still as death, the wailing child held tight. The scalding fear and confusion in her gray eyes triggered in him rage and pain and then, finally, the calming blackness of emotional death.

He made his voice hard and flat. "You mustn't sneak up on me like that, Adeline."

He waited until she exhaled the breath she'd been holding. Finally, after what felt like a lifetime, she turned toward him. Her braid swung like a rope. He thought to pull her to him, run his fingers through the woven gold, untangle each strand. A vision born of desire and pain flowed full-blown into his head, thickened his loins. He imagined her hair spread on a soft pillow, gray eyes looking up at him in trust and healing welcome.

She stared hard at him. "You all right, Jeremiah?"

"I'm no better than yesterday, no worse than tomorrow. Give me Billy Boy." He reached for the child with arms that had moments ago meant to kill and maim.

She did not move, only studied him the way a mama bear will study a hunter caught too close to her cubs. He exhaled hard into the cool morning, met her gaze through the veil of vapor his breath created. Her smile was tentative but she moved toward him.

"I'm fine now, Adeline. You just startled me before. Please. Give me the boy."

"Don't let him spill that now," she said of the pap-boat she'd fashioned of an old teapot.

She adjusted the pudgy baby in his arms, kissed first the child and then her warm mouth touched Jeremiah's forehead, her hand flitted at his shoulder.

"Good morning to you, Jeremiah," she said as though this were an ordinary morning, as if he had not, moments before, lashed out from a battle fugue and nearly struck her and the wide-eyed child. "Breakfast'll be ready in a few minutes."

He looked down to cover his relief at her trust in him.

"What is she feeding you, Billy Boy?" he swirled the brownish contents of the pap-boat.

"Don't call him that. His name is William. After Pa. Names that fall on a child have a way of sticking for life. His name is William."

"The babe has drunk goat's milk since his first suck." He tickled the child under the chin and the baby cooed and waved his arms. "You're naught but a tiny billy goat," he said to the baby. To Adeline he said, "Soon as Billy can walk, I've no doubt he'll be following that nanny around the yard baaing maaaamaaaa."

Adeline's laugh always reminded him of church bells—tinkling, ringing, building to the fine, clear joy of a new day.

"Well, now," she said, "today I've spiced his milk with a little venison broth, could be he'll be chasing after deer next."

His gaze met hers at the instant her eyes clouded. Was she seeing the Indian woman named Fawn, Niabi, the child's mother she'd tried so hard to save? Did she carry with her the image of the woman lying dead, wrapped in a ragged trade-blanket, the infant strapped to her still chest?

"You rescued her child," he said.

He'd lain drugged and woozy, listened while a mere girl had not so much argued with an Indian brave over the fate of the child as instructed the Osage on precisely what he was to do, and do quickly. Why the warrior had agreed to her plan he did not know, though he suspected strongly that despite all the shaman talk of fate and co-joined spirits, the Indian was motivated by the same lust that spiced his own blood.

Adeline stared across the dirt yard, appeared to watch the rising sun push night shadows from the eastern mountain tops. Montega strode from beside the house, his arms filled with wood like an offering to some pagan goddess of fire. Jeremiah shook his head at his own mental fancy of tribute to sensual deities. He nonetheless glared hard at the Indian. The brave turned his face to Jeremiah as he moved up the steps of the house on his two good and sound legs. The sly savage winked, his grin wide.

"Thank you, Montega," Adeline said. "You can put the wood down 'side the stove. I'll have breakfast ready in a few minutes. Did you get back this morning? I didn't hear you ride in."

Adeline touched the Indian's brown arm as he passed in a gesture Jeremiah hoped was that of a sister to a brother. Montega followed the girl into the cabin, but he stopped just shy of the door to give Jeremiah another wide smile.

"I arrived in the night." The Indian disappeared from view into the house. "A fat turkey waits in the barn for plucking."

"You'll stay a while then?" Adeline's voice light and casual.

Jeremiah bounced Billy Boy on his good knee. Cursed himself for a fool. The girl was more comfortable conversing with a savage who had scalps dangling from his waist than with an educated white man. And why not? Montega hadn't just attempted to strike her and the child because she'd committed the grave sin of approaching him without calling out his name first to lead him back to reality.

"What say you, Billy Boy? Is this lovely day more real than the phantoms that haunt me from the shadow of the woods?"

The baby blinked at him, slurped from the pap-boat's spout, his hands kneading the rough wool of Jeremiah's shirt.

From inside the cabin came the voice of Montega. "It is no good for me to stay here. Brings trouble for you and for me."

Jeremiah smiled, repositioned the warmth of the baby against his chest. The child cooed up at him, his eyes at half-mast, the kneading slowing in direct proportion to the emptying of the pap.

Sun melted the morning fog, heavy mist becoming trailing fingers of vapor and then thin threads of translucent light. The child snored, soft and warm against Jeremiah's chest. Montega joined him on the porch, stood just behind him and out of sight.

"Come around here where I can see you, Indian."

Moccasins on wood plank made no noise that Jeremiah could discern.

"Cooped up here with the healing of that leg is bringing out your civilized side, white man."

Montega squatted beside the chair, reached a hand to stroke the back of the child's fist. "The bluecoats are making another sweep through these woods. Keep the woman close while I am away."

Jeremiah turned his head and studied the ragged scar on the face of the Indian, the flat, black eyes and the hook of the nose. He hated to admit it, but without Montega's help, he and Adeline and the baby would not have survived the winter. The Indian had brought herbs that helped in his healing, deer and rabbit and wild plants that kept them fed. Most importantly, on their first morning at the farm, Montega had stolen a nanny goat from behind Kate's Brothel and carried the bound animal across his saddle, delivering it to a grateful Adeline and a starving infant.

The Indian spoke softly. "Brett James is in Freshwater. The man asks about Adeline."

"So, he's alive."

"For now he hides in town. He is the last of the men who ruined Niabi. If not for the child I would kill him now and take my chances with the soldiers." Montega bared his teeth in what might have been a smile. "Heal quickly my friend. When you are on your two feet, my way is clear."

"We're less than a day's ride from Freshwater," Jeremiah said. "Stay. The bastard will come to us."

"I thought to do this, but Jessie and Frank James are in town also. Word is, come Monday, they rob the payroll train headed for the Kansas City stockyards. Brett James will not come for the girl until after."

From the cabin came the sounds of thick plates being laid on a table, the heavy iron door of a pot-bellied stove opening and closing, a hymn sung by a young woman who deserved to make her way in the world without the interference of evil men.

Jeremiah shifted the child in his arms. "I hope you're right. I have but two shots left for the Colt and the mighty Henry packs the same one bullet it has held since I took the rifle from its dead owner."

He cursed himself for a fool for not either killing Brett James when he had the chance or avoiding the altercation entirely so he could have followed through on his plan to buy ammunition before leaving the town of Freshwater last fall. No time for replenishing supplies when one crawls out a window in the dark, squat-walks across a roof and shimmies down a corner post.

Montega stared out at the day, now bright with sun on the dripping tree limbs.

"I trade skins and meat for information. With Federals roaming the town and the woods, threatening any who help me, ammunition is not easy to get. I meet a soldier soon. He may trade for what we need."

Jeremiah watched a sparrow scatter light from the wet leaves of a gnarled oak. "You and I," he said "are joined by the woman and by the child."

Montega's laugh startled the dull-brown bird and it sent a spray of sparkling light into the morning.

"You and I," the Indian said, "are joined by the desire for revenge and the need for death."

"Come, breakfast is ready." Adeline paused before stepping within arm's reach of Jeremiah. He met her gaze, watched her pause until he nodded, acknowledged he was in this world. Her skirts swept the plank floor. She lifted the sleeping child, laid him to her shoulder.

Jeremiah gritted his teeth in anticipation of the pain, used his cane to lift himself from the chair. Once on his feet, he rode through the throbbing ache in his leg by studying the yard. The long-eared nanny staked at the edge of the clearing paused in her chewing to cast a round eye at him. Just after Christmas, Montega had ridden in on the stallion and, for three days, the roan had covered the bay. Now the two horses grazed side-by-side, the urgency of their previous coupling seemingly forgotten. Jeremiah fingered the hilt of his knife, prayed Montega was right and Brett James and his thieving relatives did not come before the Indian returned with ammunition for the rifle and pistol. Right now all he had for defense was a sharp knife, an Enfield musket and a burning desire to die fighting. He prayed to a vengeful God that was enough to protect Adeline and the child.

Chapter Eighteen

The stiff hairs of the goat's rounded side tickled Adeline's cheek. Steam rose from the bucket at her feet and the rhythmic squirt of milk at each pull of the teat sang a familiar morning melody. Jeremiah's deep voice filtered through morning fog, came to her from across the yard, from inside the cabin. Adeline could not hear William, which meant the baby was greeting the day with his usual good nature.

She trusted Jeremiah to care for the child, knew the preacher would die before letting anything happen to the boy. And, yet. Each night she woke to inhuman screams from his room. Terror and longing so sharp that the sound echoed in her mind long after the only noise in the cabin was wind moving through the trees outside, the fire settling and cracking in the stove. He spoke in his dreams with someone named Grace, bellowed the name Gil and hollered out for a sergeant. Some nights he seemed to fight an endless battle, his voice hoarse the next morning with night-time commands to take cover and that ever-present rebel yell that raised the hairs on the back of her neck and left her staring at the ceiling until dawn touched her bedroom window.

Baby William, warm against her breasts, accepted these nightly screams, as though the terror that seeped through the thin partition between the rooms were just another part of life. It was only when Jeremiah moaned and pleaded, called out for Maggie, that the baby stirred. 'Course it was on those nights that Adeline clung tight to the infant, wished Pa had taught her a curse word or two.

Over five months ago now, they'd arrived at the cabin with Jeremiah dosed on some herb Montega mixed with whiskey and poured down his throat before lashing him to the travois. Montega had packed the wounded Jeremiah inside, laid him in the room where her brothers Robert and John had slept for as long as she could remember. Those early nights, she slept on a cot beside Jeremiah, the baby in a blanket-softened dresser drawer at her feet. She bathed the preacher in cool water to bring down the fever, watched lantern light dance on a dull silver locket and small blue bottle on the nightstand at his head, and prayed he'd come back to her.

On the worst of those long nights of prayer and longing, Jeremiah cried out again and again for Maggie. Yet when finally he came to himself and she asked about this 'Sweet Maggie', he brushed her hand roughly from his brow, turned his head and ordered her from the room. She did not ask again.

The goat spooked, jerking Adeline into the present and nearly spilling the milk from the bucket.

"What's the matter with you?" She ran her hand gently along the nanny's sway back, the hair coarse under her palm. "We're almost done here. Stand still now. William needs his breakfast."

The goat calmed some, though the animal appeared anxious this morning, probably eager to get to the soft grass that had, just this week, begun to sprout along the edge of the clearing. The steady squirt of milk into a nearly full bucket, the play of a breeze in the newly greened trees, the rhythmic breath of the goat, soothed Adeline, returned her thoughts to Jeremiah.

As hard as she tried, she could not keep all his rules straight. It was like living with a haint. Or, no, it was like living with two different men in one body. That wasn't quite it either. It was confusing, that's what it was. She couldn't seem to figure how to move and talk—just be—around him without setting him off.

A week ago he'd pushed his beans and cornbread away half-eaten, mentioned how, as a boy, he'd loved his ma's venison stew. Last night, she'd cooked a thick stew of venison and the few potatoes Montega had taken in barter. She meant the meal as an apology for having startled him into striking out at her earlier in the day by approaching him quietly from behind. Something she knew not to do. He'd made it clear she was to get his attention before coming near him, that she was not to sneak up on him. He'd instructed her gently to call out to him before coming within arm's length.

Yesterday, in her enjoyment of the first spring-warm morning of the year, she had forgotten. His attack was terrifying, fast, seemed to her as instinctual as the fanged strike of a cottonmouth. An inch or two closer and he'd have struck her or the baby. She had stood on the front porch, William screaming in her arms, her heart wild in her chest.

She stayed away from him the rest of the day but that night, to help them both forget the incident, she'd cooked his favorite meal. Venison Stew. He ate two servings and she thought she'd gotten it right. For once.

She was happy watching his pleasure in the meal. "Is it as good as your mama used to make?"

His face closed.

He answered in that flat, dead tone of his she had come to dread. "It tasted fine, Adeline. Just leave it at that. It's not your job to bring back the dead."

A blackbird's call broke the morning quiet and the goat bleated and jerked hard at the rope that staked her.

"Whoa, now, nanny. What's gotten into you?"

The milking post stood just a few feet from the cabin. Adeline had dug the hole and set the milking stake herself. From under the wide branches of the big hickory tree, she could see the cabin's front door, hear William if he fussed. On mornings when Montega joined them, the spot also allowed her to milk the goat some distance from the barn where the Indian slept.

The Osage had kept all of them alive this last winter with his bartering and his hunting.

Even so, she fought with her instincts to flee each time he came near. The way he smelled of bear grease and dirt and some other, baser, earthy scent that affected her in a way that stirred shame and fear. The way he moved like a wild animal, slow and confident. It was as though he was a natural part of these woods while she—who had grown up on this land, whose pa had worked this farm for almost ten long years—in the Indian's presence, she became the intruder.

When she'd tried to talk to Jeremiah about her fear, he'd read to her from one of his books, some preachy line about how we shouldn't distrust a man because he had bad manners and his skin was dark. Which was all fine and good, but she'd seen the way the preacher stiffened just a bit, watched Montega as if he were a wolf come to call.

Jeremiah yelled to her from the porch. "This child is eager for breakfast."

Over the back of the goat, she watched him hold the baby against his hip with one arm while leaning heavy on a polished hickory cane with the other. Even crippled up and moving slow, he gave off a feel of menace. Like Montega, he brought to mind some critter you didn't want to turn your back on.

So why was she so attracted to the man? Why were her dreams wet with need for a saddle-preacher lost in a private battle between good and evil?

He lowered himself onto the porch chair, lifted the baby high over his head. She was flooded with unease. The memory of the dream she'd had again last night settled over her like a thin sheet of ice.

The archangel Michael, luminous, wings spread wide, the tips golden with light. Michael, looking past her, as though she did not exist, at something over her shoulder. She turned. Always she turned, though even in the dream, she knew what she'd see, understood she should run. Yet, each night she twisted her body, looked behind her to see the fallen angel. Lucifer. His arms raised to the starry sky above him. The devil brilliant in rage and power, surrounded by a red glow that sparked blue and orange and purple in a distorted halo.

She looked up then, in the dream, into the eyes of the devil. Jeremiah's face grinned at her. Legs heavy, she stumbled back. Mouth open in a silent scream, she felt the presence behind her then of the guardian, of Michael. She fought to turn her face to God's most glorious angel, struggled against the numbness that froze her in place, gazed up, finally, into the fallen angel's eyes, into the irresistible attraction of Jeremiah's laughing face. She woke tangled in wet sheets, desire a hot slick of sweat on her body, heavy with need and fear.

The nanny skittered, jerked away, came close to kicking over the full bucket between her back legs.

"Whoa now, settle down girl." Adeline rescued the milk, grabbed at the goat's halter.

A warning shout from Jeremiah turned Adeline around to stare into the woods. At the clearing's edge swayed a monster. Huge and furry, strings of drool hanging from the half-open mouth, the animal's beady eyes stared at the nanny who struggled under Adeline's hand. The bear snuffled, shifted his weight from shoulder to shoulder. Like a swaying boulder. With teeth. And claws.

"Leave the goat and walk toward me, Adeline."

Was Jeremiah insane? William needed the goat's milk.

The rope's knot slipped and tangled under her fingers, but finally the goat's lead was loosed. Milk bucket in one hand, the other tight on the nanny's halter, Adeline inched toward the porch.

"Take William inside, Jeremiah." She gained another step toward the cabin.

"Damn you, girl, turn loose the goat." But his voice was already coming from inside the cabin.

She heard the baby wail, the mechanical click of a bullet settling into the chamber of the Henry rifle. Adeline gained another few steps. The goat bleated and struggled, wild to get away, into the woods.

"Leave the bucket and the goat." Jeremiah's voice came low, flat, and nearly irresistible to deny. "Walk slowly toward me, Adeline."

She dragged the animal another foot closer to the porch.

A noise behind her like a thunderstorm. She turned to the sound. The bear charged directly at her. Growling. Roaring. The ground became dust beneath the beast's heavy, powerful body. Adeline stared into the bear's fury, struck dead-still by the animal's power, the muscles that moved under the fur like rippling water.

The goat twisted, fought against Adeline's grip. Adeline dug in her heels, jerked at the nanny's halter. The bear stopped, rose upon hind legs, swatted the air and filled the yard with a sound like a mighty wind. A rifle shot rang in the air. Adeline pulled and tugged at the goat, earned another couple of feet toward the cabin. The bear dropped to all fours, turned its massive head away from the goat and glared at the man on the porch.

"That was the Henry's last bullet, Adeline." Jeremiah's voice low and calm, as though he were murmuring to a fevered child. "If he charges again, I cannot get to you in time to help."

From inside the cabin, William screamed in outrage.

The goat, as if suddenly overcome with an understanding of the situation, trotted toward the porch. Adeline ran beside her.

The bear growled. Swayed. Stayed where it was. Ten feet, no further, then up the steps and she and the goat were inside the relative safety of the cabin.

The baby's wails stopped. From his cradle, William blinked his eyes at the sight of Adeline and the nanny.

From the porch, Jeremiah's cane thunked on the planks, his voice came loud and empty.

"Be gone, bear. Go on back to the woods. I've not the strength to protect you if that girl gets ahold of your hide. She'll likely strangle you with her bare hands to protect that half-breed child. Get now!"

The front door closed. Adeline began to shake. Jeremiah pressed himself to her back, pried her fingers from the goat's halter. His arms encircled her, his heart beat strong against her back.

"Set down the milk bucket, Adeline. Go to Billy Boy. I'll stake the goat."

Her shaking stopped as suddenly as it had begun. A calm that felt like safety, like heaven, settled over Adeline. The bucket was, all at once, heavy in her hand. She set the milk on the table, went to William, lifted the baby from his bed, and carried him to the window. The bleating of the goat echoed strangely in the confines of the cabin. Outside, the bear snuffled at the far corner of the barn, massive head swaying on wide shoulders. Jeremiah's cane tapped closer.

He dug his fingers hard into her upper arms, pulled her tight against his length. "Dammit, Adeline, when I tell you to do something, you do it!"

The bear swatted at the barn once, then seemed to lose interest. The animal lumbered away, wide rump disappearing into the woods.

She turned to Jeremiah, the torment on his face terrible to see. His jaw clenched hard and she could not tell if he shook her or if he himself trembled so violently that the movement carried through his fingertips and into her flesh. For a moment, the time it takes to draw a breath, no more, his dark eyes revealed so much pain and sorrow and despair that she very nearly dropped her gaze from his. Then he squeezed his eyes shut, ground his teeth so that she feared he would break them in his mouth.

Adeline did not flinch.

Over the dark, silky hair of the baby trapped between them, she studied the slight bump at the bridge of Jeremiah's nose, the thin scar that sliced his cheekbone. She waited until he opened his eyes and looked into her face.

"You ever call this child a half-breed again and, I swear, it's you I'll strangle with my bare hands!"

His eyes widened, flashed anger and then his laughter competed with the goat's bleating.

She lifted her face, his mouth soft and greedy on hers. The child bawled between them unheeded for the time it took to wipe away all caution, to seal her fate to that of this wounded veteran.

"Feed the boy," he said when they broke apart. "God help me, Adeline, if it be the death of us both, I cannot resist much longer."

She watched him hobble away, barely heard the words, just as he shut the bedroom door. "Please, Lord, let no harm come to this child."

Adeline smiled, thinking he meant to call down protection on the boy.

Chapter Nineteen

"**A**deline?"

He hated the thump of the cane on the cabin's plank floor, the scrape of his left foot, each dragging step a reminder of his infirmity. Once he warmed up some, poured a cup or two of coffee down his throat, the leg would be oiled up enough that he could walk without the cane. A few more weeks and he'd ride on out of here. Get on with his life. See if the Lord, that bully and trickster, saw fit to speak through him once more.

"Adeline!" Where was that girl?

He set a half-empty pot of coffee on the wood stove, threaded a piece of kindling through the iron handle. Heat hit like a solid force when the door swung open. He fed the fire and pushed himself to his feet, knees popping like the split oak he'd just laid on a bed of red embers.

"Adeline!" That girl would be the death of him.

Her bedroom door stood open. The bed empty. No girl. No baby.

His heart beat quickened. Breath caught in his belly.

Damn that woman!

His cane caught on the leg of a chair as he hurried to the front door, the sound of the slatted back hitting the floor like a shot behind him. He flung open the door, stared out into the empty yard. His vision filled, crowded with images. The bloody fangs of a grinning brown bear. Brett James plunging between Maggie's pale legs. No. No. Not Maggie. Adeline. Adeline had abandoned him. Grown tired of waiting, tired of him. Adeline.

Panic hovered.

He squared his shoulders. Three seconds, no more. That's all the bloody past had cost him. Three seconds. Enough time to get him killed. He cocked his good ear toward the woods searching morning sounds for danger.

A door slammed shut inside him, graced him with numbing calm. A line from The Last of the Mohicans stilled his heart and quieted his mind.

I have listened to all the sounds of the woods, as a man will listen whose life and death depend on the quickness of his ears.

Leaves rustled, the sound drifting down from the tops of trees. The bleating of a goat, the soft nicker of a horse—these normal morning sounds drifted to him muted from inside the barn. He gimped down the porch steps, stood in the brushed dirt of the yard, and swept the area with his eyes, section by section. The edge of the woods. The corral.

The day's first light was silvery, the edge of the eastern mountain tipped in lilac.

Dawn was a good time for attack. Enough light for the enemy to move into position, enough shadow to confuse his eye. They would expect to find him groggy, stumbling from his bed as the Federals at Seven Pines had scrambled for weapons on another purple morn.

He stood again in the mist of that cold morning, his vision filled, for a killing instant, with the view between the Enfield's sights. Like coming up out of cold creek water, sucking air down into hungry lungs, he slipped naturally into his real world. Relieved, and shamed by that relief, he nonetheless embraced that one killing instant, an endless vision, an eternal loop of misery wrought by the press of his finger to a small curve of metal.

His first look at the sergeant, framed in the deep V of the musket's sights, his suspenders flopping at his hips, coffee cup in hand, eyes wide and testifying to his confusion and fear. Jeremiah's aim was true. The Enfield's minie tore through the sergeant's face, sprinkling bone and gore over—

"Jeremiah?"

He twisted to the voice. His bad leg betrayed him, dropped him to the dirt.

The toes of her boots were wet with mud. A breeze pressed her skirt to her legs. The milk bucket dangled from her hand, caught a shard of lavender light and blinded him for a split second, the way the sun will find the blade of a bayonet and trick the viewer with its beauty. She squatted awkwardly beside him, the baby asleep in a sling against her breast.

"Jeremiah? Are you all right?"

He struck at her hand when she offered to help him stand, watched her face transform from joy, to something else, something that resembled fear and sadness and worry and anger, all mixed together into one ugly mask.

"Where were you, Adeline?" He fumbled in the dirt, found his cane. "You just walk away? Don't take a gun with you, don't say a word to me."

He got the cane under him, pushed himself to his feet. His heart might just explode in his chest. This woman was surely sent by God to ruin him. Last week the foolish girl spent all one afternoon cooking a stew of venison because he mentioned casually that it was his favorite meal. A savory trap to imprison him in domesticity. A ridiculous attempt to cage him and demand he perform with intimacy and kindness. Stupid woman. She'd do better to catch that brown bear and teach him to sing.

"Maybe you're right to go off by yourself." He spoke slowly, fed the rage and terror that churned in his belly. "Might be best for all of us if you just got yourself eaten by a bear. You *and* that Indian brat. Or taken by your old fiancé. Could be that's what you're hoping for, huh?"

His words shattered her face. She dropped the bucket. Mayapples poured like water in a glittering yellow-green pool onto the dirt.

He knew he should shut his mouth, walk away. Understood he was deliberately destroying something precious and beautiful. Felt this knowledge with a clarity he'd only ever felt before in battle.

"Could be a rough fuck from the likes of Brett James is just what you're looking for. Pass you on to that fat whore when he's had enough of your whining. You and Maggie and all the rest. You talk a fine game of love and nurture. In the end, you're all whores, seizing what a man offers while pining for what he can't give."

She turned her face from him, bent to retrieve the bucket and he knew he'd won another bloody battle, knew he'd driven her away and narrowly

missed the trap hidden in the love of a good woman. He put his back to her, headed for the barn. Time to saddle the bay, begin his preaching circuit, see what babies needed burying, what young fools needed marrying.

A glint caught the corner of his eye an instant before a blow struck him in the back of the head. He threw his hands up to protect himself. The cane slipped away and he was down again, on his side in the dirt of the yard. Something shiny parted the air over his head.

The bucket! The bitch was beating him with the metal bucket.

"Who . . . ." She swung at his head. "Is . . . ." A rain of yellow fruit fell. "Maggie?"

The metal edge of the pail hit the side of his head. A slice of pain and then warmth flowed from a cut just above his ear. She flung the bucket at him, stood wide-legged, the baby screaming at her breast. Dust rose in little red tornadoes around her boots as she stomped to him, kicked the cane out of his reach.

"You, Jeremiah Jones, are a coward. Afraid to face your own demons so you push me away, make me the enemy, call me a . . . a . . . bad woman."

Tears burned his eyes. This girl, this Adeline, God help him, she shimmered in his vision like death masquerading as salvation. She bloodied his head with a milking bucket but refused to say the word whore. Six months with him and he'd transformed a naïve, innocent child into the shrew that stood over him now. Any second now she'd commence to kicking him. Wouldn't surprise him if she broke his damn ribs before she was finished.

Laughter bubbled up in him.

"Don't you dare laugh at me." She stamped her foot. The wails of the baby were high pitched, building to the hysterical, the unstoppable cries of a child desperate for warmth and love and attention. "You tell me who Maggie is or . . . or I will get that Colt and shoot you with the last two bullets."

He lay on his side, the dirt coarse under his cheek. How fitting it would be to survive four years of war and die at the hands of a mere girl. His belly shook with mirth. He opened his mouth and released the laughter of the absurdity of life out into the morning's brightness.

He watched her stride across the yard and into the cabin. The door shut with a slam that threatened the window glass. He surrendered to laughter. Knew this emotion, like all others, would pass of its own accord. He waited until his aching belly produced no more than fluttering ripples. Then he rolled to his back and stared up at the clear blue sky, studied the way the tops of the trees laced the clearing at the edges with a hundred shades of green. Took him a minute to place what all that moving light reminded him of.

A private name of Mark Hanson from Charleston had found a kaleidoscope in the saber-scarred pouch of a union major at Chickamauga. The thing wasn't as long as the stock of an Enfield and about as big around as that rifle's barrel. They'd taken turns passing the instrument around, holding it to the light and grinning at the magic conjured by that little tube.

From inside the cabin the baby's wails became sporadic crying and then soft snuffling. Jeremiah pictured Adeline, perched on the side of her bed, the baby, Billy Boy, sucking goat's milk from that ridiculous pap she'd fashioned from an old tea pot. He painted himself into the picture, let himself settle beside the pair—young mother and satisfied babe. He imagined the warmth of her body, the way she would form herself to him, take his need onto herself.

The vision, like the magic of the kaleidoscope, was only a moment's fancy.

He pulled himself back, smothered desire with anger, fed the fire with fear, and blew expertly on the tiny flame until it roared into rage. On his hands and knees he crawled to where Adeline had kicked his cane. It was a chore to get the stick under him, push himself to his feet. If she thought to tame him while he was infirm, trapped here in this cozy cabin, she was sorely mistaken. He limped to the barn. It was a good day to hoist himself onto the bay, begin to ready his leg for the spring circuit.

The curry comb made smooth swirls in the mare's coat. The horse nickered in greeting when the barn door swung open behind him throwing a wide slant of purple light across the stall.

"Tell me who Maggie is or, I swear to God, I will shoot you in the back."

"No, you won't," he said without turning. "The bullet would go through me and into the mare. You may hate me enough to kill me, but you'd never harm the horse."

He was grateful she could not see the wide smile that stretched his face. Horse or no horse, the anger in her voice warned him she'd pull the trigger.

"Tell me who she is, Jeremiah. I'm a good enough shot to hit you in the head and miss the animal entirely."

He faced her then, laughed out loud. "It took you four bullets to hit Brett James on that ridgeline and then you didn't do enough damage to kill him."

The pistol shook in her grip. Sure looked like she'd lined him up in her sights just about right. Serve him right to be shot with his own weapon because he was too foolish to carry it on his person.

"Who is Maggie? You've got three seconds before I put you out of your misery."

"Well," he said, "this is an interesting way to spend the morning, but I'm about done now with the entertainment."

Her finger moved from the guard to the curve of the trigger.

"Good to see you listened all those nights I demonstrated how to shoot."

The Colt held steady, she did not blink.

"You win." He sealed her image to memory. May as well complete what he'd started, end this child's attempt to teach this particular bear to sing. "I'll tell you about Maggie. But, child, like most desires, I believe you'll find that the attainment does not satisfy in the manner you had hoped."

She dropped the gun a few inches, kept her finger inside the trigger guard.

"Maggie," he said calmly, "is the last woman I killed."

Chapter Twenty

S **unlight, pale with** the day's newness, streamed through the thin curtains of the bedroom. Adeline absently traced the squares of Mama's old quilt with her finger. Tears and morning light swirled the colors, turned the faded patches to shimmering jewels.

The sound of the metal edge of the bucket smacking against the side of Jeremiah's head echoed in her ears. Just last week, after the bear wandered into the yard, she convinced herself the man had feelings for her. And then she came home today, happy, skipping like a stupid child through the woods, anxious to return to Jeremiah with her surprise of Mayapples. Found him, on this spring morning perfect in its clear, warm light, in the middle of some kind of fit. Screaming her name. His eyes darting from place to place, as though searching the woods for enemies. Accusing her of horrible, awful things. She had been a fool to think he cared for her.

And then, that one word on his lips—Maggie—and a hot, boiling, red mist had fallen on her. She hadn't felt that kind of anger since she was a child. Believed that with ten years of morning and evening prayer, the temptation to ignore the Lord's command to leave vengeance to His hand had been overcome. The echo of that milk bucket opening a gash in the side of Jeremiah's head told a truer tale. The remembrance of the curve of bright red that appeared an instant before blood began to mat his dark hair spoke of her failure to overcome anger.

And still, she was not sorry for the swinging of that bucket. No more than, all these years later, she regretted her actions on another spring day.

She couldn't have been more than six or seven when Mama forced her brother Robert to carry Adeline with him to the cabin of his friend, Daniel Olsen. The Olsens had a new litter of pups and Adeline coveted the runt, a speckled female with one eye brown and the other blue. Stiff grass and sharp stones poked the soles of her bare feet as she followed her brother through the woods. She plugged her ears with her fingers to drown out Robert's fretting and grousing over his fate in having a whiney baby sister who always got her way. Even so, Adeline heard the trouble long before the Olsen's makeshift cabin came into view.

In a weedy patch of garden, Daniel's pa stumbled in lopsided circles. His voice echoed loud and strange so that, in another setting altogether, Adeline might have mistaken his piercing shouts for speaking in tongues.

Robert took her hand. "Stay still, Adeline."

The mother dog, with dragging teats, slunk from behind a sloppy pile of chicken manure and compost. Tail between her legs, the dog skirted away from the reeling man. The speckled runt followed her mother. Adeline's vision slowed the scene. The pup looked up, tail wagging, wiggled her way to the staggering drunk. Mr. Olsen stopped dead. Adeline watched in horror as the man took aim on the approaching pup.

His kick lifted the surprised pup off the ground and slammed her into a fence rail. The dog's yelp split Adeline open, emptied her of all but a hot, red mist that made a tunnel of her vision. She jerked her hand from Roberts and, surely her feet must have touched the ground with each step, but it seemed to her, even now, all these years later, that she simply flew across the distance, propelled herself into the fat belly of the man.

The surprise of her attack, coupled with the extreme drunkenness of her target, knocked him flat onto his back. When it was over, when Robert and Daniel pulled her kicking and screaming from the man's chest, her hands were bruised, the big toe of one bare foot bent sidewise at an angle that let her know it was going to hurt bad before she made it home.

The anger that claimed her that day was like one of mama's hard slaps—a stunning surprise that knocked her from one reality to another. If Robert and Daniel had not been there, she'd have kept at the kicking and beating of the man who kicked that speckled pup. She would not have stopped as long as he drew breath.

Baby William fussed in his sleep. The quilt's colored squares rippled in the morning light. The memory of that day perched on Adeline's chest like some vulture from the past, waiting patiently to peck at her eyes, ruin her for all time.

"No man will take you for his wife if you cannot control your temper," Mama had lectured as she spread salve over Adeline's knuckles, set the bent toe straight with one quick twist.

Pa had hugged her to his wide chest, told her to commit to memory Romans 12:19, sow the words of the apostle Paul so that they put down deep roots into her soul.

Never take your own revenge, beloved, but leave room for the wrath of God, for it is written, vengeance is mine, I will repay.

Adeline swung her legs to the side of the bed, sat up and stroked the soft cheek of baby William. Billy Boy, Jeremiah called him. For ten years she'd repeated St. Paul's instruction to herself at each rising and each lying down and never again had anger risen up in her like a hot, red tide. Until today.

Mama'd been dead going on a year, but her voice was clear in Adeline's mind, the tone scalding. "You should be ashamed of yourself, Adeline. Beating a man with a milk bucket? What has gotten into you, girl?"

Adeline rose from the bed, walked the two steps to the window and stared out at the shadows at the edge of the woods. She'd die before she allowed a man to treat her like some animal. Talk to her as if she had no worth whatsoever except as a balm to his own needs. If not for her, Jeremiah would have died on that ridgeline. Brett James's bullet his final injury.

"If not for you, girl, he'd never have taken on those men to begin with," her mama's voice taunted.

Jeremiah wasn't right in his mind. That was the problem. That bloody awful war had ruined him. He ranted and tossed and cried out each night in his sleep. One second his face softened with the feel of the baby in his arms and the next he'd push William back at her, limp away on his cane and she'd not see him until mealtime. My Lord, the man had even twisted things in his mind to where Brett James was still alive, as if she hadn't killed the man dead, watched the blood bloom on his chest, seen him roll down into that hollow with her own two eyes.

Adeline turned from the window, and sat again on the bed. She laid her hand on the baby's chest, felt the slow rise and fall of each breath. The idea of Brett James still alive made her stomach flutter and her hands shake. Why was she letting Jeremiah's crazed words build such fear in her?

Where had her life brought her? What would she do if Jeremiah left? Each rare moment of closeness between them—a soft look as the baby reached for him, or brief instant when firelight warmed their faces as she mended and he sat, bad leg stretched in front of him, one of his books open in his lap—each small intimacy seemed to require him to lash out, push her away. Each day she rose with the intention of not repeating a past mistake, promised herself she'd not ask for praise at a meal well-prepared, would take care not to approach him from behind or take him by surprise. And each day, she found new ways to trigger in him a rage that frightened her and further angered him.

While milking the goat this morning, she had thought to search the nearby woods for mayapples. Surprise Jeremiah with jelly for his biscuits. He had slept especially poorly last night. His cries and screams had not quieted until dawn's thin promise lined the jagged top of the mountain. She let the man sleep, fed William on the porch, the air warm and bright with the smell of spring. Once fed and his diaper changed, she'd tied the baby to her, collected the milk bucket and gone off to enjoy a morning of gathering what Pa had called the natural blessings of the woods.

She had judged the harvest correctly. The fruit was ripe and ready for picking. Humming an old hymn, she'd returned from a short stroll wondering if she had enough sugar for jelly to find Jeremiah wandering the yard like a mad dog. It hadn't helped that he'd fallen when she called his name. Her hand still stung from where he'd slapped away her help.

From her position on the bed, she rubbed her hand, heard boots pound hard on the front steps and then the front door scrape open.

Adeline held her breath. If he came to her, what would she say? What would she do? Her mind jumbled and swirled with desire and fear and anger and need. If Jeremiah left, how would she feed and protect herself and the baby?

He thumped across the cabin floor, the tap of his cane marking each step.

She could go to him. Ask gently, without a trace of anger, for the story of Maggie. Say she only wanted to know because she cared for him and knew from his nightly screams and pleadings that this woman was important to him. Maggie. Just the name brought back the anger. How many hours had she sat beside him and stared at that silver locket with the woman's picture folded inside its heart shape? Who was this woman? Was she really dead? Adeline did not believe for a moment that Jeremiah had killed her. He could not have killed her. He'd flung the lie at her only to drive her away.

The door to his room creaked. A drawer scraped open.

She pictured him there, just on the other side of the wall, rummaging in the dresser. Would he come to her?

Footfalls traced his path back through the cabin. She heard him pick up his pistol from the table where she'd dropped it on her return to her room.

He's leaving! Get up. Go to him. Now.

The slam of the front door.

She would not beg him to stay. Would not!

The mare's hooves thudded in the bare dirt of the yard.

An empty sound pounded in Adeline's chest, grew dimmer until she was left with her confusion, and pain, and with the child. She was left with the child and the uneasy feeling that Jeremiah's accusations had somehow resurrected Brett James .

Chapter Twenty-One

The sour stink of night sweats washed over her with the opening of the door. Adeline stepped inside Jeremiah's room. The dresser drawer creaked as she inched it toward her, breath catching in her dry throat. Two leather-bound books laid atop one another. She ran a finger over the words *James Fennimore Cooper* spelled out in gold letters across a dark cover.

Relief slowed her heart, surprised her some. She'd spent all day yesterday and all the long hours of last night telling herself she didn't need him. Was better off without a man wounded beyond redemption. Was, in fact, happy he'd ridden away like a coward, left her alone with the baby. Good riddance to bad rubbish, as Pa used to say.

Staring at the books that told of Jeremiah's eventual return, promised he'd come back to her, tears stung her eyes and throat. Her knees weakened and she lowered herself to sit on the edge of his bed, lifted the novel and laid it beside her.

The second book was a journal, tied with a rawhide twist that creased a faded leather cover. The diary weighed little in her hand, pressed a heavy burden on her mind.

To read someone's private thoughts was akin to thievery. She'd been taught better than to snoop. Remembering Pa's voice comforted, even as the message convicted.

He that passeth by and meddleth with strife belonging not to him, is like one that taketh a dog by the ears.

Adeline laid her hand to her cheek, felt again the sting of Ma's own brand of teaching when she was caught squatting outside the open window, straining to hear her brother Robert's talk of Emma Lou, the girl he married quick-like the following spring. The words rang clear as though Ma stood right beside her, eyes blazing. *The business of menfolk is of no concern to you girl. Stay out of your brothers' room.* This very room. Where Jeremiah now slept. But, with Jeremiah, who parsed out words like a stingy man counted pennies, well, how else to know his hidden heart?

She lowered herself to the edge of the bed, fingers already working to untie a swollen double knot. She opened the leather cover, smoothed her hand over the first yellowed page.

For my son, Jeremiah Jones. My prayers and love are with you always. Your mother, Ellen Massey Jones.

Under this inscription, written cross-wise of the page in a darker ink and in Jeremiah's hand sprawled the words:

I request of the finder of this journal that the book in its entirety be sent to Margaret Mary Owen of Fayetteville Arkansas. May God bless you for your kindness.

She wiped damp palms on her skirt, heard again the nightly moans, the timbre of his voice as he called that name.

Adeline carefully turned the first page.

10ᵗʰ of September, 1861

My dearest Maggie,

It was over two months ago I left you standing alone in the woods. My intention was to write each day, but it has taken me this long to put pen to paper. I think of you each day. Wake in the dark to the memory of your warm mouth pressing mine. Surrounded by sleeping men, the woods are lonely on those nights. And yet, in asking you not to write, to live your life as though I will not return, I believe I have followed God's instruction.

Men talk of this war ending in a few months. Even Colonel Rust speaks of teaching the Yankees a lesson and being home in time for next spring's planting. But it is all bravado, persuasion needed to keep men marching toward Virginia where we are to meet up with the rest of Lee's army. It requires neither a graduate of West Point nor a scholar of history to know that this will be a long and bloody fight.

There is every chance I will not return. The keeping of this journal is, in truth, for me and not for you. Like the locket I carry in my pocket, the writing is a way to hold you close, to carry your memory and countenance with me into the dark days ahead.

This morning dawned clear, the air brilliant with promise. My regiment, the Third Arkansas Infantry, is bivouacked at Travelers Repose. There is a rumor that tomorrow at this time we will marching along Staunton Road which lies just to the east of us, headed into our first battle.

But this morning, possibly the last for some, men rub sleep from their eyes, or set to scraping whiskers from their cheeks, or scratch letters to loved ones. Wind from out of the west billows the canvas of tents and sun flashes on the metal of a strange assortment of weaponry. The smell of coffee and wood smoke mixes with the tangy smell of over a thousand unwashed men. The nickering of horses and mules drifts from the make-shift corral. The rattle of pots and the occasional loud jest of one man or another adds to the general organized confusion of an army preparing for another day's march. In the midst of this cacophony, I am back in a summer green woods, wishing I were the kind of man who could have accepted what you offered, pressed you to me in a physical good-bye that might have sustained us until my return.

Adeline marked her place with a finger to the page. A smile curled the corners of her mouth. Perhaps he had not, then, slept with this woman. She stared out the bedroom's four-paned window into the spring day, tilted her head to the rustle of leaves in the tops of oak and hickory. She might be only sixteen but she knew enough of the ways of men and women to know that an unfulfilled longing could be buried in the rich ground of new passion.

She dropped her gaze back to the open book on her lap.

Colonel Rust's headquarters squats to my left, recognizable amongst a sea of similar tents by its larger size and by the St. Andrews Cross snapping in the wind over the center peak.

The soft close of the front door raised Adeline's head. Startled, palms instantly wet, her heart thumped fast and hard.

Feet padded across the cabin floor.

She pressed the journal closed, fumbled with the leather twist, gave up and slipped the book, untied, into the top drawer.

A rhythmic song, a low vibration, thrummed at her ears.

Relieved, Adeline smiled and did her best to appear casual as she strolled into the main cabin.

At the door to her room, the powerful stink of bear grease was an assault and, hand to her nose, she stepped back a few feet.

Montega stood at the foot of her bed looking down. Boxed in with a rolled quilt and two soft pillows, William slept on his knees, his diapered bottom in the air. The baby's head was turned toward Adeline, thumb firmly in place. The child's rapid sucking told her it would soon be time to warm goat's milk.

"The child is well." Montega turned, met her gaze.

Adeline dropped her hand from her nose.

"He's crawling now." She forced a smile. "Jeremiah says it'll not be long before William will have no need of the pap, be chasing after the goat to get breakfast fresh from the tap."

Her face heated in shame. Why had she found it necessary to remind Montega of Jeremiah's presence in her life? To share this crude, teasing observation as if revealing an intimacy? It wasn't as though she was afraid of the Indian. Not precisely afraid.

"I bring ammunition. A few rounds for the rifle, caps and balls for the Colt." He continued to look into her eyes.

She was certain he knew of her fear, sensed her reaction to his smell, her uneasiness at the manner in which he stood—balanced lightly on the balls of his feet.

"The wolf and raven are very different creatures." His words flat, lifeless, he did not shift his gaze from her face.

Jeremiah said that, if you ask an Osage if he thinks it'll rain, he'll begin his answer with the Indian equivalent of "In the beginning God created the heavens and the earth." Adeline smiled but did not share this insight with Montega.

"Yes, very different." She smiled to let him know she was teasing. "The raven has feathers while the wolf has fur."

He did not return her smile.

"These two animals have different powers." He paused stone-faced until she nodded. "Both live in the same woods, but even their smell is different, one from the other."

Adeline's face burned with heat.

"Yet, in a hard winter, the wolf and the raven, they strike a bargain. When the wind turns against the hunter, the raven will lead the wolf to a deer hiding in the woods. In return, the wolf allows the bird to eat from its kill."

"So," Adeline asked, "in this story, am I the raven or the wolf?"

The cabin was silent but for the crackling of logs in the stove and the soft suckling of the baby, his thumb firmly, wetly in place.

"You keep both the raven and the wolf alive," Montega said. "You are the deer."

She felt as though she'd been slapped. Her throat burned with shame, while her chest swelled in anger.

"In a bad year," the Indian said, "the deer that survive are those that never for a moment forget they are hunted."

Adeline pushed past Montega, scooped William to her breast and swept through the cabin and into the yard. With the baby fussy and warm against her, she pulled open the trapdoor to the stone-lined root cellar, lifted the milk bucket in one hand and carried it to the cabin. Montega watched from the door of her room while she heated a pap and, arranging a chair so that her back was to the Indian, fed the baby.

"Brett James may ride this way," he said from behind her, each word like a pebble dropping into a creek, small and separate one from the other.

Fear rippled through her. She refused to turn and look at him. Adeline swallowed hard, gripped the baby tighter to her breasts. Had Jeremiah's words conjured James?

"James is dead." Her voice quivered.

"You shot him, but he did not die." A sliver of sun from the partially-open door sliced Montega.

She hugged the baby in the hopes of slowing the shaking. All these nights she had comforted herself in the dark with the knowledge that James lived only in her dreams. Was *everything* she believed a lie?

"You did not think to tell me this until now? That this man who hunts me is alive?"

The Indian shrugged and she wished for something to throw at his greasy head.

"The James gang robbed a train near Kansas City, took gold and paper money meant for the stockyards."

"When?" Her voice, meant to be hard and flat, came from her mouth like the soft peep of a new hatched chick.

"Four days past," he said and then, "There is meat in the barn. A sow bear."

The pap slipped from William's sucking mouth in her hurry to turn toward Montega.

"What? You killed the bear?" As though this were the news that speeded her heart.

He stood squarely, watched her. "Bluecoats killed the sow. I traded skins for meat and fat."

The baby's screams of outrage at having his meal interrupted grew louder. Adeline readjusted the spout of the tea pot, waited for William to resume his contented sucking.

She looked up at Montega. "Three days past we had a bear come right on into the yard."

"Yes. I saw sign. A big male. Your bear has a crippled shoulder. He will return to you."

"To me? He was hungry, came to make a meal of the nanny."

The Indian shook his head slightly side-to-side. "The spirits have bound this bear to you."

Her life wasn't hard enough? A baby to feed and protect. An outlaw, ex-beau who refused to die and was rumored to be looking to exact revenge on her. A half-crazy soldier who intrigued and terrified in just about equal measure. An Indian who first kidnapped her and then stuck around to keep them all alive through the winter. And now, this same Indian tells her she's joined, through some kind of savage destiny, to a large, toothy animal?

Chapter Twenty-Two

Jeremiah leaned low over the neck of the mare, pushed her hard in the day's gloaming. The horse's shoulder muscles bunched and released. Warm flesh carried him up from the twisting path he had traveled for the last hour. It was the animal that found the smooth rock ledge along the face of the mountain for which he searched.

Caution demanded he dismount, walk the mare along the narrow trail. Instead, Jeremiah laid his cheek against the horse's warm neck, her mane a veil striping his vision of flying hooves. He urged her on, and the mare obeyed the pressure of his knees on her heaving sides, foolish in her loyalty and obedience, sparks flying with each beat of her shod feet against the hard rock path.

The mountain, cool and flat, pressed in on the left. On the right, warm air whispered from the surface of the river a thousand feet below, a chasm of emptiness, a siren call to death. Jeremiah straightened in the saddle, tightened his thighs, lifted his arms and turned his face to the cold stars of a cloudless night.

A terrible cry rose up in him, echoed in the emptiness. The horse moved under him, carried him toward his destination even as he flung curses and then pleas into the blackness.

"My God, my God, why hath thou forsaken me?" The words of the Psalm provided no comfort.

He threw rage and terror and desperation into the dark void. His mind swirled with images. Battle. The smell of dead horses burning in hastily-heaped pyres. The screams of the dying. His arms ached with the memory of the killing thrusts of a bayonet into living flesh. He saw Maggie, sinking lifeless to the plank porch. Adeline, the pain of his betrayal on her young face.

"Adeline!" His plea sliced the night. "My need will ruin you."

The mare slowed, then stopped, her breath loud in the sudden silence of her stilled hooves. Jeremiah bowed his head, tears warm on his face. The horse tossed her head, turned into the cold mouth of the cave. Her sides heaving with the long effort, the horse simply stood.

Jeremiah's bowed his head. "There is no mercy. God, you are a liar. A cheat."

Stone walls flung the words back at him.

"What fool am I?" Laughter smothered hope. "To call upon a spirit that is naught but the invention of men desperate to find meaning in a world gone mad?"

He slid from the horse, laid his cheek against the animal's neck. Flecked with the foamy sweat of her efforts, the mare stood solid, took his weight without complaint. His bad leg, numb for hours, struck with a pain that exploded up into his lower back and dropped him to the cold rock floor of the cave. He did not bother to rise, but collapsed unto his side, sank into physical pain and sweet, black oblivion.

When he came to himself, the mouth of the cave framed the dark, jagged edge of the mountain on the other side of the river. A lone star, caught in a deep V of ancient rock, drew his eye. He tightened his jaw to the pain, dragged himself up so that he sat, butt flat on the cave's stone floor.

"It's over." His words a last prayer. "Why go on even one more day? Answer me, you coward." His final plea no more than a whisper.

In the cold light of the beckoning star, he imagined himself running, boot heels clicking, saw sparks fly from his spurs as they had from the metal shoes of the mare. Every muscle in his body felt the leap as he flung himself into the empty darkness.

The mare pushed between him and the mouth of the cave, blocked his view of cold release. She lowered her head, bumped him hard in the chest.

"You'll find your way home, girl." He grabbed the animals halter, used her as leverage to pull himself to his feet.

The horse jerked her head away and then swung back and slammed the hard side of her face into his chest. Knocked off balance, his wounded leg took the weight poorly. Jeremiah screamed in pain, fell back onto the cold ground, bad leg twisted under him.

"Goddamn you, horse! I've not time for this."

The mare's warm nose nuzzled the side of his face.

Jeremiah wrapped his fingers around the leather bridle, pulled himself upward.

The horse tossed her head. The white foam of sweat flew in a speckled glow, like lightning bugs in the blackness around them. On his knees, Jeremiah clung to the horse.

"What's gotten into you? Stand still, God dammit!"

The mare's warm nose was, again, soft against the side of his face. Her lips nuzzled, one instant, wet and warm, and the next moment, her teeth nipped hard. His ear burned with pain and warmth flowed from the side of his head. Stunned, Jeremiah, held himself completely still for one breath. One breath only. Then, on his knees, he collapsed forward, pressed his head to the ground.

His words muffled against the cold foundation under him, slow and by rote, but flowing still, came the voice of the psalm.

"You have answered me."

Jeremiah fell then into a misty vision where Gil and the sergeant and sweet Maggie laid hands on him. Gil's cold palm, pressed hard to his outer thigh, drew pain and heat from his wounded leg. The bony feel of the sergeant's missing jaw, the wetness of the Yankee's exposed mouth and tongue, branded Jeremiah's chest, seared his flesh as hot vaporous poison rose into the cave's blackness. Maggie's soft palms stroked his forehead, smoothed his brow, her breath a comfort in his ear.

A still, small voice, like a salve of mercy, flowed over Jeremiah then.

For I have not despised nor abhorred the afflicted. Nor have I hidden My face from you. But when you cried to Me, I heard.

He surrendered himself, sank into a warm balm of peace. Slept.

He woke to the nickers of the mare, opened his eyes to the animal silhouetted against the dawning day. A voice, sharp and clear in the morning light, instructed:

Rise up. Gather yourself and follow a new trail back to Adeline. Go quickly now, else all be lost.

Jeremiah clenched his jaw to the pain, dragged himself back into the saddle and obeyed the voice of a God in whom he did not trust nor dare disobey.

Chapter Twenty-Three

Light pooled on the cabin floor. Adeline spooned thin mush into William's greedy mouth, gazed out the room's only window. Jeremiah had been gone three days now. Maybe he wasn't coming back for his precious books. Or for her either.

Framed in a dusty pane of imperfect glass, the trunk of the hickory tree rippled as though under moving water. When she was little, Adeline would stare hard at that magic and then, able to stand it not one second more, she'd race outside, squeeze her eyes hard and then pop them open, only to see an ordinary tree, its trunk perfectly still, breeze ruffling only the topmost leaves.

Pa laughed at her each time, quoted from The Book.

When I was a child, I spoke as a child. I understood as a child. I thought as a child. But when I became a man, I put away childish things.

For now we see as through glass, dimly, but then face to face. Now I know in part, but then I shall know just as I also am known.

And now abide faith, hope, love, these three; but the greatest of these is love.

The baby bounced on her lap, his open mouth chasing the spoon in her hand. She smiled, laid her cheek to the top of his warm head.

It was so hard to know just what the Lord instructed. Was she to hold close the love she felt for Jeremiah, cling to her hope that he would one day return that love? Or was she meant to put aside such childishness and trust in the Lord to protect her and the child, the two of them alone here on the very edge of the wilderness?

What if she could get away? Go west. Maybe go all the way to San Francisco. Folks said things were different out there. Wide open with opportunity for anyone willing to work hard and take a few chances. Adeline imagined herself in a sweeping skirt of silk, a saucy hat perched on upswept hair, dainty shoes with impossibly pointy toes, William laughing in a big-wheeled carriage with a shady parasol.

Well, *sufficient onto the day is the evil thereof*. If she didn't get the garden in soon, they'd starve even before winter set in. William bounced on her lap, slapped his hands on the table and chortled at the sound of his little palms on scarred wood.

"You're a happy boy this morning." She smoothed his dark hair, soft as corn silk under her palm. "Let's you and me finish breakfast and then we'll get to work clearing that fallen oak limb from outta the garden."

William blew mush in a sticky spray across the table top. His belly laugh spread a smile across Adeline's face.

"So, I suppose you're done with breakfast then." She wiped his face.

Ma used to swat Adeline's bottom for clowning at the table or, when she got older, a slap to the back of the head generally ended any horseplay. But Pa always grinned, said how a little fun never hurt a soul. Be nice to have either of her parents around to answer questions about how to raise this young'un. Seemed like, most days, she just made his raisin' up as she went along.

She sat the baby on the floor. He grinned up at her, then leaned forward onto his hands and knees, swayed a second and then crawled toward the speckled light peeking through the hickory leaves and dancing across the plank floor.

"It'll take me two minutes to straighten this mush mess. Then you and me, we'll hitch up ole Hector and get to work moving that fallen branch outta my garden. How's that sound to you, Billy Boy?"

The baby ignored her and she grinned at her use of that particular name for the child. She maybe didn't need Jeremiah, but it was a fact that she did miss the ornery man. Missed his deep voice and the way he sat in the evenings, his bad leg straight in front of him, lantern light falling across one of his precious books. The very air itself seemed alive with his presence on those nights, her body drawn toward him the way metal filings are drawn to a magnet.

Well, enough mooning over a man with moods that changed as fast as the weather on a day in early spring. One minute, a clear blue sky that filled the heart with longing and the next pellets of hail big enough to knock a body to the ground.

Adeline lifted the baby from his game of chasing light, changed his diaper and, while he struggled and fussed, wrapped him securely in a length of cotton. She bent at the waist and struggled to position the child against her back while he kicked against the bindings and screamed as though being murdered. Finally, sweat already tickling her spine, she managed to tie William to her back.

In the barn she gathered the shovel and ax, careful not to rub up against the blades of either tool. Sharpening was one of the few jobs Jeremiah could do with his bad leg. He took the job so seriously she feared he'd wear every slice of metal on the farm plumb away before he healed up. A hidden cardinal chireeped from the fluttering leaves of the lone maple beside the corral. Adeline lifted her skirt, tucked the bunched hem into the fabric of the baby sling tied at her waist. The ax in one hand, shovel dangling from the other, she danced a peculiar bobbing step across the yard, an attempt to calm the baby whose loud objections to confinement made her head throb.

Pa used to say *take care of your tools, Adeline, and they'll take of you.* She leaned the ax and shovel against the trunk of the oak that shaded the south end of the garden, protected from the morning sun, and returned to the barn for the mule. On her back, the baby bounced, cried himself into a fit and then, finally, as she led the mule to the garden, fell into a bout of hiccups that ended in sleep.

It took a hot, sweaty effort to rig the trace to the mule, but finally Adeline stood panting, her booted feet ankle-deep in rich garden dirt. Linked to the fallen oak limb, the mule stood passive, head down in the warm, mid-morning air. Dust clogged Adeline's nose and coated her damp skin. She stared west at a line of low, black-bottomed clouds sweeping in from the west, teasing with the hope of rain. At the mule's head, one hand on the leather lead, the other behind her cupping the baby's bottom in an attempt to shift his weight more comfortably on her back, Adeline was overcome suddenly with the feeling of being watched. She stood dead still and scanned the forest. Dropping the lead, she turned in a slow circle, eyes darting, searching for anything out of the ordinary.

Nothing. No sound but the breeze in the tops of trees newly-leafed with green. No movement but that of the mule, his warm head pressing hard against her chest.

"Enough of this foolishness now," she said, as much to herself as to the animal beside her. "Gee up and then I'll get these lines off and you can spend the rest of the day in the shade. Come on, now, gee."

The mule leaned into the traces. The oak branch inched forward, a wave of black dirt gathering along the limb's front edge. The baby shifted in his sleep, his weight tipping Adeline off balance for just a moment as she tugged at the mule's halter, looked back over her shoulder at the branch.

What was that?

She pulled the mule up short. The rhythmic sound of a horse coming hard off the ridgeline lifted Adeline's head.

Jeremiah! She wiped dirty hands on her dress front, struggled to untangle the hem of her skirt from where she'd tucked it at her waist, pushed loose hair back into the messy knot at the back of her neck. Of course the man would return now. When she was coated in dirt and sweaty as a hog. Not a thing to eat in the house but goat's milk and day-old biscuits.

Man and rider emerged from the woods into the yard. The white, lightning-bolt blaze of the horse's face slammed her heart against her chest. Sun glinted from the dull gray-blue of a pistol barrel pointed in her direction.

Brett James sat the horse, a lazy smile on his face.

"Well, now, lookee you." His voice casual and mean. "Working like a darkie in the heat a the day."

The barrel of the gun jerked sideways. "Come on over here to me, gal. Ain't you happy to see your fiancé?"

"You got no business here, Brett James." Adeline could not look away from the eye of the pistol. "You and I are done."

His laughter caught her heart in her throat. She shivered, took a deep breath and met his gaze.

"We ain't nowhere near done, girl." The look on his face playful, his voice hard. "Get on outta them clothes now. I've not rolled in the dirt with a nice piece a slash for some time. We gonna have us some fun."

Anger, cold and solid, settled over Adeline, coated and froze her fear to a tight, hard knot that sunk to the bottom of her belly.

"That's real big talk for a man with no trigger finger and two bullet holes in him from the last time we met up."

He slid from the horse's back, the animal tossing its head and leaning away as a horse is wont to do when its rider is not to be trusted.

James's grin was lopsided. "You think I don't know, you think the whole town don't know you're fucking that crazy preacher and that savage both? You taken 'em both at once, or you bedding 'em one at a time?"

Heat flooded her chest, rose up and claimed her face.

"You got one minute," he said. "Then you better be nekid in the dirt with them legs spread open. Else that papoose you got strapped to your back like as if you're some kind of squaw? You ever see what a bullet to the head does to a little Indian brat? It takes all the starch outta his mama, I guarantee you that."

He strolled toward her, his boots silent in the soft dirt of the garden. Adeline backed away, edged toward the shade of the oak.

"I'm gonna start to countin' now." He grinned, wiggled his eyebrows, as if flirting at a church social. "When I get to ten, if you ain't all nekid and smiles, the brat's dead."

His eyes narrowed and she reeled back from the raw evil revealed.

"One."

She needed to say something, anything, to distract him. But her dry mouth stayed shut, her mind frozen in anger and terror. She took another step back.

"Run and I promise the sight a that half-breed's brains will be the best part a your day. We're at two now, gal, and you're still wearing all them filthy clothes."

He was less than twenty feet away now. If she turned to run, he'd have a clear shot at William. She put her hand to the top of her dress, opened the top button, inched toward the shade.

"Too slow." He closed the distance between them, his hand ripping her dress and camisole before she could back away.

Just as she had done when kidnapped by the Indians, Adeline felt as though she were looking down on herself. She saw a young girl, standing at the edge of an old garden, breasts rising and falling in panic, while she looked into the soulless eyes of a man intent on ruining and then killing her, killing her child.

Into this tunneled view intruded the scream of a horse. The mule tossed his head, pulled at his lines. The shriek of the horse, the movement of the mule, returned Adeline to her body. A deep growl rumbled from the yard behind them, turned Brett James toward the sound. Deep in her belly Adeline felt the vibration of instinctual fear mix and blend with the knowledge that Montega had been right and God had provided salvation.

The bear, monstrous in its power, stood on its hind legs. Tiny eyes squinted. Wide mouth opened, issued another roaring warning.

Adeline ran to the oak tree.

Brett James fired his pistol at the bear.

Her hands closed over the smooth handle of the ax. The power of the tool pleasingly heavy, its weight swinging out in a little half-circle as she turned back toward James.

The pistol fired again.

From a distance, as though in a dream, she watched the bear drop to all fours, shift from one paw to the other, big head swaying.

Adeline's boots touched the ground, surely they did, but she felt light as air, as though she flew toward the man who would kill her and her baby. She lifted the ax high on the backstroke. James turned. His eyes wide in surprise, fear. Then, as the blade swung forward strengthened by every wrong, every terror, every pain she had ever endured, Adeline sliced a path through the air. There was an instant, a moment, when the dark eyes of Brett James reflected for one split-second on the knowledge of his own death.

Someone screamed.

The blade struck just above the collar of James's shirt at the side of his neck. His body continued its turn toward her. Blood, so much blood, like paint thrown from a bucket. A bloody arc that glistened in the air, hung for an eternity before falling to the dirt. She tugged at the ax and a scarlet veil misted the air, a second bloody half-circle that hung, hung as though time itself stopped and then fell in a new-moon pattern onto the soft ground.

It took long seconds for James to fall, for his body to collapse into the dirt. The screaming went on and on, joined with the frantic cries of a baby. Adeline stood, ax raised high, looked down at the man who lay at her feet, blood darkening the soil around a gash that cocked his head oddly to one side.

The man opened his mouth. Gasped. Blood gurgled in his throat. A hand closed over her ankle. She brought the ax down through the screams, through the cries of the baby, through the panicked braying of the mule, straight down she swung the ax, sinking the thin blade through the soft flesh of his throat, through the bone of his neck, through the last of her fear.

The wooden handle sunk deep in the rich dirt of the garden, separated head from shoulders.

Adeline staggered back. Her vision filled with the image of a hen racing headless in the dirt, Ma already striding across the chicken yard, waiting patiently for the stupid fowl to recognize its own death.

She stared at the body pouring blood into the black soil at her feet. The baby's cries grew louder, more desperate. From far away came the thunk and clack of wood against wood, the sound like cicadas on a summer night that lull and invade dreams, but do not wake the sleeper. It was the bear's roar, a thundering growl that finally released Adeline from her trance, lifted her head from the dead man at her feet to look into the animal's beady eyes.

William continued to scream.

At the edge of the garden the bear rose like a mountain, close enough to see that one huge front paw was minus a nail. One long, sharp claw out of ten, missing. The animal's musky stink mixed with the smell of rich dirt warming in the day's heat, the scent of blood that reminded somehow of the metallic heat of a blacksmith's shop, the sharp tang of her own sweat. The bear dropped to all fours, swung one front leg forward, hesitated. Adeline clutched the ax handle tight, took one giant step backward.

The baby's cries grew louder, more frantic.

"It's going to be all right." She spoke to William, and to the beast swaying toward her, and to herself too.

The rhythmic thunk, thunk, thunk began again. She turned her head from the bear's stare, followed the sound to the mule, still tethered to the oak branch. The oak limb was caught, hung between the stump of an old pine tree and a flat-topped chunk of granite Pa used to use as a natural bench to sit, smoke a hand rolled cigarette and *survey his domain.*

The mule's eyes rolled, exposed a wide circle of white around dark irises.

Adeline flipped her gaze, her full attention, back to the approaching bear.

"I'm gonna back outta here now." Her mouth dry, throat closed, voice cracked.

She stepped away from the bear, inched her way toward the mule. Montega's prediction returned to her then, whispered confidence in her ear.

The spirits have bound the bear to you.

Be more comforting if she knew whether that meant the two of them, girl and bear, had some kind of covenant, or if the premonition told that she was bound to end up in the beast's belly.

"I ain't gonna hurt you." As if the bear was concerned that *she* would harm *it*.

She took another step to the side, edged closer to the corral.

The baby's screams had grown lower, intermittent, the crying of a child exhausted, dropping, finally, into sleep.

The bear raised his snout to the breeze, stopped his forward movement.

"Just let me get this mule unfastened and into the barn."

Every muscle commanded her to run. Every instinct said ease away slow.

The bear swung his shaggy head away from her, shuffled into the garden, lowered his snout to the body of Brett James.

Adeline slid backwards, step-by-slow-step, to the mule. She sliced through the traces with the ax, and hurried Hector to the barn. She did not look back toward the garden. Did not dwell on what the snorts and grunts and thumps and wet noises coming from that direction might mean.

Chapter Twenty-Four

Thin strips of widow's lace raced a gibbous moon. Night flowed into bluish light and back again into deep dark. With the face of the moon hidden, the mare pushed through blackness so absolute as to be solid. Jeremiah laid his face against the horse's neck, watched white foam flow from the mare in a veil of effort. He gritted his teeth to the throbbing pain of his leg, ignored the hot tip of a knife that sliced up from the calf into the base of his spine.

Dark, wind-frayed streamers tore and the moon blessed his path. The mare stumbled and he knew he should dismount, leave the trail, search out water and rest.

Go quickly now, else all will be lost.

It would do no good to run the horse to ground. He'd not make a quarter mile on his bad leg. Truth be told, he wasn't sure he'd last long enough to reach Adeline even if he could keep the mare on her feet.

Clouds cavorted across the moon, plunged him again into black night. The mare slowed to a walk. Jeremiah loosed the reins, closed his eyes and gave the animal her head.

I am the Lord. I will not fail or forsake you until the work is finished. The voice a whisper, like smoke in bright sunlight the words filtered upward, scattered in the night.

Jeremiah was thrown forward, lost his balance, as the horse pointed her nose downward into a ravine to their left. There was a lovely moment of peace when Jeremiah accepted the pull of giving up, of letting himself slide to the ground and simply lay in the dark until he died.

At the same moment, below the man and horse—but close, touching close—a wolf's howl tore the night. That piercing song of joy and hunger turned the mare to the right, straightened Jeremiah in the saddle and erased all pain from his leg. A second howl from the ravine, like a finger of terror that reached out a claw in the darkness and stroked his cheek, and Jeremiah turned the horse back to the path.

The blue light of a moon, freshly freed and naked among the clouds, lit the trail. The mare heaved herself out of the ravine, her hooves a staccato heartbeat on the path over the mountain and to Adeline. Infused by this new terror, Jeremiah leaned over the mare's neck. He spoke soft, encouraging words to the exhausted animal, promised her rest and oats and spring water fresh as a new dawn.

For hours, as the moon played chase with the storm clouds sweeping in from the west, each time exhausted horse and rider lagged, the piercing howl of a wolf spurred them on, awakened in both a strength neither knew they possessed. Finally, Jeremiah looked up from the pounding hooves of the mare, raised his eyes and watched a shimmering line of gold trace the jagged peaks of the familiar mountain to the east and knew a few minutes ride would bring him back to Adeline.

A pistol shot shattered the morning quiet.

The sound bounced through the thick woods that separated him from the farm, carried fear like shrapnel to pierce his gut, bind him in pain and carry him forward.

Branches, bowed low with new growth, slapped at his face. The mare faltered, recovered and ran on. Neither man nor mare hesitated at the ridgeline. The horse's stumbling gait plunged them down into the hollow, parting a sea of spring grass that brushed the animal's belly.

Then, as though everything before that moment had occurred in a vision, the horse came to a stop beside the closed doors of the barn. The mare stood, head low, sides heaving, flecked in sweat. Jeremiah lifted his head in desperation, swept his gaze over the empty yard, knew he'd come too late.

The air reeked with the stink of blood and entrails. The Colt shook in

Jeremiah's hands when he pulled it from his belt. He cursed himself for a fool and a coward even as he slammed fear and rage into a battle-scarred box. The pistol steadied in his hand. No chicken pecked the dirt for bugs. No goat tore grass or tender leaf. No mule brayed a greeting. No woman or child greeted his return. Jeremiah's heart slowed, he forced himself to look toward the garden, toward the source of the rank smell of death. The muffled sounds of feeding came to him then, resurrected his rage and terror.

The bear's open mouth dripped with viscous red that stained from snout to ears and darkened the fur of the wide chest. The beast raised its beady eyes to his, swayed once, back and forth like the pendulum of a clock, lowered its massive head and returned to rooting in the bloody remains at its feet. A scream tore from Jeremiah's throat, the Colt jerked in his hand and a shot exploded in the unnatural quiet. The bear raised a huge paw, scratched at the side of its shaggy head as though brushing away a mildly irritating insect.

Jeremiah fired his last round.

Behind him, the door to the barn slammed.

The bear lifted its snout. A misshapen, bloody, human head hung from the animal's mouth.

Jeremiah bellowed, slid from the mare, fell in a heap. From the woods rode an antlered buck deer astride the roan stallion he'd stolen from Maggie's dead husband. Shots exploded. Soft hands caressed his face. Warm breath touched his ear. A woman's voice soothed.

"Jeremiah? Can you hear me?"

The deer squatted beside him, spoke with a human voice.

"Adeline and the child are safe."

Jeremiah struggled to free himself from the heavy blackness that pulled and tugged at his mind, enticed him away from the confusing images that whirled his vision. He felt himself lifted, carried, looked up at the antlered, talking face.

"The bear is gone. Your woman safe. You rode hard, my friend."

"Wolves." Jeremiah struggled to warn of the wolf pack that had pursued him and the mare. "Wolves close by."

The deer-man laughed.

"No wolves here in many seasons. A bear is trouble enough. Sleep now. There are no wolves and the bear, now fat with the meat of Brett James, will trouble us no more."

Cool hands stroked his face, removed his clothes. He floated in and out of sleep, dreamt of a full moon that raced torn clouds above wolves and bloody bears. At the blurry edge of consciousness, a woman murmured as though in prayer.

Later he woke to a searing pain in his leg, the bed wet beneath him, heard the woman's voice.

"Can you save the leg?"

Jeremiah claimed the voice then, saw corn-silk hair, freckles across the bridge of a nose, gray eyes—Adeline.

"I will hold him. You must cut." Another voice said. A male voice. Jeremiah fought his way through the haze in his mind. He knew that voice, did not want the owner around Adeline.

"What? I can't . . . ."

"You must. Or he will die. The fool has rebroken the leg. The poison is strong in him. Cut from here . . . to here. Deep. Until the knife point hits hard bone."

A weight fell upon him. A heavy, hard mass that smelled of dirt and bear grease. A figure rose up from the fog of his mind. The Indian. Montega, bare-chested, dark eyes triumphant.

"Do it now. Hurry."

A searing pain, like none he'd ever known, pierced his leg. Pain so exquisite, so intense, so all-consuming, that it canceled every moment he'd ever experienced. Pain that focused, balanced his mind, his body, and his soul on its blade tip.

A scream tore his throat, carried him to every battlefield tent-hospital he'd ever hurried past.

A smell, rotten and putrid, the devil himself, loosed into the air.

Chapter Twenty-Five

Adeline stared, mesmerized, her face reflected in the river of gold. Coins were scattered across her scarred kitchen table as though washed up after a flood, or thrown by some mighty wind. A bound stack of paper money rested to the left, tied with a length of rawhide with a rough square knot. The open front door caught the last of the day's sun, a stream of dust motes danced, flitted over the treasure like tiny insects.

Her heart fluttered her chest, breath caught in her throat. She hung the empty saddle bags over the back of a cane chair. Stood silent and still in the cabin where she had once been an innocent child. The wavering trunk of the oak tree framed in the window drew her attention. Adeline raised her eyes to the image of this magical childhood comfort. The head of Brett James grinned at her through the paned glass. From James's ragged neck flowed strings of blood and hacked meat, the white of broken bone and the tallow-yellow of gristle.

James winked.

Adeline grabbed at the heavy saddle bags for support. Her hand slid over the cool leather. Her knees became jelly. She fell against the wooden chair, slid down the cane back and sat, her butt flat against the plank floor, her legs splayed in front of her like a ragdoll.

She had killed a man. Chopped off his head with an ax.

In a nightmare, she relived the moment almost a year before when James sat beside her in a pew, the smell of late summer heavy in the air. She saw again the exact slant of wavering light across her lap from the church's one window. Felt the heat that built and grew between them as Pastor Coleman droned on about the last days. She turned her face toward James. Stared at the glisten of saliva on his slightly overlapping front teeth. His suspended head dripped gore and white bone. James grinned at her.

Adeline screamed, fell sideways onto the floor and curled in a tight ball. Shaking took her, as though a mighty hand grabbed her by the heart and shook and shook and shook. The fit went on and on until she was no more than a whimpering animal. From far away she heard a calm, flat voice proclaim, *Do not fight fair, Adeline. There is no fair.* The trembling lessened. She swallowed the truth. Knew she'd kill James again if given a chance. With each of those bloody, slicing strokes she had become someone different, someone who would never again be as hopeful or as fearful as she had been that morning.

She sat up, smoothed her skirt over her legs. Almost, but not quite, touching her left foot, William rocked on his hands and knees, his eyes wide and staring. Adeline opened her arms and the baby crawled to her, covered her face with tiny hands and wet kisses. She hugged the child to her and the remnants of her shaking fit passed over.

Salvation and escape winked at her from the dull gold river that flowed across Ma's old kitchen table. She saw herself, one daintily shoed foot stepping from a carriage, a man in a derby tipping his hat, offering his arm. William, fat with health, bouncing in her arms. She wiped sweat from her face. The grit of dirt scratched her skin, brought her all the way back to the moment.

The money must have come from the James gang's robbery of the train headed for the Kansas City stock yards. The gold glittered like magic on the scarred wood table, brought a flood of danger. The James gang might not care a hoot about losing their distant cousin, but Jessie and Frank would come looking for Brett's share of the gold and greenbacks.

Into the soft curve of William's ear she whispered, "We're going to see the Pacific Ocean, Billy Boy."

A low moan from her brother's old bedroom told her Jeremiah was waking. He'd need tending. Montega had held him while she sliced open the preacher's leg from ankle to thigh, pus and black blood pouring from the swollen flesh. She had spent an hour or more cleaning the wound with warm water steeped in some herb the Indian called simply Spirit Salve. The leg would either heal or kill. It was in the hands of God.

From the garden she could hear Montega sinking a sharp-bladed shovel deep into rich, soon to be richer, soil. William patted her cheek with a small hand, a drool-coated twenty-dollar gold piece held to his mouth in the other fat fist.

Adeline pushed herself to her feet, unfolded the tiny fingers and retrieved the shiny coin from the boy, setting off a red-faced squall. She sat William on the floor and he squeezed his eyes closed, opened his mouth in a scream. The child drew a long, ragged breath and the bleat of the nanny came to him through the cabin's walls. He smiled, clapped his chubby hands.

"Da da da!"

"More like ma ma ma," she told him. "But close enough."

The ordinary moment closed the door on Adeline's shaking remorse. She had no doubt the grinning head of Brett James would follow her for a very long time, but for today, for right now, there was work to do.

Two steps carried her to the front door, which she pulled firmly shut before sweeping the money back into the saddle bags. Hope and fear tangled, a mixed up mess in her belly. A cold knot of fear clutched, bent her double, even as her heart beat hard in excitement.

Jeremiah moaned again, louder this time. The wooden bed frame squeaked, revealed his tossing and turning.

William crawled to her, tiny fists grasping her skirt, and pulled himself to a standing position. The baby grinned at his own accomplishment, rubbed his face into the folds of calico.

"You're a clever boy," she told the child. "But right now I need to find a good hiding place."

She disentangled chubby fists from her skirt. William sat with a padded thump and then tilted forward onto his hands and knees, his hiccupping sobs following her into their room. Her heart beat so loudly she feared Montega would hear its pounding rhythm from the garden, abandon his filthy work to investigate the drumming beat. The saddle bags heavy in her arms, she stood, awkward with uneven weight, searched the room for a place to hide the unexpected treasure the Indian had carried in to her from James's black horse.

Under the bed was too obvious. If the James gang came for their gold, where would they not think to look? She knelt beside the steamer trunk grandma and grandpa Mitchell had carried with them from England. The saddlebags beside her, she lifted the heavy lid and removed the bridal ring quilt. Under her ma's last gift to her, her fingers smoothed the folds of a wool blanket washed so many times the cloth was soft and thin as paper. Under every treasure, in a much mended calico bag with a drawstring, she found what she was searching for. The bags contents, rags and ruined panties, scattered around her in a blood stained puddle, Adeline folded and worked the saddle bags to the bottom of the empty sack. She remembered how ma had given her the drawstring bag on the day, as a naïve twelve-year-old, she had run from the outhouse, certain she was dying. Her heart threatening to kill her with its pounding, she covered the saddlebags, hid the gold, under the soft cotton requirements of what ma called The Curse.

She returned the now-heavy calico bag to the bottom of the chest, covered it with the blanket and quilt and closed the lid. The baby edged his way along the bed, slapped his hands onto the mattress and filled the room with belly laughs.

"Come here, happy boy."

Still on her knees, she held her arms out to the child who sidestepped his way along the bed and threw himself, warm and smelling of soap, against her breasts. She hugged him to her, slipped a hand under his shirt and tickled the roundness of his belly. The baby collapsed against her in a fit of giggles and she lifted him squirming to her face and kissed his rounded tummy over and over in an ecstasy of joy and relief.

If her insides trembled and shook and her knees threatened to fail to support her each time she saw the fan of blood flying from the ax, heard the sickening thunk of sharpened metal sinking into flesh and bone, tasted again the hot iron and slaughterhouse smell of what she had done, she pushed the images deep inside, concentrated on getting through the next hour. Deep in her belly, where terror loves to dwell, she knew she'd relive those few moments in the garden over and over for the rest of her life. But, for now, William needed tending and she had money, enough money to get her out of Arkansas and to a better life.

"The work is done." The voice came from directly behind her, startled a yelp from her even as William raised dimpled arms to Montega.

"Good." She cleared her throat. "Good. Thank you for . . . for . . . taking care of that." She forced herself to meet his gaze, swallowed the dry lump that choked her throat. "Won't the bear return for his . . . meal?"

His hands and arms still dripping water from his wash-up at the outside tub, Montega lifted the child into his arms, watched as Adeline pulled herself from the floor and arranged her skirt so the folds half-hid the trunk at her feet.

"Your *wasape*, your bear, will not return." He studied her face, a smile tipping the corners of his mouth.

"That beast is not my bear. Why do you speak such hokum?"

"Your ignorance does not steal the truth, only hides it from your spirit, blocks your view of the message."

She tilted her head to the side, licked dry lips.

Montega lifted the baby to his shoulders, arranged chubby legs to hang down his chest, the Indian's hands firm on the boy's calves. "You show great foolishness. *Wasape* was sent as your protector, just as *shonke*, the wolf, guided Jeremiah in the night."

She dried her hands on her skirt, pushed past man and boy, strode across the kitchen to the oven. A square cast iron skillet in hand, her eye fell on a round, gleaming object on the floor near the table's edge. Quickly, she raised her eyes from the evidence of her deceit.

"You've gotta be hungry after all that . . . that work. There's biscuits left from this morning and I'll stir us up a batch of red-eye gravy."

The toe of her boot covered the coin.

"The child and I will wait on the porch. Give you time to serve us. Time to hide that gold coin with the others from the saddlebags."

Adeline jerked her head up, stared into the grinning face of the Indian.

Chapter Twenty-Six

From the kitchen came the familiar sound of a heavy cast-iron frying pan being laid on the pot-bellied stove. Jeremiah shifted his weight in the bed, enjoyed the way the smell of grits and meat gravy mixed with the breeze from his open window—the scent of early summer blending with the smells of breakfast. He imagined the tender green of new growth in the garden. The dark, sword leaves of corn. The curling tendrils of scarlet runners. The deep, rounded leaves of okra. The fine, white roots of all that good food growing fat and strong on the miserable flesh of Brett James.

Jeremiah smiled. His leg ached cleanly now. The swollen, pulsing poison vanquished with the slice of Adeline's knife. He had awakened yesterday morning, clear headed and filled with a calm peace that refused worry. Adeline sat by his bed, the baby asleep in her lap. He had watched her rock Billy Boy, the baby's head pressed against her breast. This was no longer the desperate girl who had stolen his horse. No. This was a young woman, sure and solid, capable and not easily persuaded from her chosen path.

A voice in his head laughed. *Should have had her while she was vulnerable. This one, now, she ain't gonna put up with your shenanigans.* Jeremiah recognized the sentiment, searched the room for the sergeant. Found only the fresh breeze of a summer morn. He had not been visited by Gil, or the sergeant, or Maggie either, not since he rode away from the cave, trusted the mare to bring him home.

It was then he remembered the wolves. The dark of the night, when the moon hid her round face. The roiling, clenching of his gut with each howl. The surge of energy from the horse. The terror that filled him with a strength he did not know he had. The endless ride through stripes of blue moonlight and darkness as black and heavy as the grave.

"Think you're up to eating at the table?" Adeline question brought him back to the present.

She stood, framed in the open door of his room. Light from the window shimmered on the pale gold of her hair. A streak of white flour marked her cheek and wisps of hair, darkened with sweat, hung damp on her neck. She wiped floury hands on the apron tied at her waist.

"It's been what?" he asked. "Almost six weeks since you sliced my leg to the bone from hip to foot. Guess that's time enough to heal."

His face hurt with his smile. He was reminded of leather, badly kept, that splits and cracks when bent at an unfamiliar angle.

She shook her head. Light scattered around her head, like water will fly from a shaking dog after a swim. Delighted with the mental imagery, Jeremiah laughed out loud. The sound, honest and clear, a novelty which brought up more laughter. Adeline's smile seemed hesitant.

"You want help settin' up?"

A soft breast pressed to his arm as he leaned into her, the smell of her skin inviting as the breakfast that awaited.

"Sure. I could use some help."

She turned her back on him, returned to the kitchen.

"Montega." A smile in her voice. "The invalid would like to try eatin' at the table. Can you help get him in here?"

Jeremiah was perched on the edge of the mattress when the Indian appeared at the door, the crotch of a young hickory tree balanced lightly in one dark hand.

"I don't want that damn thing." He nodded toward the crutch, his breath stolen with the effort to swing his legs over the side of the bed and sit. "Where's my trousers?"

Fresh with washing, his pants laid folded in the rocker Adeline had dragged beside his bed. Montega tossed the pants to him, the essence of sunshine and the breezes of the forest rising from them. In his mind's eye he saw Adeline bent over a washtub scrubbing the heavy cotton with lye soap and that worn-in-the-middle brush of hers. The homey smell comforted at the same instant fear shivered him.

He glanced up at Montega, pasted on a smile. "Goose walked over my grave."

The Indian did not blink. "Many years past, in the time before your people invaded our land, Dancing Brave tried to tame young shonkes— wolves—he took from the den of their dead mother."

"I am not in the mood for Indian legends. Not this morning. Get the hell out of my room while I dress."

Montega did not move from the doorway, stood, arms loose at his sides, watched as Jeremiah fought with his pain, struggled with light-headedness, and, finally, got both feet in pant-legs.

"Dancing Brave fed these wolves choice bits of meat, brought the animals into his tent and kept the shonkes warm against his squaw in the winter."

Jeremiah exhaled, then raised his butt off the bed enough to slide the pants up and button the waistband.

"Let me guess," he said to the storyteller, "in return for being rescued, the wolves ate the kind and gentle Dancing Bear along with his wife?"

Montega crossed his arms over his chest, bare but for a deerskin vest, stained nearly black with use and hung with the vertebrae of small animals, a dozen or so trading beads and what looked suspiciously like at least two, maybe three scalps braided into a greasy knot and tied with a gingham bow.

"Your mind seeks pain," Montega said. "One wolf pup crept under the tent each night, preferred to sleep outside. We found him one cold morning, only the tip of his nose above the snow."

"The lone wolf," Jeremiah said, "meaning me. Insisted on running from comforts offered and ended up out in the cold, frozen. Is that your message?"

"No message. I only share with you an interesting story about a wolf."

Jeremiah lifted himself to his feet. Sharp fangs sunk deep into his foot, the snake of pain began to swallow the leg. Jeremiah sat down hard on the bed. At the edge of his tunneled vision appeared a length of smooth hickory. He tucked the fork of the wood into his armpit, pushed himself to his feet. His jaw clenched. Breath shallow and hard-won, he waited out the pain.

Jeremiah looked up in time to see a fleeting smile on the brown face. He waited until air became easier to draw into his lungs and pain retreated a little. Then, one slow, dragging step at a time, he worked his way past the Indian and to the kitchen table.

Adeline set a steaming cup of coffee in front of him. The smell of chicory soothed. Montega passed behind him on silent moccasins, took his able body out the front door.

"I can't figure what to do with the horse." The sound of her voice an enticement. A trap.

A heavy plate appeared, the sweet smell of biscuits and butter rising to him. A bowl of thick, yellow grits was set to his right while he still smeared his biscuit.

"What horse?" Even as he spoke, he remembered the wide mouth of a bear. A head. Dull, dead eyes.

She lowered herself onto the chair across from him, a cup of coffee in one hand, a half-eaten bowl of grits in the other. From her bedroom came the sound of a waking, fussing baby. She spooned grits into her mouth.

"Brett James's horse," she said around the mush.

"It's coming back to me," he said. "That old bear that was nosing around after the nanny? He ended up killing James?"

"Not exactly." She slurped coffee.

He wasn't ready to eat, waited for his stomach to cipher its way through the pain brought on by his little stroll from bed to table. Small sips of coffee provided time to study the woman across from him, enjoy the way her throat moved with the swallowing of breakfast, the dove-gray of her eyes and the solid manner in which she sat in the old chair—back straight, feet flat on the wood floor.

If he could get rid of the Indian, he'd a mind to sweep the breakfast dishes to the floor, lay her round bottom against the table and claim her for his own. Trouble was, that's exactly what he'd be doing. Claiming her.

His trouble was not the swelling of his loins. Lust was easily remedied. He feared his feelings for this young woman. The soft plumpness of her forearms, the way she stood over a chore, one hip cocked to the side, the baby balanced perfectly against her.

He gritted his teeth.

"What does that mean?" he asked. "The bear didn't exactly kill James? I saw the beast leave with the head." He did not tell her of his panic, terror, a pain worse than that of his damn leg, when he thought the body the bear feasted upon was hers.

From the porch came a throaty chuckle.

Jeremiah twisted in his chair, set off the pain in his leg again. Damn that Indian.

"The bear helped some with gettin' rid a the body," Adeline said. "But was me what killed Brett James."

He watched her finish her coffee in two gulps, the fussing baby growing louder with each passing moment.

"You shot him?"

She stood, gathered her empty bowl and cup.

"Turns out all that sharpening of blades you did when you was laid-up come in handy."

"Adeline? You stabbed him? Did he not have a gun?"

"He did. No trigger finger on his right hand, thanks to you, but it appeared he'd learnt to shoot just fine with t'other." She looked him square in the face, her eyes flat gray stones flecked with pale moss green. "I kilt him with the ax."

"You killed a man with an ax?" This little bitty girl? "But. I saw the bear."

"You ain't listenin'. I was workin' the garden with the mule. Removin' a big oak limb what had fallen 'cross my intended corn patch. James come at me with a gun and . . . and bad intentions. The bear reared up behind him, turned James's mind long enough for me to reach the ax. Once the man was kilt, I didn't see no reason to fight the bear for the meat."

From the porch came loud guffaws, the shuffling of soft moccasins on wood planks.

Adeline swept past Jeremiah, strode into her room where Billy Boy was working himself into a good fit.

Jeremiah bit into a biscuit, washed the first buttery bite down with coffee. The front porch squeaked and Montega stepped around the table and sat in the chair Adeline had just vacated.

"Is she okay?" he asked the Indian.

"I heard a shot. By the time I got to the cabin, James was dead. Reminded me of how a squaw'll take out after a rooster who's raked her with his spurs once too often. Looked like she hit him from behind." Montega ran a finger along the side of his throat. "The blow knocked him down, stunned him some. Once he was on the ground, the second swipe took off his head."

Jeremiah pictured the ax raised high above Adeline's head. The whistle of the blade through the air on its downward strike. The shock of impact, the head falling to the side, surprise still registering in the eyes. He held the Indian's stare.

"She did what she had to do," Jeremiah said.

"She did. Now you and I must hide the horse and fight off whoever it is comes looking for the gold she stole."

Chapter Twenty-Seven

Naked, knees pressed to her breasts, steamy water lapped gently at her navel with each breath. Adeline rinsed the last of the soap from her back. The August day had been hot, but the evening had cooled nicely. The warm water felt good. The presence of Jeremiah on the other side of the wall tingled her skin, hardened her nipples and stained her breasts with heat. The man seemed drawn to her and repelled by her in pretty near the same exact strength, like a magnet that can't figure out if it's pushing or pulling. As the hunk of iron being knocked about by his indecision, she was getting mighty tired of his confusion.

She'd turned seventeen last month, knew very well what she wanted. Jeremiah, as her husband, in her bed. The two of 'em raising William and making more babies. And there were moments when she knew without a doubt that he wanted the same. But then, other moments, generally immediately after the air heated between them and their bodies leaned toward one another, when Jeremiah seemed disgusted with the very thought of her. He'd stomp off into the woods, or saddle the mare and she'd hear him for hours riding rings around the cabin.

Last week she'd met him at the door after one of his circling rides.

"If'n you're so dang eager to ride out, then go. The baby and I don't need you here."

He had lifted his hand, stroked the side of her face and she had been undone.

He quoted scripture then and his voice vibrated in her belly, made her think of the purr of a cougar.

"For the law is spiritual, but I am carnal. What I do, I do not understand. What I want to do, I do not. But that which I hate, that I do."

Adeline shivered, remembering the slap of those words, the way she had stood watching the chickens peck in the last of the day's light.

"It ain't scripture I need, preacher," she had murmured.

Done with her ablutions, the metal sides of the tub pressed into her palms as she pushed herself up, lifted high one foot and then the other, stepped out of the cooled water. A breeze billowed the curtains at the open window. Her skin puckered like a plucked chicken. Adeline dried quickly, pulled her best nightgown over her head. Buttoned to the neck, the hem exposed her ankles and, with a single-minded purpose that made her wonder at herself, she left camisole and drawers folded on the shelf, the soft cotton of the gown like a flowing hand against her skin.

Did Ruth not lie at the feet of Boaz? Did not Beersheba ensnare David with her body? 'Course, that story didn't work out all that well, but still. Adeline was done with waiting.

On the other side of the wall, Billy Boy sang his night-night lullaby— soft humming that meant he rubbed the ragged edge of his favorite blanket along his lower lip. Montega had left yesterday, lit out up north to find the small band of Cheyenne he'd traded Brett James's blazed gelding to three months ago. He meant to collect more of the ammunition they'd promised. The Indian's absence left her alone in the cabin with Jeremiah. She ran her hands over the thin cotton that clung to her body like a second skin.

In the main room, Jeremiah would be reading. He might be studying the bible. Lately he'd fallen back on reading the Lord's word. A line or two all he seemed to get through before either sitting quietly in thought or slamming The Book shut and disappearing outside in a cloud of curses. He called it talking to God but it appeared to her more like arguing with the devil. She pictured Jeremiah in the rocker, long legs stretched in front of him, book open in his lap, his mind filled with thoughts of her bathing in the next room. She'd bet one of them twenty dollar gold coins that's just what he was thinking on, too.

Now that his leg was almost healed, a dozen times each day she looked up to see him watching her, a hunger in his eyes that struck the flint of her own need. Each night her body ached with the effort of not going to him. She smoothed the thin nightgown over her thighs, opened her bedroom door and stepped into the cabin's main room.

Jeremiah stood, gazing out the window toward the fingernail moon that peaked over the Boston Mountains. He kept his back to her, did not turn. His reflection wavered each time his warm breath met cool glass.

Adeline's heart pounded in time to her plea.

Lord, forgive me for my boldness, but if you cannot help him, I will.

Her bare feet left wet prints on the cabin's plank floor. In the glass he raised his eyes, watched her approach. Close enough to touch, close enough that she fancied the narrow distance between them threw sparks into the air. He turned to her, so close now his shoulder brushed her hair in the movement. She slipped her arms around his waist, pressed herself to him. The hardness, the wide strength of his chest against her breasts seemed ordained.

His black eyes flashed. The scar that trailed his left check appeared to crawl in the flickering candle light. He brought his mouth to hers, his tongue hot and probing, his hands like hungry beasts cupping, pressing at her breasts, thumbs hard against her nipples.

She was afraid. Frightened by his urgency, frozen by her own desire. She struggled against him. He forced her back against the chinked wall of the cabin. His manhood hard against her belly. Hot hands probed high on her thighs. His tongue deep in her mouth gagged her, brought back the incident at the church picnic with Brett James.

She struggled. Fists pounded against his chest. He imprisoned her wrists, dropped his mouth to her breasts. Protected by only the thin cotton gown, she cried out at the warmth of his mouth, the panic and desire that rippled from deep in her belly. She shivered, rose up on her toes to meet him even as she fought against the rough possession of her body.

Jeremiah moaned, leaned away, the air instantly cold between them. Her upper arms hurt with his rough grip. This was not what she wanted. He slammed her hard against the wall. She cried out, struggled to turn away from him.

"No! Stop it!"

He pushed himself away, staggered back, and limped from the cabin.

The door stood open to the night. His voice from the yard sliced and cut her, brought hot tears and choking sobs.

"Damn you, woman! Get thee behind me, Satan!"

Adeline sunk to the floor, her knees once again pressed tight to her breasts, hope and desire replaced by anger and shame. Now what? Now what would she do?

Chapter Twenty-Eight

Jeremiah leaned back against the rough wood doors, waited for his eyes to adjust to the warm dark of the barn. The smell of hay and horse piss and oiled leather welcomed him. He trembled with the effort required to resist the temptation to turn, allow the pull of lust to draw him back inside the cabin. Damn her. She asked of him what he could not give.

His loins throbbed with the need to strip her of that thin gown, plunge into her warmth. But to bed Adeline was to seal an implied pledge he could not keep. A promise that would force him to leave, to saddle the mare and ride away. Abandon the stupid woman to those who would come for the gold.

"You always was right good at foolin' yo'self." Gil stepped from the shadows, a stalk of hay protruding from his mouth.

The sergeant strolled from the empty stall beside the mare's. "Ah, leave the man be," he said to the young man in tattered blue. "It ain't time for thinkin'. It's time for drinkin'. Where'd you hide that bottle, Preacher?"

"Ah, yes," Jeremiah sank easily, gratefully, into the familiar company of ghosts. "I had thought the phantoms of war vanquished. Driven away by wolves and divinely-inspired livestock, perhaps even by the hand of God himself."

Loud guffaws erupted from his belly, shook the dusty air.

"I see now the ghosts were merely biding their time, waiting in line behind the fevered pain and the euphoria of pain's absence."

The mare whinnied and the nanny, bedded in the same stall for company, bleated. A chorus of animal laughter. How appropriate. He was, after all, no more than an animal. The spark of humanity long extinguished. And what did it matter? *Vanity, vanity, all is vanity.*

The flat of his hands against the barn door, eyes adjusted to the dark, he pushed himself into the shadowed barn. Strode to a narrow shelf and lifted a small wooden box onto the workbench below. His fingers found an awl, a ballpeen hammer and a rusted pair of tongs. The whiskey was wrapped in an oil-stained rag at the bottom. The scent when he uncorked the bottle, instantly slowed his heartbeat, settled his nerves.

Jeremiah lifted the whiskey, prolonged the anticipation by turning the trapped amber in his hand. The bottle twirled slowly, in and out of the moonlight that striped the barn, the liquid amber hidden in darkness and then hazed in the dust that thickened the blue light filtering between the planks of the barn's walls.

"Open the dang bottle and let's get to the drinkin'." The sergeant appeared beside Jeremiah, laid a cold hand on his shoulder. The rotting stink of the ghost's breath, the jaw long ago lost to Jeremiah's Enfield, opened in the striped darkness, grew larger, and larger still, until Jeremiah feared he himself would disappear into the grotesque darkness.

The bottle dropped from his hands, glass shattered, a woman, once beloved, whispered from the depths of the barn.

"Adeline is strong, Jeremiah. This woman can survive your love."

Jeremiah twisted toward the voice. "Maggie?"

Her skirt flowed around her ankles. She floated, in and out of the light, until her warm, sweet breath blessed his face. He fled the barn. The night air, thick with the coming of rain, wrapped its warmth around him, stole his breath.

His knuckles rapped softly on the door to her room. "Adeline?"

He heard the rustle of bed covers, the squeak of the mattress against its wood frame.

"I need to talk to you, Adeline." He should apologize for his earlier roughness, explain the potent combination of lust and fear her awkward attempt at seduction lit in his belly. The words stuck in his throat. He stood, stiff-backed, ignored the ache in his center, the desire for understanding and acceptance that ate away at his gut, shut his mind hard against emotions of any kind. Both joy and grief hid in the same locked box.

"Yes," she said, "what do you want?"

She had not given permission for him to come inside, but she had not turned him away either. He twisted the knob and stepped into the room.

The baby in her arms, a human shield between them, she sat, fully clothed on the side of the bed. So, he had frightened her sufficiently that she felt it necessary to sleep in her dress and, by the look of it, her camisole and drawers and possibly an iron-toothed chastity belt.

He pushed the room's only chair against the wall, as far from her as the space would allow, lowered himself onto the wooden seat.

"I'm sorry to have frightened you." There. The words were spoken. Now, the two of them could move on.

A single candle threw yellow light across the side of her face. She sat stiffly on the edge of the bed. Her eyes looked lavender in the flame and he imagined he saw lightning bolts fly from those purple irises. He felt certain that, if she had access to a gun, she would shoot him through the heart. He shifted in the chair. The Colt was at his waist, but he wished he'd thought to check the location of the Henry. The woman wasn't much of shot, but at this range, even *her* aim would hit flesh.

"I know about the gold, Adeline." The best defense is a good offense, a good lesson of war.

"You don't know nothing. You're what Pa used to call an educated fool." Her voice cold, the force hard enough to stir the sleep of the child in her lap.

Well, perhaps his apology hadn't had quite the effect he had anticipated. It appeared she wasn't quite ready to forgive his roughness.

"The gang may not care about the disappearance of Brett James," he said. "But they'll eventually determine where he died. They'll come for the gold."

She stared at him, ignored the tears that ran in a steady trickle down her cheeks to drip off her jaw, fall onto her breasts. God, he hated when women cried. And this, this stoic acceptance of the tears, as though cursed with the knowledge that any encounter with him would always result in hot tears of pain? This was killing him.

He lifted himself from the chair, meant to sit beside her.

"Don't," she said. "Do not come any closer." From the folds of her skirt she drew a cleaver. A blade he'd sharpened himself and with which he'd seen her, just this week, chop the head from an unruly rooster in one swift flash of metal.

He lowered his ass back onto the chair.

"Look, I said I was sorry." He swallowed. This woman frightened him more than going into battle single-handed against a dozen enemies. Hell, all an adversary in battle could do was put him out of his misery. But this woman, she was determined to force him to look deep into the muck of his soul.

"You don't know anything about me." His voice rose in anger and frustration. "You think you do. You believe all that soft, intuitive woman's knowledge has given you some kind of window into my heart." He fluttered his fingers in the air. Fought back the fear. "You have no idea of the beast that lives in me."

"You're a fool, Jeremiah Jones."

The baby stirred in her arms and she lowered her face to the child's, pressed her lips to his cheek. She lifted her gaze to him, the tears flowing now like a steady stream of anguish, dampening her dress front.

"I have no more time for fools," she said.

He forced himself not to look away.

"Montega's heard rumors that Frank and Jessie have already left Arkansas, are living large in Texas. The rest of the gang is milling around Fort Smith, and they know Brett James was bent on taking you for his prisoner when he rode off. I will not leave you until I've dealt with the James gang."

"You want to help me?" She stood so suddenly the baby jerked in his sleep, Jeremiah flinched backwards in the chair. "Get out. Leave me the Colt and go. I was doing fine before you showed up."

He stood, leaned over her in a deliberate attempt to intimidate.

"You stole my horse! Hell, woman, I rescued you from Indians, got shot defending you from Brett James. Shot! Five years of war, and nothing but a couple of flesh wounds. A week in your company and I'm damn near killed. And you have the unmitigated gall to tell me you were doing fine before I showed up?"

She bent and laid the baby in his makeshift bed, straightened and stepped into Jeremiah, backed him against the wall of the tiny room.

"Leave the pistol on the table. Go on! Ride off into them mountains. Lift your arms, but not your heart, to a God whose love you cain't accept. Go to your burying and marrying and to your . . . your fornicating women."

"My what?" He lifted his hand, slowly, gently as though petting the soft coat of some wild animal whose heart flutters just under the skin. Her tears wet his hand. She did not step away but she did not lean into him either. He softened his voice.

"Adeline?" He waited for her to look into his eyes. "It is because I care for you that I must leave you."

Her hand sliced at him so fast he was still wondering whether or not she'd dropped the knife when the stinging of his cheek told him it had been only her open palm. But it was what came next that cut him to the bone.

The little horse thief laughed.

Chapter Twenty-Nine

Dawn stained the mountain gold and pink. Adeline stripped the nanny of the last of her morning milk, scratched the goat between her nubby horns. William, bowed legs wide, one hand on the bottom rail of the corral fence, squealed with the discovery of some bug or splash of light. His day's first miracle.

"Whatd'ya find, sweet boy?"

The baby turned to her, his mouth a perfect O of delight, a struggling grasshopper gripped between his finger and thumb. The bug wiggled free, landed on his bare foot. The baby clapped his chubby hands, forgot his grip on the fence. Squatting so that his bottom was only inches from the ground, he shuffled forward—one step, then two—toward the escaped grasshopper.

There was a shaky moment when he realized he was not holding onto the rail, an instant when he hesitated, wavered, and then, confidence lost, sat flat in the dirt of the corral. His face twisted into a cry. Before a sound could escape, the hens spotted the grasshopper. The entire flock of sixteen hens, head's bobbing, dust rising around them in a yellow cloud, raced toward the bug.

William's eyes widened. From his level, his bottom in the dirt, the hens must look like feathered monsters, racing right at him. Adeline stepped between the baby and the chickens, tossed a handful of corn from her pocket and scooped William into her arms. The hens ran in circles and then waddled off in a frenzied search for the thrown grain. William stared after the birds. His laughter came from his belly and, despite her shame and anger over what had happened last night with Jeremiah, Adeline smiled.

She had risen before dawn from a sleepless night. In the lantern light, the coffee pot slipped from her hand, knocked against the wooden table. She stood still, did not even breathe, dreaded the opening of the door to Jeremiah's room, the look on his prideful face. When, three lifetimes later, another ragged snore came from his room, she set the pot back on the table and went to the crying baby.

The bucket of milk dangling from one hand, Adeline struggled to balance William on the opposite hip. The baby bounced in her arms, clapped his dimpled hands.

"You think those hens are funny, do you?"

He patted her cheeks with his hands, grinned, exposing four front teeth.

"Me and you are gonna take the nanny just up the hill to a new grazing patch. That goat has cleared every leaf from aroun'st the cabin."

Be good not to lay eyes on Jeremiah today. Her chest heated with shame just thinking of what she'd done the night before. What had she been thinking to offer herself to him that way? Sitting in the tub, it had seemed a fine way to let the man know she was ready to join with him. Preachers taught to wait for their blessing before coming together, but heck, most times a man of God weren't around to pray over a couple. Besides, Jeremiah was a preacher his own self. All's he had to do was lay hands on her and she'd be his.

She blushed at her thoughts. Just the kind of thinking that got her in trouble last night.

Adeline stood the baby on his feet in the yard, opened the door to the root cellar and set the bucket against the cool dirt of the wall. She should go back in the cabin and gather a biscuit or drumstick leftover from last night's dinner. 'Cept there was no way she was going to risk running into Jeremiah. Not yet. Maybe not ever. He was probably hiding in his room, just waiting for her to leave so as he could saddle up and make his escape.

The memory of his hands on her breasts pushed her from the cabin. Might be there was something wrong with her. She'd wanted him last

159

night. Or thought she did. Until his tongue gagged her and his hands tore at her clothes. Maybe that's just the way sex was between a man and a woman. It wasn't like she hadn't seen the bloody bites on a mare's neck after a visit from a stallion. Heck, a rooster'd knock a hen to the ground in his enthusiasm for his job.

She'd been raised in a two room cabin with five kids. Plenty of times she'd heard the sounds of baby-making coming from Ma and Pa's room. But, Pa used to come up behind Ma while she cut biscuits, or washed dishes. He'd lift the hair from her neck and nuzzle. Ma would scold him, but she'd smile and blush and, that night, soft moaning would come through the door of their room. Adeline smiled remembering once when she'd surprised them, skipped into the cabin when ma was cutting biscuits. The two broke apart when they saw her, but ma had left two perfect floury handprints on the backside of Pa's pants.

From inside the cabin came the sound of morning coughing. Next would come the sound of boots being pulled on with a small groan, hard heels meeting the wood floor. Adeline ran to the corral, untethered the goat and, knowing the nanny would follow for the handful of grain in her pocket, hurried back to sweep William into her arms. She was half-way up the hillside when she heard the front door of the cabin slam.

She worked her way along a deer trail, weaving around tall oaks whose gnarled branches were hidden in the whispering leaves of early summer. It had been almost six weeks since Montega had found any trace of the bear, her bear as he insisted on calling the beast.

"Your spirit bear is gone." His arms were crossed over his chest, the fletching of the arrows in his quiver sticking up over his shoulder, the bow itself showing its tip over the other.

"It weren't a spirit what ate Brett James."

She had grown tired of Indian hokum. Sometime between late night feeding and months of caring for an invalid, the whole twisted mess of feelings she had for Jeremiah, and Brett James's head laying in the new-turned dirt, staring up at her—well she'd just about given up on magic and miracles. Besides, she had gold and greenbacks now. Hidden in a place no man would think to look for it.

The goat bleated and William twisted and squirmed in her arms. She had stopped carrying him in a sling the way Montega had shown her. Nothing to do with Brett James calling the boy a papoose. William was starting to walk now. It was best to give him freedom to explore. She bent, set the child on his feet. William stood knee-deep in old leaves, palms turned parallel with the ground, a look of joy on his gap-toothed face.

The nanny lifted tiny hooves, each dainty step crackling in the dead leaves of the forest floor. The goat made her way to William who swayed on the balls of his feet, watched her approach as a saint might wait upon the Lord. The goat pressed the flat of her head into the baby's chest and the child fell backward, buried in brown leaves and twigs and new green growth. The laughter of the boy mingled with the bleating of the goat.

Adeline sat on a mossy log. Jeremiah was right. Billy Boy had an unnatural attachment to that goat.

How would the child's life be different if she used the money to take them west? How would her life be changed? Three years ago she had stood beside Ma at the mercantile and listened to a man traveling on the stage from Philadelphia tell of a city clear across the continent. San Francisco it was called. A place with shops and carriages and tall houses that crouched on steep hills. Half-hidden in fog most mornings, he told of streets where ladies with parasols and boots with tiny pearl buttons strolled from shop to shop, the Pacific Ocean spread out like a jeweled quilt below them.

William, one fist gripping the goat's stubby tail, pulled himself to his feet.

"Ma ma." The boy smiled at Adeline, his dark eyes sparkling.

She grinned, shook her head. "You talkin' to me, or to the goat?"

A shot rang out from the cabin below. One flat shot, like a slap, that seemed to reach into her chest and stop her heart, kill all thoughts but one.

Jeremiah!

Adeline tucked the boy tight to her chest. She ran toward the cabin.

Chapter Thirty

It was the braying of the mule that told him they were coming. Jeremiah set the fork beside his plate of half-eaten eggs, wiped his mouth on his sleeve.

Perfect timing. Adeline and the boy were gone, hiding in the hills from the madman in their midst. Montega had not yet returned from his second trip to the northern Cheyenne but on his first trading trip he had procured enough ammunition to fight off a small army. Jeremiah meant to go out with guns blazing and knife bloody.

He assumed an offensive position in a straight-backed chair on the front porch. The Bowie nestled snug in its sheath at his waist. The Henry laid across his open knees. Already he could feel the weight of the sixteen-shot rifle pressing against his shoulder, his trigger finger itchy with the day's promise. The Colt was tucked snugly into his belt. Though if he had to draw the pistol, his time on earth might well be done.

The braying mule could be heard in the pasture, hooves thudding dully in belly-high grass. From far up the hillside to the left came the bleating of a goat. Adeline's hens scratched and clucked in the dirt of the yard. The smell of the sun on well-fertilized dirt came to him from the garden. The morning was without a cooling breeze, the sky that washed-out hue his mother called summer blue. Jeremiah was aware of all this in the way a man walking a thin plank over a deep crevice knows the sound and sights and smells of life are all around him. He knows these things exist outside the placement of his feet on the narrow wood, but they are of no importance, except as they pertain to his next step.

Jeremiah grinned at the men riding in a triangle pattern, approaching from the east. The point was a fat man in a battered hat riding a skinny bay. The rider to his left wore the coat of a Confederate Colonel and to the fat man's right, sitting a sway-backed paint, a tall man grinned with a mouth empty of teeth. Strung out behind and to either side of this formation, four additional enemy sat a motley assortment of horses.

None of these men was either Frank or Jessie James. Which meant Montega's intelligence had been correct. The leaders of this band of thieves had meandered off to enjoy their loot. What he had here were the misfits and dregs of the outfit. The cowards in a gang of bullies.

He watched the riders clear the woods, a clotted knot approaching his position on the porch. The horses in mid-step, thick dust rising to the fetlocks of the animals, Jeremiah stood.

His first shot took off the top of the fat man's head. The preacher smiled at the way the man's hat hovered in the air for the split-second it took the body to fall to the side. The horse of the man behind the point screamed and fell, pinned the rider under the struggling animal. The curses of men mixed with the screaming of the injured horse. On the far left a man raised a pistol. He wore the hat of a union officer, the looped gold band woven now with a length of purple silk and marking it as stolen by a disrespectful fool.

Jeremiah fired a second shot and the man dropped his gun hand, a red bloom spreading across his right shoulder. Jeremiah squeezed the Henry's trigger and the fool fell to the side, one boot heel hung in the stirrup, the horse running in wild circles.

Heat lashed the Preacher's cheek. The sound of a shot pitched him to the side. Jeremiah charged screaming into the milling horses and men. The Henry kicked against his shoulder. Warmth flowed into his shirt collar. A horse reared. Something knocked him to his knees. He looked up into a toothless face, the man's finger already on the trigger of his pistol. Unable to raise the rifle's long barrel with the necessary speed, Jeremiah fired into the belly of the man's paint horse. The horse swayed, struggled and collapsed.

Jeremiah stood in the midst of terrified horses and dust and screams, felt himself complete. The toothless rider of the paint struggled to free himself from beneath his dead horse. The preacher fired again. When Jeremiah lifted the pistol from the man's hand, slid the gun into his own belt opposite his Colt, the man did not object. A scream of desperate joy and wild freedom tore from Jeremiah's mouth. He turned in a circle, the rifle an extension of himself. Cocked and squeezed the trigger, cocked and squeezed, in a motion as smooth and easy as drawing breath. Shot after shot, the gun kicked against his shoulder in an ecstasy of killing.

The trigger of the Henry clicked and Jeremiah dropped the rifle, drew the Colt from his belt. Horses rolled eyes ringed with white, blew terror from flared nostrils, slammed against each other in panic. Jeremiah swept his eyes over the battlefield. All enemy accounted for. Seven men and two horses down.

Movement. To his left. Flat on his back, blood pooling at his belly, an enemy lifted a pistol in a shaky hand. Jeremiah fired and the man was no longer a threat. Pistol at ready, Jeremiah stepped from body to body, tipped each casualty onto his back with the toe of his boot. Twice more he fired, stared into lifeless eyes. A moan and he swung the pistol's barrel to the right. Two steps and he looked into the toothless face of a man splattered with the blood and guts of his paint horse.

"My God, man, we only come for the gold. We meant you no harm."

Jeremiah stared down the barrel of the pistol, pressed the trigger and watched the spark go out in the man's eyes.

The sound of crying, the snapping of branches turned Jeremiah's attention to the hillside. Adeline crashed through the underbrush and into the yard. Baby pressed tight to her breasts, she stood dead-still, stared at the scene around her. Two horses, huge and dead, four more flecked in fear, reins trailing, paced in a tight, nervous cluster. A dapple-gray mare ran the fence line, her panicked neighing mixing with the braying of the mule. Seven men sprawled on their backs, their legs and arms and heads in unnatural poses, blood darkening the dirt under them.

She lifted her eyes from the carnage.

"What have you done?"

He shrugged. Grinned. "We had visitors."

Chapter Thirty-One

A **deline did her best** to steady her hands, concentrate her mind on the task before her. She wrung a bloody cloth in the warm water of the basin. The bullet had sliced the right side of Jeremiah's face. The stark line of exposed bone along cheek and skull made her queasy. She dabbed at the purpled flesh, concentrated on not vomiting. Dark blood still flowed from the place where the top of Jeremiah's ear had been an hour before, when she left to go up the hillside with the goat and the baby.

"Leave it be, Adeline. It's naught but a small inconvenience. We need to make a plan. In this heat the bodies will draw buzzards by this afternoon. The carrion eaters will draw the curious, and the curious will bring the law."

It was the matter-of-fact way he spoke that sent her through the door to lean over the porch rail and pour clumps of yellow grits and long green ropes of bile into the dirt. Already the yard stunk of careless death. Not butchering. Butchering done right was sticky with blood and soft with the mush of flesh and muscle under your hands, but it did not smell of guts and fear and waste.

She kept her eyes down, refused to look again at the men and horses stiffening in her yard. The excited clucking of chickens pecking in the blood-softened dirt sickened her. She hoped her hens had not yet found the soft eyes and open wounds warming under the summer sun. Adeline turned her back on the dead, refused the trembling that threatened to shake her until she lay down and stopped breathing, ceased fighting once and for all, to find her way in this life.

Jeremiah met her at the door, slipped his arm around her waist. She struck out with the flat of her hands, flailed at him like a frightened bird beating useless wings against a toothed predator. His touch unleashed hot, sweet rage that rose up in her. She struck his chest with pounding fists. Again and again and again she struck. Jeremiah did not move, did not even seem to breathe. Merely stood, as though waiting for her to come to her senses.

"My . . . God. Did you have to . . . kill them . . . all?" Her words started in piercing screams, ended in panting moans.

"I judged so, yes."

He led her to a chair, sat beside her. From his shirt pocket he withdrew a brass star in a circle of silver, laid it on the table between them. Adeline stared at the badge, struggled to make sense of its presence. She traced her finger along the brown muck coating the words inscribed into the silver. Her finger came away sticky.

"I need you to listen carefully, Adeline."

"You've ruined us with your killing." Her voice dull, less accusation than statement of fact.

"It wasn't me that kept the stolen money, woman."

The force of his words sobered her, slammed her back into the reality of a yard full of bodies, at least one of which had, just this morning, been a lawman. Now the Texas ranger was a meaty treat for her hens.

Adeline stared into Jeremiah's face, his gray eyes rimmed in blue with startling specks of silver circling the black irises. Dead men in her yard and she focused on the color of their killer's eyes. She looked away from his face, stared out the window at the sway of leaves in the old hickory, the distorted, double-image of the tree a comfort.

"What happened when they rode in?" She did not turn her gaze from the wavering tree trunk.

"I killed them."

Her heart beat slowed. Tremors gone, hands steadied.

"How'd ya know they meant trouble? Could be they only wanted water for their horses or a bite to eat?"

His laughed, coarse and mean. A short, hacking blow of a laugh.

"They rode in from out of the east. The sun behind them."

She shook her head.

"There is no natural trail approaching this cabin from the east, Adeline. They deliberately skirted around so I would be blinded by the rising sun as they rode to battle."

"Battle?" My Sweet Lord, this haunted man would be the death of her. "The war is over, Jeremiah! Why must everything be a battle to you?"

He lifted the bloody star from the table, turned it in his hand.

"I don't know that it must, Adeline. But certainly, it is." He lifted her wrist, placed the metal star in the palm of her hand. "And the war is only ever over for civilians like you who wander clueless through a landscape enriched by the blood of battle, heap one bad decision upon another in desperation or pride or greed, and then stand, hip-deep in the muck and consequences of your own choices, and decry the morals of the warriors who come to your aid."

His eyes were dark now, almost black with intensity. He folded her fingers around the points of the badge.

"*You* stole the gold." His voice flat now. Dead. "Those men out there, lying dead in your yard, they did not come as lawmen, they came as thieves and murderers and rapists. I did make a mistake when they rode in. I will admit to that error."

She squeezed the badge until silver cut into her flesh, lifted her other hand and wiped away a thin stream of blood that trickled from under the white cloth pressed to his head, just below what remained of his ear.

"What would you do different?"

"It was a strategic error to vacate the porch, go among them on foot and cede the high ground."

She stared at him. His tone was that of a farmer who sets his foot on a nail keg and ruminates on last season's crops. *I'da done better to plant the corn afore that last winter rain.*

The star slipped from her fingers. She withdrew her hand from his cheek, pressed both palms against her open mouth, as though trying to hold what was left of her safe inside.

He patted her knee. A smile lifted the corners of his mouth.

"Rage is a detriment in battle, Adeline. Remember that. When that bullet grazed my head, I relinquished all thought but one."

She swallowed hard, forced herself to look into his face.

"Did you fear to die?"

His eyes crinkled at the corners with his smile.

"I feared to leave you and the child alone before fulfilling my mission."

Adeline stood. Still seated, Jeremiah raised his arms, pulled her to him, laid his head to her breasts. The hickory tree swayed and wavered, its double trunk as real as the warm breath of the man she held against her. He wrapped his arms around her waist. The world stood still and she imagined herself as an old woman, still holding this one moment in memory—a single pearl on the dirty string of her life.

"Collect what you need for the boy." His voice muffled in the folds of her dress, the swell of her breasts. "We'll ride within the hour."

He ran his hands up her back as he stood. The small space between them filled with power, the way the air after a lightning strike raised the little hairs on the back of her neck. She closed her eyes and tilted her face to him. His lips were soft on hers, gentle. Her hands rose of their own accord, circled his neck. His mouth demanded more and she parted her lips and rose up on her toes to meet him.

He hands moved to her arms and he pushed her away.

"No time for this, Adeline. Collect the boy and . . . don't forget the gold."

Chapter Thirty-Two

The woods, dense with dust and the powder of rotting leaves stirred up by the horse and mule, tightened around Jeremiah. Earth and decay pressed in upon him. Squeezed. Suffocated. The leaves of hickory and oak drooped in the breathless heat of late afternoon. Adeline, with Billy Boy in a sling strapped to her front, rode drag on the mule. Jeremiah's mare bobbed her head, arched her neck and tried to twist around and see behind her each time the ornery mule pulled within rump-biting distance.

The reins shook in Jeremiah's hands. It would be best to stop soon, build a small fire to cook mush for the child and then move on again, ride under the full moon for as long as the woman and child could travel.

It wasn't the discovery of the bodies he feared. It would require two days, maybe three, to organize a posse. No, it wasn't flesh and blood men that trembled his hands, it was the inevitable visitation of ghosts that came after battle, when the work of killing was finished and the mind woke from its numbed slumber.

Each battle carried one defining moment. An image that branded itself upon his soul, burned to the bone. This night, and many after, he would relive one momentary flash of light. The all-consuming moment of realization when the bullet had creased his head and he saw, not his long sought death, but a blinding vision of Adeline.

An eternal moment. Freckles across the bridge of her nose more clear than the blood speckling the churning legs of the horses all around him. Adeline turning from the stove, morning light a haloed blessing to the white-gold of her hair, a smile of greeting for him. For him. Opening his eyes in the dark to her powdery scent, the softness of her skin when she came to him in the night, her words leading him back from whatever nightmare had swallowed him.

That moment, her scent and touch all around him, that was the moment he would relive forever. The instant he knew that, like David with Bathsheba, he had allowed himself to gaze too long upon that which he could not claim without sacrificing his soul. In that blinding flash of light, when the bullet creased his head, fear—not of death, but of leaving this woman unprotected—had overpowered reason and he had waded into the middle of battle with no more thought to strategy than a green recruit.

He pushed the arc of his boots against the stirrups, straightened his legs and twisted his body to look behind him. Pain shot up his bad leg, from ankle to hip, radiated in a band of white heat, from lower back to navel. Jeremiah swallowed the pain, smiled at Adeline.

Soft humming floated like the whir of insect's wing. Adeline fussed with the baby, stroked the boy's dark hair from his forehead. She looked up. The corners of her mouth tilted. Her eyes met his gaze. He nodded, turned away and let himself settle back into the saddle.

This was not the desperate child who'd stolen his horse eight months ago. Nor was she anymore the cringing girl he'd rescued from Indians. Behind him rode the young woman who'd fought her way from under a rapist, brought a stone down upon his head and left him for dead. This was the mother who had faced a bear for the sake of the child to whom she now murmured and hummed. The formidable comrade who had killed an armed enemy with an ax. An ax! And not just killed him, but separated his head from his neck.

Jeremiah smiled. In his mind, he saw a wrinkled sack, no bigger than his fist. Had it been Fredricksburg? Yes, Fredricksburg. It was that time of evening when long slants of weak light laid a final blanket over the earth.

The Union colonel was gone when he and a private from Winslow opened the tent flap with bayonets, stepped into the gloom. A camp table was all the Federals left in their quick departure. The cross of the folding table's legs trapped the sun's final light and he thought of Jesus and his suffering. All that remained on the solitary table was a small, brown bag, tipped on its side. Spilling from the open top were candies as brilliant red as new blood.

He and the private had split the sugary treasure. The private ate his share by nightfall, said he might be dead by morning, better not to waste the treat. As it turned out, that was sound thinking on his part. A sniper picked off the boy from Winslow less than a week after Lee sent Burnside packing at Fredricksburg.

Jeremiah had rationed his seven candies, their presence in the pocket of his jacket a solemn faith in his survival. The last piece a consolation at Appomattox. They were hard on the outside, those shiny red sweets, like gems that sparkled in his palm. In his mouth, each jewel rattled against his teeth, dissolved slowly, exquisitely, until just when he had forgotten to anticipate it, the soft, gooey center was exposed.

He thought of the way Adeline had melted against him after the bear attack. The warmth of her lips, the little gasp when his tongue found the ribbed top of her mouth. He saw her staring at the scene in the yard this morning. The way her eyes widened and she'd clutched the baby so tightly to her breasts the child had squirmed in her arms, screamed his displeasure.

Jeremiah heard again her words. *What did you do?* Not just an accusation, though there was some shocked blame in the words to be sure. *What did you do?* The question more the seeking of guidance a private will seek from a seasoned sergeant.

We're surrounded by bluecoats, the powder's wet and there's no help coming. What now, Sarge?

His smile widened. Could be it was wishful thinking on his part, pretending she'd responded as a lower-ranking soldier to a respected leader. The truth was, him getting her away from that cabin had been more like him following orders from a commanding officer. A somewhat overwhelmed and confused officer, but one locked and loaded and taking no prisoners.

It had been a fight to get her to leave the damned goat. The boy would have to survive on mush for a day or two. The child had four teeth. He could gnaw a slice of jerky almost as well as Jeremiah. Then, she'd fretted about the hens. Fussed over the horses even after he assured her that, without the gold and stacks of paper money in their saddle bags to weigh them down, the animals would find their way back home just fine.

He'd rather lead a battalion of new recruits than this stubborn woman who had no more idea of chain of command than that goddamn Indian, Montega.

Still, she'd not fainted. Not drifted into a sleep-walk like he'd seen so many young men do in the aftermath of battle. Only vomited the one time and, even then, she'd wiped her mouth and got back to the business of what needed doing.

"How's the boy?" He turned his head, kept his back straight, his throbbing leg motionless in the stirrup.

"Fussing. We'll stop right soon." Not asking, hell, not even suggesting.

He shook his head. Best to go ahead and pull up, get the child fed. Not like the woman was suggesting anything he hadn't already planned on doing.

"I'll let you know," he said.

Silence pierced his back like shrapnel.

"Be soon, though. Don't worry. I'll find a good spot to build a little fire. But then we got to get back on the trail."

"I wa'dunt worried."

He wasn't looking forward to telling her the next part of his plan. Tomorrow she was going to report the killings. Just her and the child. She'd swear to whatever sheriff she could find that he had lit out from the cabin headed due west into Indian country and she had saddled up and headed for the safety of Fort Smith alone.

Once she'd done her duty with the sheriff, she was to take the stagecoach to Kansas City and from there a train to St. Louie. From there, he prayed, she'd put herself and the boy on a train to the west coast. With luck, he'd convince her that returning to the cabin alone was suicide by marauding Indians or, more likely, by winter cold. The woman talked about living in San Francisco like it was a front row seat on the second coming. With a satchel of stolen money and gold, now was the time for emigration.

He would head southwest. Alone. It wasn't like he had ties to this woman. He'd saved her life. Brought her more pain than she needed. His throat tightened and he swallowed hard, stared into the dusty underbrush. Time for him to find another battle. Texas might be just the place.

Chapter Thirty-Three

Adeline rocked gently from side to side, stroked circles on the child's mush-round belly. Her eyes had long ago adjusted to the thick darkness of the woods. She sat flat on the forest floor, her back pressed against the smooth trunk of a maple tree, the baby a warm comfort against her chest.

The wind blew a cloudy veil across the full face of the moon and, beside her, Jeremiah shivered.

His voice came from out of the darkness, like an unexpected breeze. "We need to talk about where we go from here."

She laid the sleeping baby beside her, turned to study the profile of the man. He was building up to one kind of nonsense or another. Adeline sat quietly until Jeremiah turned his face to her, his eyes darker than the night around them.

"We need to split up, Adeline."

Adeline leaned forward from the waist, brushed the lobe of his good ear with her mouth. She held perfectly still, her mouth so close she could touch the soft swirl of his ear with the tip of her tongue. Though his words made her ponder more on biting than licking.

"No," she whispered.

His sigh warmed her neck. Wide hands folded on his bent knees, one gripped the other as though wrestling some small, fierce critter.

"Listen to me." He raised his hands then, gripped her shoulders, held her away. "Tomorrow you're going into the next small town we come up on and report to the sheriff what I've done. Tell the law you saddled the mule and rode for help the minute you returned and found the men dead in your yard."

"Where you planning to be while I'm talking with the law?"

"Tell the sheriff I headed west after killing the men. Say you watched from the trees while I searched the dead men and their horses for the gold. The sheriff won't suspect you, Adeline. It will never occur to the man that a sweet little thing like you has the money stowed in the saddle bags of that ornery mule. I'll be in Texas long before the posse gets to your place."

The heat from his hands burned through the sleeves of her dress.

"That why you rode off up the mountain afore we left home? Set down a line of tracks to lead the law in the wrong direction? You been planning all along to ride away and leave me?"

"You have the money now, Adeline. You don't need me. Hell, I've been a burden to you since Brett James shot me from my horse. Take the stage to Kansas City. The train'll get you from there to St. Louis. Go to San Francisco like you've been chewing my ear about for months. Make a new life for yourself and the child."

The air between them was warm with their breath.

"I ain't leaving you." She leaned into him. "We'll meet up after I fill the sheriff with lies. Take the train out west. Together."

He released his grip on her arms, with his finger traced a tear from cheek to chin to the top of one breast and then, across the swell, to the other. A hot line of desire hung her breath in her throat.

"Listen . . . now." His voice like he'd forgotten how to breathe. "Riding from here to Texas . . . too hard . . . on the child."

She lifted her face, exposed her neck, leaned against the hot trail of his mouth on her throat.

"William's strong." Above her a ribbon of stars lit the night. "The child's known nothing but love since I took him from his mama's pyre." She pressed his face to her breasts, arched against him. "It's you needs lovin, Jeremiah Jones."

"No." A moan.

"Yes." The one word both plea and demand.

There was then a moment when the world hung, like the morning sun on the peak of Bear Mountain, balanced between possibilities. Then, Adeline was flat on her back, Jeremiah's silhouette blocking the stars and the moon and all the night sky. His mouth greedy on hers. His hands hot, flowing rivers pulling her down into a whirlpool so thick, so powerful, there was nothing for her to do but let the need take her where it willed.

He claimed her then as his own. Or so it seemed to Adeline. She arched up, beyond the pain and the fear of the first time, lost herself to their co-joined desire, cried out her love for him. At that moment, Jeremiah seemed to disappear, his spirit lifted from his body, leaving only animal need.

He turned his face from her. His hands stopped their journey from aching breasts to lifted hips. Desperate to meet his rhythm and need, she clung to him, arched her body higher to draw him back into himself, return him to her. Jeremiah's body completed its task, even as clouds raced across the moon's face and hid the stars.

He rolled off her, turned his back, left her to watch the moon race the clouds.

Chapter Thirty-Four

D **awn touched** the eastern mountain with thin fingers. Jeremiah's back warmed with the day's first light. The mare trotted, head up, turning occasionally to look back as though she missed the ornery mule and the fussy baby. Or, perhaps, he put his own feelings onto the animal.

Last night he had ignored Adeline's hand on his back, the murmurings of affection she was too young, too inexperienced, to know were no more than a product of the physical act that had passed between them. He waited until her breathing slowed, then rose without looking back, and fled through the tree-striped moonlight.

From his left, the shrill whistling call of a whippoorwill split the morning and the mare lifted her head and nickered.

He pulled the horse to a stop. Studied the shadows from which the birdcall came.

The Indian rode from out of the sumac and shrub oak, his face grim. "You have been busy, my friend."

"Stop at to the cabin?" Jeremiah's mare neighed a greeting to the stallion.

Montega pulled in beside the mare and the animals touched noses. The mare rubbed the length of her long face along the underside of the stallions arched neck. The stallion ducked his head, pranced in place, all but bowed in greeting.

Montega stared straight ahead, ignored the dancing stallion. "Shame to have shot the horses."

"How long you been following?" Jeremiah cut his eyes to the Indian.

Montega did not turn his head, kept that stoic Indian mask firmly in place, stared out over the land like a shaman.

"Long enough to come by some knowledge of why kidnapped white women so often prefer life with their Osage captors."

Jeremiah hand dropped to the butt of the Colt at his waist.

Montega touched the reins to the stallion's neck.

The mare, with no encouragement from Jeremiah, kept pace with the stallion. The four, two nuzzling horses and two silent human riders, moved across the gentle slope of the land. The rising sun sent long pools of wavering silver-gray forms ahead, as though the shadows themselves rippled the tall grass. Jeremiah thought to rein the mare ahead, put some distance between himself and the Indian, but figured he'd pushed his luck about as far as it would go with ordering around romantically-inclined females. Best leave the mare to her reunion with the stallion.

He fished in his shirt pocket, withdrew a circle of thin steel and brass, handed the badge across to Montega. The Indian ran his finger along the deep indentations in the star's center.

Montega laid the pocked emblem in the palm of Jeremiah's hand.

"The Rangers were disbanded in '65," Jeremiah said.

The Indian laughed. Sounded like a cross between the howl of a wolf and the braying of a sick donkey.

The Osage's laughter stopped as abruptly as it had begun. "You're a fool you think that means every lawman in Texas won't come for you."

Jeremiah turned the badge in his hand, let the morning light play over the dull brass circle and the tarnished star at its center. He imagined a triangle of mounted men riding fast across a grassy plain toward a lone man sitting a mare at a ragged tree line.

"Death stalks us all." He dropped the Texas Ranger's badge into his shirt pocket. "You interested in a recon mission? Ride into the next town, Renegade is the name if I'm not mistaken. Scout the local law. Meet up and report on which direction the posse heads?"

Montega stared straight ahead. "My interest is the woman and the child of my blood. In my years with the blackrobes I learned well the white man's hatred of all things outside their understanding. I fear an unmarried woman with an Indian baby will not be welcomed."

Montega pulled back on the right rein and the stallion tossed his head, turned away from the mare.

Jeremiah spoke over the snorting of the horses, the creaking of the saddle leather. "We'll meet up at—"

"I will find you," the Indian called over his shoulder.

The mare fought the bit for a moment, but settled quickly under his hand, moved smoothly into a gentle trot. The day's heat stirred a breeze that swayed the grass and cooled his face while the rising sun sent a trickle of sweat down his spine. With luck, he and the mare would sleep warm and well-fed tonight.

Laurel? Was that the school teacher's name? Tall and lean. Warm redhead with thighs like a vise and fried chicken even better than her loving. Laurie? Linda. That was it. Linda. Be a nice treat to spend some time in the company of an older woman who knew how to love a man without asking for his damned soul in return.

"That there's an interesting turn a phrase, Preacher." The sergeant walked calmly beside him, kept pace with the trotting mare with no apparent effort, daylight shining brightly through his missing jaw. "'Cause you surely are determined to damn your soul to hell."

"I've nothing to say to you."

He glared at the apparition. Sweat collected at the collar of Jeremiah's shirt and he rolled his shoulders in the sun's warmth. He clucked to the mare and the staccato of her shod feet pounded faster over the prairie.

The sergeant kept an easy pace at his side. "Suit yourself. You always was a slow learner."

The jawless ghost vanished and Jeremiah rode on. He adjusted the horse's direction slightly to avoid a dust devil that swept the tall grass up ahead and off to his left. The dervish shifted its direction, swirled directly at him. Jeremiah rubbed his eyes. Sweat gathered at his waist. The mare slowed, veered away from the small tornado of sharp twigs and small, hard stones.

Jeremiah squeezed his eyes tight, popped them open in an attempt to clear his vision. A face appeared in the eye of the dust devil. A face with long, dark hair that swirled around green eyes and a wide mouth that, the last time he kissed it, had tasted of almonds and death. He kicked the mare's sides, turned her nose to the north. His knee ached with riding through the night. Be best to hole up for the rest of the day. Put off for a spell his reunion with the tall redheaded schoolmarm. Besides, could be Montega would need to find him sooner rather than later. Be good to know what the local law had in mind before deciding which direction to ride. Be good also to assure himself the girl and that papoose hadn't run into trouble in the little town of Renegade. Montega was correct. An unmarried girl clutching an Indian baby to her breasts wasn't likely to receive a warm welcome.

Chapter Thirty-Five

Adeline folded the remnant of Mama's old quilt over William's sleeping face, pressed the child to her breasts. A gray-bearded man in a straw hat with the brim bent nearly to his chin leaned against the rock building, watched her slide awkwardly off the mule and tie the animal to the hitching post. The man coughed and spit into the street. A silver star pinned to the faded cotton of his shirt-front caught the afternoon light, told her she'd found the person she was looking for.

"He'p ya, ma'am?" His words gurgled through tobacco juice.

Behind her the mule brayed his displeasure at this last stop before the stable.

"Are you the sheriff of this here town?"

Adeline had no idea what town she was in. Once Jeremiah had put the Boston Mountains behind them, she was lost. Truth be told, anything outside of a days' ride from the cabin was new territory to her. She'd liked to have stabled the mule, gotten a room and a soak in a hot tub before facing the law. But, if her story was to stick, she'd need to feign a bit of panic and her exhaustion might just help with this charade.

The man spit a brown glob into the dirt street, swiped his mouth with his sleeve.

"I'm the law he'ah in Rampage, if that's what you's askin'."

"Rampage?"

"Rampage, Arkansas, yes ma'am. What can ah do fer ya?"

Adeline shifted the child in her arms, swayed on her feet, did her best to appear stunned and of need of help from this disgusting man. The odd thing was, the second she pretended weakness, her knees became jelly. She steadied herself on the hitching post to keep from falling.

The sheriff stepped to her aid, extended a dirty hand. His yellowed nails left half-moon indentations on her wrist when she pulled away.

"Come on inside now, Missy. Set yourself down."

He led her into a rock-walled room about the size of her bedroom back home. His laceless boots shuffled on plank floors. An iron-barred cell barely big enough for a narrow cot and a slop bucket squatted in one corner of the narrow space.

She lowered herself into a high-backed chair, wondered which was the actress and which the real Adeline. The strong, steady young woman doing what needed to be done to save the child and herself. Was that the real Adeline? Or this younger, past version of herself, begging rescue from yet another man?

This morning she'd awoke to find Jeremiah gone. The gold his mare had carried gleamed in the morning light—a well-balanced load ready for her to throw over the wide rump of the mule and get on with her life. Out of the mountains she'd known most of her life and surrounded by wide open spaces, the sun came up in an explosion of color. She'd forced her way through thick sumac and tangles of wild grape, stood barefoot and ankle-deep in a fast running creek and rinsed the last of her innocence from the inside of her thighs.

She'd allowed herself a moment's thought then, wondered if Jeremiah rode now with the blood of her innocence sticky on his manhood. Later, she would let herself feel the anger and razor-sharp hurt that begged to cut and gash at her exposed belly. But not just yet. She had waded wide-legged for balance, careful to place her bare feet carefully on each slimy stone, scooped up William from where he sat studying a water bug and got on with the plan.

The sheriff removed his floppy hat, spit toward a brass spittoon. His chair squeaked as he leaned forward with his arms resting on his desk. He cleared his throat.

"Ya don't mind me sayin' so, ma'am, ya look a might ragged."

Adeline blew through her mouth, made herself meet the yellowed eyes of the man behind the desk.

"Yesterday . . . or . . . maybe it might could a been the day afore . . ."

Panic rose from her gut. She saw Jeremiah walking calmly from body to body, firing into the heads of the two men that still drew breath.

"Men . . . seven men. Came to my cabin seeking to do me harm."

That was the phrase Jeremiah had instructed her to use. *Seeking to do me harm.* In this one way she would do what he had told her to do. Certainly those words sounded better here in this tiny office of the law then the truth. *They come for the gold I stole off 'n the man whose head I chopped off with an ax.*

"The men got to squabbling between em, fightin' over who was to . . . ." She lowered her eyes, was surprised to feel hot tears slide down her cheeks. "Well, sir, who was to have their way with me first is what I believe they was fightin' 'bout."

The sheriff extended a plaid, snot-stained handkerchief across his desk.

"No, thank you, sir."

She shuddered, rocked from side-to-side, prayed William would not wake.

"Go on now, ma'am. You's safe he'ah now. Tell what happened."

"I run, sir. While the men was fightin' amongst themselves, I run to the barn, saddled the mule and rode outta there."

"So you just rode away? Didn't none a them bastards . . . 'scuse me, ma'am, didn't none a them scoundrels touch ya?"

Adeline rocked forward and back again in the chair. Forward and back.

The sheriff cleared his throat again.

"That's fine then, ma'am. Looks like you got a fine young'un thar. Where 'bouts is your husband, ma'am."

She raised her eyes, looked deep into his, told the truth as she knew it.

"He done rode off a while back, sir. I ain't sure he's comin' back."

The sheriff took in her muddy boots, torn skirt, her tears. He cleared the phlegm from his throat, spit at the spittoon.

"You got he'ah, ma'am. That there's all that matters. You got away."

She nodded, grateful for his misunderstanding of the tale.

"I'd like a bath now, sir. Please." Shaking claimed her, rattled her teeth. Whether from the lies or the realization of her true situation, she did not know. "If you direct me to where I might get a room for the night."

"Yes, ma'am. That'd be Miss Ruth's boarding house at the end of the street. I'll walk on down thar. Make sure ya get settled in. Take your mule on over to the stable."

"No!" The word came out louder, stronger than she intended. She blew breath from her mouth, slow and steady. "I'm sorry. I just . . . I'd rather . . . I'm sure I'll find Miss Ruth's just fine, sheriff. Thank you for your kindness."

She stood, prayed he'd take her refusal of help as a product of the rape he imagined she'd endured.

His boots knocked against the legs of the desk as he pushed himself to his feet.

"All right, then. That's fine, ma'am. Where 'bouts is this he'ah cabin a yours? I'll round up a few men, ride on out there. You never know. Could be the rascals is holed up there, eatin' your grinds and restin'."

"The closest town from our place is Freshwater."

He jerked his head up. "Freshwater, Arkansas?"

"Yes, sir. I know I come a long way. I don't rightly know which direction I even rode. I just kept ridin', kept goin' till I come to this here town, this . . . Rampage." She made herself look into his face, watch while he ran the tip of his tongue in a circle around the brown-stains of his mustache and beard. "I just rode 'till I couldn't go no further, sir. Hoped I'd come far enough me and the babe would be safe."

He cupped the air under her elbow, led her to the door.

"You got plans where you'll go from he'ah?"

"I got me a sister in Kansas City. Thought I'd take the stage up that direction come mornin'."

"That's a fine idea, ma'am. A right fine idea."

Outside he offered to hold the baby while she swung up onto the mule. Adeline shook her head, clung so tight to the child that William woke and bellowed his displeasure and, for a moment, she thought all was yet lost. But the boy quieted as the mule swayed, slept soundly all through getting the mule settled at the stable and the few moments it took to pay too much to a woman with hair the blue-gray of a gun barrel and climb a curving staircase to a room and bath, saddle bags banging against her thighs at each step.

In the night, she woke on Miss Ruth's lumpy mattress, the baby snoring softly beside her. She pushed back the rough sheets, stood at the room's small window and looked down at the street below. The street where tomorrow she would board a stage for Kansas City, leave everything she'd ever known behind her.

A flat-sided moon the pale gold of new-churned butter hung in a bed of stars. She felt again Jeremiah's hot mouth on her body, the pleasure mixed in pain when he'd entered her. She swiped at her cheeks, dropped her eyes from the sky to the dark street below. The batwing doors of the saloon just across the dirt street swung open, throwing yellow light out onto the walkway. She recognized the sheriff by his floppy hat and the way he took the time, even with a prisoner handcuffed in front of him, to lean over the raised wood sidewalk and spit into the street.

She recognized the prisoner by his easy stride, by the red feathers woven into his scalp lock, the gingham braided scalps tied to his buckskin vest.

Chapter Thirty-Six

Jeremiah pressed his spine to the scaly bark of a hawthorn, listened to the small night sounds of the woods at his back. He swept his eyes over the open grassland in front of him. The hobbled mare tore great chunks of grass from the land, the soft sound of her chewing a comfort to him. Though he'd taken the time before bedding down to sweep the area with the blooming branch of a dogwood, the fallen thorns of the hawthorn found new tender skin each time he shifted his body. The tree's flowers released a smell like rotting flesh and the night buzzed with the busy work of insects swarming over the enticing odor. The protection of the newly-fallen tree at his back provided adequate compensation for its sharp thorns and disgusting smell.

Jeremiah stared up at a wide swath of silver stars in a milky trail, adjusted his hip slightly and found another thorn. He had bedded down with the expectation of a visit with Gil and the sergeant, anticipated their ghostly presence as soon as night claimed the day. A single star burst across the velvet sky and he smelled gunsmoke and the burning bodies of dead horses, saw the face in his sights, lit by muzzle flashes, the boy's lips blackened with gunpowder, his teeth clamped on the powder cone.

Dead leaves rustled behind him. He smiled, waited for the private to join him in the night. The sound moved past him and, in the crescent moonlight, a pink-nosed skunk turned his head, met his gaze and moved on about his nightly business. Jeremiah abandoned hope of sleep, sat with his back against the hawthorn and stared out into the night and contemplated on where life had deposited him.

He chuckled in the dark.

So it had come to this. Alone but for ghosts and now even his ghosts had abandoned him. He probed his mind, like the tip of a tongue pressing at a bad tooth, did his best to call up an image of Maggie. A second star blazed a path of light across the sky, died and was gone. No picture formed, no vision appeared. He sat alone under the dome of heaven.

Adeline and the child would be fine. She had the money. Gold bought great protection. Of course, it also carried grave danger. Still, this was not the naive young woman who had shook with fear of him when he lay down behind her on that first night in the cave. The corners of his mouth twitched. This was a girl who had killed a man with an ax. Truth be told what he ought to be feeling guilt over is the turning loose of that young woman on the unsuspecting citizens of the little town he'd sent her into.

Rampage. He was nearly certain the tiny town of misshapen rock and make-shift log buildings was known as Rampage. He'd passed a night or two there, ridden through on his preaching circuit. If memory served, the sheriff doubled as the owner of the mercantile. It would be many days before the inept law of such a small community could ride to Fayetteville, organize a posse and make their way to where seven men laid bloating in the sun, the sky above them by now a circling sea of dull-black buzzards.

He saw her then, a vision of Adeline lying on her side, the yellow light of a nightstand candle dancing across her sleeping face, the child, Billy Boy, tucked in the soft curve of her body. Her brow creased in dreams, heat wetting the soft curls at the back of her neck. Reflected in the four-paned window at her back he saw his own weeping face, and was overcome with a premonition that, once again, he'd rejected love, abandoned salvation.

Shivering overtook him. Hollow, emptied of faith or belief enough to call out to God or ghosts or the past, he closed his eyes and surrendered to sleep.

He woke sitting up, his back still pressed to the hawthorn, a thin pink shimmer along the eastern horizon. The mare lifted her head above the belly-high grass, nickered a greeting, whether to him or the new day, he did not know. No breeze stirred leaf or grass. Time balanced between day and night.

A still, small voice entered Jeremiah, like warm breath exhaled directly into his soul.

"Return to me, and I will return also to you."

He rose stiffly, his bad leg a cold ache, tears hot on his face.

An hour later he and the mare parted the grass like a yellow sea and he prayed to a living God, pleaded that he not, once again, arrive too late.

Chapter Thirty-Seven

William squirmed in her arms. The child hated his head covered.

"Hush now, sweet boy." She lifted the blanket just enough to touch her lips to his cheek. "Go on back to sleep."

The collar of the new dress scratched at her neck. It had been a mistake to buy the fancy one with the lace neck, but the fabric, like mossy water flowing over smooth stones, had just worn her resistance down to a nub. With gold in her pocket for the first time in her life, the silk dress was a luxury she could not resist when she stepped inside the mercantile yesterday afternoon.

Now she admired the way the dress picked up the morning light, took the time to cock her new green hat with the shiny feather just so on the side of her head before stepping into the sheriff's office.

"Well now." The sheriff set his coffee mug on his desk, swallowed, and smiled at her. "Glad you stopped on over to say goodbye afore catchin' the stage this mornin'."

He swept breakfast crumbs to the wood floor, wiped his mouth with his sleeve and stood to greet her. A heavy white plate, yellowed with egg yolk and smeared with grease, sat next to a bone-handled pistol turned on its side, the eye of the barrel pointing at a Winchester rifle leaning against the desk.

She stepped to the side, bounced the fussing child in her arms, kept her eyes from the man in the cell to her left.

"Morning, Sheriff. I... um ... I see you got a prisoner." She turned then and for the first time since entering the room, lifted her eyes to Montega's.

The Indian shook his head slowly from left to right, turned his back on her and sat on the thin mattress of the cell's cot.

The room smelled of rancid bacon, tobacco and morning urine from the honey pot in the corner. Dust motes hung thick in a narrow band of morning light from a small window high on the wall of the cell. Adeline knew what Montega was telling her. But she'd contemplated the situation all throughout the sleepless night and could not board a stage and abandon the man who had kept her and the child and Jeremiah alive all winter.

"What you got him locked up for?" She gave the sheriff her best smile.

He came around the desk, laid his greasy hand on her elbow.

"That ain't nothin' for you to fret 'bout . You go on and get yourself on the stage and to your sister up thar in Kansas City. This here Indian ain't goin' nowheres."

"But what's he done?" William struggled in her arms and she pinned his arms at his sides, rocked him from side to side.

"This un is gonna hang for the murder of a man down south a he'ah."

Adeline pulled her arm from under the sheriff's hand. She turned toward the man, tried not to grimace at the string of yellow yolk hung in the bristly gray of his beard.

"That ain't right," she said. "I know this man."

The sheriff adjusted the strap of his overalls, stared at her.

"Ma'am. This Indian killed a man whose wife is still missing. Cabin burned to the ground, mules found wandering the countryside. Killed the man awright. Rode into town big as you please on the roan stallion what belonged to the dead man."

Adeline turned to stare into the cell at Montega. He refused to meet her eye, sat like a stone, like the earth itself, silent and still on the cot. The child fought to break away from her, screamed his outrage at being confined in her arms. She needed to think this through. Jeremiah had traded that roan stallion to Montega in exchange for her life. If a man had been murdered, it wasn't the man in the cell who had done the killing. It was going to take some time to figure what to do.

"Could be I've made a mistake." She bounced the child in her arms.

"But ain't it possible the Indian came by that horse some other way?"

The sheriff patted her arm like petting a dog, smiled and shook his head.

"He done it awright. Hidin' in the hills, stealin' from honest folk. These he'ah Indians is takin' advantage of the white man's good nature. Time they was dealt with proper."

Best not to show her hand until she had a plan. The screams of the boy grew louder, his struggle to break free of her arms more vigorous. Since learning to walk, William had no use for being carried.

"I'll let you get back to your morning then, Sheriff. I guess I was mistaken about knowing the redskin you got locked up."

"You ain't thinking proper now with all you've been through, that's all. I'll walk you on over to the mercantile. The stage'll be comin' through in a hour or so. Best to get yo'self a ticket."

The sheriff set his hat on his head and reached for the door.

William squirmed in her arms, flung the blanket from his face. His screams died mid-cry when his dark eyes fell on Montega.

"Da?" William pointed a pudgy finger at the Indian in the cell. "Da da."

The sheriff stared at the smiling child in her arms. The man's eyes widened, he dropped his palm from her elbow, slid a half-step back.

"That thar's a half-breed Injun, Missy." His face hardened like meat left too long in the heat of summer, dried and cracked along the edges. "You wanna tell me what in tarnation you're doin' with that papoose?"

The Good Book taught the truth would set you free. Adeline had her doubts in this here situation, but couldn't rightly come up with a better plan. She set William on the floor, watched him toddle, giggling, to Montega. The look of disgust on the sheriff's face was just about to rile her.

"White men raped his mama." Rape wasn't a word used by respectable young women, but how else to say the truth clearly? "I took the child to raise as my own."

William pressed his face through the bars of the cell, stretched his arms inside.

"Da. Da. Da."

"That his spawn?" The sheriff jerked his chin toward the cell.

Adeline swallowed hard, stunned by the change in the man—from kind and gentle protector to an oily cauldron of hate and disapproval. She'd seen lust on the faces of men since she started to fill out her camisole when she was twelve. Lust didn't bother her none. But the expression on the sheriff's face, like she carried some contagious disease and sought to deliberately sicken the community, this was new to her.

She stamped her foot, moved between William and the sheriff and glared up into the hatred.

"I done told you. The child's mama died givin' birth. She was ruined by white men. The man you have in jail is the boy's uncle."

"Ah, huh. That's a fine story, Missy. 'Cept that boy ain't in on the lie just yet. Get yourself out a my town, girl. You still he'ah by nightfall and I reckon you and that buck'll be havin' a family reunion in jail."

She turned her back on the sheriff, scooped William into her arms. Montega stood, hands at his sides. He dropped his chin, cut his eyes to the door. Told her to go as clearly as if he had spoken. William kicked his pudgy legs, grinned, and reached toward the sheriff's floppy hat.

"Da? Da, da, da."

Adeline swept past the man, stopped with her shoulder against the door.

"The boy seems to recognize you, Sheriff. Where was you when his mama was raped?"

She pushed outside, blinked in the bright light. The time for secrecy gone, she set the boy on his feet, his hand firmly in her own. The door opened behind her and she turned to see a green gob of spit land on the hem of her new dress.

"That stage ain't for Indians and whores. You got 'till I've had my morning constitutional to saddle that mule and get outta this he'ah town. I generally get feeling frisky once I've dropped a load. I'll come looking for ya."

Chapter Thirty-Eight

The stable air pressed thick with hay-dust that seemed alive in the beams of morning sun streaming from the loft. Jeremiah led the mare who tossed her head, no doubt hoping for a rest after their two-day ride, dreaming horsey dreams of a rub down and a bag of warm, sweet oats.

"Not yet," Jeremiah spoke to the horse.

"What's that, sir?" A red-headed kid with the makings of a black eye just beginning to swell trotted beside Jeremiah, the boy's voice like a mosquito in his ear.

Jeremiah strode slowly, back straight and eyes searching. He rubbed the soft nose of the mare and took in every detail of Rampage's stable. The smell of sweet alfalfa mingled with the earthy stink of manure. The red roan stallion urinated a stream as strong as a spring creek, the sound of the steady flow splashing on hay-covered wood coming to Jeremiah a few seconds before the smell. The animal tossed his head, nickered to Jeremiah's mare. The mare pranced in place, quivered under Jeremiah's hand. Adeline's mule was not at the stable, nor had the animal been in front of the run-down boarding house he'd passed.

The stable boy rubbed gingerly at the edges of his bruised eye.

"A dollar a day ta board the horse, sir. I'll take right good care a her for ya."

"Has the stage come and gone today?" Jeremiah studied the boy, the nervous shuffle from one foot to the other, the hand that kept going to that swelling eye.

"Yes, sir. Couple hours ago. It ain't due back he'ah now 'till next week Tuesday."

"That's quite a mouse you got there." Jeremiah nodded at the boy's eye.

"We had some 'citement 'round he'ah the last couple days." The boy bounced on the balls of his feet. "Last night the sheriff done arrested him a murderin' Indian and this mornin' a yellow-haired whore and her half-breed was run out a town."

"That so?" Anger slowed Jeremiah's heart rate, focus filled the void in his center. He smiled.

"Ain't I seen you 'round he'ah afore?" The boy's head bobbed on a skinny neck, the movement creating a halo of dust that glowed gold in a stripe of light. "Ain't you that revival preacher?"

"How'd you come by that eye, boy?"

"The damn whore with the half-breed kid give it to me." The boy paced side-to-side like a high-strung horse, like he couldn't decide between shame and pride at the cause of his rapidly swelling eye. "Hit me with her fist like a man! It weren't no secret. The sheriff hisself told me she'd been fuckin' greasy Indians. I was doin' that whore a favor offerin' six-bits for a few minutes with a white man."

"Son?"

Jeremiah dropped the mare's reins and advanced on the boy. The preacher tapped an index finger on the boy's forehead, waited until the kid closed his mouth and held perfectly still but for the rapid rise and fall of his shallow chest.

"You need praying over, boy. But, I do not have the time this morning to bring you to salvation."

The boy gulped, his Adam's apple a small, trapped animal in his throat.

"I'm going to take that roan stallion with me." Jeremiah's voice low and calm as the eye of a hurricane. "If I ever lay eyes on your miserable hide again? I will kill you. If you tell anyone I'm in town or that I've taken the stallion? I will kill you slowly. One bloody piece at a time. Do we understand each other?"

The boy nodded, wet himself with piss and soiled himself with fear.

A smart kid would forget the fear and the pissing himself, twist the story until he could live with his own actions. But this boy was not smart. This boy would likely spread the alarm before Jeremiah had accomplished his goal. Jeremiah sighed, led the boy to the stall furthest back in the stable, tied the little brat with rope and gagged him with a wadded rag that stank of liniment.

The stallion stamped a front foot, showed off for the mare. Jeremiah saddled the animal and then led both horses from the thick dust of the stable into a day washed clean by an earlier rain. Adeline could not have gotten far. The boy's eye hadn't yet finished swelling. If Jeremiah was lucky, he and the Indian would camp tonight with the girl and the child. He tried to remember the last time he was lucky.

In front of the small stone building that housed the Sheriff's Office and jail, Jeremiah tied the horses to a hitching post ring crusted with rust and what looked like dried vomit. A fat man in overalls and a floppy hat swept the three-plank walk across the dirt street, the morning sun gilding the dust that rose to his waist. The man pretended to be busy with his ratty broom, but Jeremiah understood that every move he made was being watched from beneath that ridiculous hat.

A woman in a calico dress and the wide-brimmed bonnet of a farm wife clutched the hand of her small daughter, passed him by on the narrow sidewalk. She did not smile, but just as she passed, the woman raised long-lashed brown eyes to his. He nodded to the woman, removed a red bandanna from his pocket, swiped at his face while running his gaze over every window, doorway and alley. A mangy yellow dog slinked from a narrow path on the right, but seemed in no particular hurry. Dry air swirled pink with dust and stunk of night soil dumped into the dirt street a few hours earlier.

He stepped up onto the narrow sidewalk that fronted the little rock building. His boot heels thudded hollow three times and his palm laid flat on the rough wood door of the Sheriff's Office. The huffing breath of the fat man crossing the street came from behind him.

"Hey! You, there." The man lumbered up onto the sidewalk. "You huntin' the sheriff, you found him."

Jeremiah turned.

Momentum carried the sheriff another step forward. Under the droop-ing hat brim, the man's eyes widened. Jeremiah held himself motionless. Morning crud clung to the corner of the man's left eye, his matted beard stunk with winter's crumbs and leavings.

"Preacher?"

Jeremiah deliberately took one step sideways, indicated with the slightest nod of his chin that the sheriff was to unlock the door. The man fumbled in the pocket of his overalls for the key.

"You ain't been by our way for a good while now, Preacher. Was startin' to think maybe you'd forgotten 'bout our little town."

Jeremiah followed the sheriff inside, shut the door behind him and took the time to hook the inside latch and drop the bar before turning to face the man. In the cell, Montega rose from the cot, stared flatly at Jeremiah, gave no hint the two had ever met before that moment. The fat man rocked on his heels, couldn't keep his gaze from cutting to the Winchester leaning against the desk to his left.

"How's your wife, Sheriff?"

Jeremiah strolled the two steps to the lever-action rifle, lifted the gun and sighted casually down the long barrel, lined up the guns' deep V on the spittoon beside the fat man's scuffed boots.

"And your lovely sister-in-law? Sally? The long-legged woman with the children that look so much like yourself. How many children has the Lord blessed Sally with now? Three? Or is it four?"

"Look he'ah now. There ain't no call for threats and such."

Jeremiah returned the gun to its resting place against the sheriff's desk, turned his mouth up in an imitation of a smile.

"The Indian you got locked up?"

The sheriff drew his tongue in a wide circle around his lips, licked at the curly hairs of his beard. "That thar Indian done killed a white man in cold blood. Kidnapped the man's young wife. Come ridin' into town as bold as ya please on the dead man's roan stallion."

"No." Jeremiah laid his hand to his knife hilt, took pleasure in the feel of the bone handle against his palm. "The stallion was taken in trade." He stared at the sheriff until the man dropped his eyes, rubbed one boot toe against the other. "Unlock your cage. Release the Indian."

The sheriff cleared his throat wetly. A muscle in his right cheek twitched and his eyes hardened for that split second when a man convinces himself he's capable of courage. Jeremiah moved into the threat, the point of the Bowie pressing into the folds of fat under the sheriff's chin while the idea of courage still flitted across the man's eyes. The sour sweat of the lawman's fear filled Jeremiah's nose. He pressed his mouth against a dirt-crusted ear, spoke slowly.

"It was not the Osage that put the stallion's miserable owner out of his misery."

The fat man's breath was ragged and loud, his eyes rolled white and Jeremiah wondered if the problem might be solved without firing a shot, the man keel over and die right here, smote by his own gluttony and greed. This blubbering man sent Adeline and the boy away, alone, into the wilderness. Jeremiah pricked the soft underside of the sheriff's neck. Dark blood trickled through creases and rolls and Jeremiah saw moonlight on the face of a sleeping girl, watched as a man rode away into the night and left her alone with a child tucked against her breasts. The knife sliced deeper. Jeremiah fought to contain the beast that rose in him, slavering with self-hatred and regret.

Montega spoke for the first time since Jeremiah stepped inside. "Do not kill him. We do not need another star."

Jeremiah backed the sheriff to the chair. The fat man collapsed onto its creaking seat.

"The keys." Jeremiah eased back on the knife point, extended the palm of his left hand to the sheriff's chest.

The man fumbled in the slit pocket of his filthy overalls, dropped a heavy iron key into Jeremiah's hand.

"You got no call to harm me now, Preacher. If'n I made me a mistake, I'm a big enough man to admit when I'm wrong. 'Sides, you got bigger trouble than me. Rangers out a Texas is looking for you, boy. I got the poster rat thar, ya see. You kilt one a thar own and I hear tell you got gold what belongs to 'em."

The thin circles of iron that hung on a rack beside the desk cut deep into the sheriff's wrists when Jeremiah cuffed the man to the leg of his desk. Jeremiah lifted a poster from beside an egg-smeared plate, folded the paper smoothly and tucked it inside the pocket of his jacket.

"You got no call to treat me this a way." Bent double, his heavy belly pressed against the tops of his thighs, the sheriff panted, twisted his neck to look up at Jeremiah.

The cell opened with a heavy clang. Montega moved silently across the plank floor like water following its inevitable path, all grace and purpose. He opened the top drawer of the sheriff's desk, removed a Colt Open Top with a walnut grip. With his thumb he popped the loading gate open, spun the cylinder, and then closed—careful to drop the hammer on the gun's one empty chamber.

"It ain't enough you handcuff me to my own damned chair, now you steal my gun?"

Montega turned his back on the man.

From behind Montega came the sharp scrape of a desk on a wood floor. Jeremiah stepped around the Indian as Montega turned toward the sound. The flat wood top of the desk flew through the air to the left. The fat man staggered up, the barrel of the Winchester rifle rising like the eye of death. Jeremiah dropped to the wood floor at the sheriff's feet. The Bowie's blade stabbed through shoe leather and flesh and bone even as Jeremiah's hand grasped the booted ankle.

Jeremiah rolled to the right, jerked hard on the ankle. The window above him shook with the fat man's fall, late morning light shimmered the sheriff's open mouth when Jeremiah pulled himself up the fallen man, used his weight and anger to drive the knife blade into the fat man's throat, pin him to the plank floor. A geyser of blood sprayed the upturned desk, the wall, and Jeremiah, who leaned into the knife hilt, finished the job he'd started. Jeremiah did not move until the red geyser was no more than the trickle of a drought-dead stream.

The preacher pushed himself to his feet, pulled his bandanna from his back pocket and wiped his face. He rolled his shoulders, wiped his knife blade on his pants.

Montega slipped the Open Top into the waist of his leather breeches. "You could not have just shot the man?"

"Too much noise." Jeremiah slid the knife into its sheath.

"The man was as big as a mountain. Every window in this town rattled when he fell."

Jeremiah smiled and the drying blood of the dead man pulled at the skin of his face. "Not going to thank me for saving you from a hanging?"

"You and me, preacher, we have not outrun death, only changed the location of our last battle."

Chapter Thirty-Nine

Adeline's braid hung heavy against her back, a warm breeze ruffling loose strands that tickled her neck. The mule plodded through tall grass that brushed the bottoms of her boots in the stirrups, the prairie stretching out around her like an endless sea. She hoped she was headed in the right direction. Northwest. Mostly north. Sooner or later she'd run smack dab into a town of one size or another. The question was whether or not she'd find that town before running out of food for William. And if she did get lucky and stumble into a town, would she be allowed to buy needed supplies and get out without some nosey Pharisee seeing the child strapped to her chest and casting that first stone?

William had fussed and fought to escape from the moment she strapped him into the sling this morning. Just as she was ready to give in and let the boy chase grasshoppers and wear himself out a bit before moving on, he had hiccuped himself into a fit and fallen blessedly asleep. He was getting too big to spend much time strapped to her chest. The boy's fat legs pumped and crawled from the moment he opened his eyes in the morning until he fell into an exhausted sleep each night. She sometimes found him, like a puppy, collapsed in a corner of the cabin or under a tree in the yard.

The feel of the sleeping boy's silky hair under her hand, the roll and pitch of the mule combined with the sun which threw long shadows onto the swaying grass beside her—all these sensations blended into a sense of drowsiness, a feeling that she and William were outside reality somehow.

Alone in a great sea of uncertainty. Adeline shook her head, rolled her shoulders to ease the weight of the sling. Best to stay alert.

She would not allow herself to think about Jeremiah. She would not! The man had shamed her. In her mind she saw moonlight laced through tree tops, felt again that moment of surrender when her body had arched up to join his and she had given herself over to him. Heard him cry out in release. Felt again the cold that overtook her when he turned his back, refused her touch.

She would not think of him!

He had left her and the child alone in the wilderness with nothing for protection but a rifle, a handful of bullets, and a two day supply of hardtack. What kind of man did such a thing? Her face burned with humiliation at her own stupidity. How wrong she had been about Jeremiah. She had thought him a hero. Thought him almost a god. Thought herself special for being loved by such as he. Maybe this was all God's punishment for that sin of pride, her willful disobedience of the Lord's commandments in lying with Jeremiah without the blessing of a preacher.

Pa taught that God's laws were not meant as stumbling blocks but as protection for his children. Adeline swiped at her wet face, thought of how she'd turned her back on those childhood teachings, opened herself to the desires of a full-growed woman. She ought to bow her head, beg forgiveness. Except if given a chance, she'd do it all again. She felt herself bound to the preacher and, God forgive her, could not turn from that difficult and wounded man.

Of course, this thinking was all fine, but chances were good she'd never see the man again. Waking on the cold forest floor, dawn the merest promise of pink on the horizon, a hungry child snuffling at her dress front, she knew herself for a romantic fool. She needed to think of the child and how to get the both of them to Kansas City alive, needed to pray they'd be allowed on the train once they got there. She would not think of Jeremiah!

The mule tossed his head, curled his top lip from the bit and brayed. Adeline twisted in the saddle, studied the open grassland behind her. Empty. Nothing but that open sea of waving grass. But the mule heard or smelled something he didn't like and unless she'd forgotten everything Pa'd ever taught her about reading the mind of a mule, that something was a horse. There was nowhere to hide in this open country. No tree or stone or ditch.

Adeline brought the mule up short, dismounted, led the animal in a wide half-circle so that the three of them—mule, woman and child—stared back the way they'd come. Fat, yellow seed-heads weighted each blade of grass, tugged at her waist, tickled her forearms and hands. She had only to squat down and unless the rider passed directly over her, he would never know she was there.

But what of the mule? Not only would the grass not hide the long-legged critter, but with nothing to tie or stake the mule to, the cantankerous animal would undoubtedly go on the attack and sink its blunt teeth into the approaching horse's rump. A sound like the screech of a giant hunk of metal scraped against hard rock rose up from the belly of the mule. He bared his teeth, stretched his neck and brayed. So much for the element of surprise.

She carried the child as far from her and mule as she could tolerate, slipped the sling from her shoulders and laid the boy in the tall grass. William slept peacefully, his dark lashes crescent shadows on soft cheeks. She thought of Moses floating among the reeds, awaiting the Pharaoh's daughter, knew if she died or was taken, this child was lost.

Adeline stomped back to the mule, yellow grass parting around her as though blown back at each stride by her anger and desperation. She could see them now. Two horses, one behind the other, floating in that great sea of grass and aimed directly at her. She pulled the Henry from its leather sheath, the lever loud in the morning quiet. Now there was nothing to do but wait. And pray. The sky was a washed-out blue, made her knuckles ache with the thought of denim scrubbed hard with lye and worn to a near white. There was no sound but the swish of grass in a lazy breeze and the cawing laugh of an unseen raven.

It was the hat that stole her ability to breathe. Wide brimmed and high domed, it was the headgear of the saddle-preacher. No more than dark silhouettes against that white sky, the riders grew until she could make out the wavering outline of a man who seemed a part of the red roan who carried him; the way the preacher's right leg stuck out away from his bay. She lifted the Henry, pressed its butt to her shoulder. The rifle's power flowed through her hands. She felt the strength in her stomach and her chest—a warmth that spread like fire, licked at her anger.

She framed Jeremiah in the V of the rifle sights. By the time he was within firing range, her arm shook, though whether from the extended weight of the Henry or anger she did not know. She swallowed, adjusted her cheek against the gun's wooden stock, refused to remember the smell of his skin, the way his hands felt on her body.

"Now, Adeline." His voice just as she remembered it, a growl that brought to mind the purr of a painter. "You don't want to shoot me."

"Oh, but you're wrong there. I do. I most certainly do want to shoot you dead."

She laughed. He flinched.

Hector snorted and brayed, lowered his head and ran at the roan. Montega slid easily from the stallion's back, secured the mule's reins. The Indian led mule and roan well away from the aim of the Henry. A small dust storm rose around the mule's pawing hooves. Montega stood in the midst of the pink haze, grass brushing his thighs, a smile on his face.

Adeline waved to the Indian, turned her gaze back to Jeremiah. "Get on down off that mare. As you pointed out once afore, I'll not risk harming a fine horse."

"My actions were in your best interests, woman. Put down the gun before you hurt somebody."

William's cry came from inside the sea of grass. Montega, one hand tight between the bridle and cheek of the mule, dropped the reins of the stallion and led the mule toward the screaming child.

Jeremiah swung his good leg over the neck of the mare, slid from the saddle. His bad leg gave out from under him and he leaned against the horse for a moment, seemed to gather himself before turning to face her.

William's cries stopped abruptly. "Da! Da! Da! Da!"

Adeline would be pure delighted when that child learned a new word.

"It may have been a miscalculation for me to leave you on your own, Adeline. I did not think of the reaction of the town folk to the child."

Heat swept her, radiated from that small pressure of metal on the calloused pad of her finger. Shaking took her. She lowered the barrel of the gun, laid the rifle carefully in the grass at her feet. Jeremiah closed the distance between them, his hands at his sides, palms facing her. She exhaled, waited until she could see the flecks of gold and green in his dark eyes. Her fist slammed into his cheek, vibrated pain down her arm and across her chest. She hit him again, felt his nose give under her knuckles.

Jeremiah backed away. She followed. He brought his hands up to cover his face. Rage roared from her belly to tingling limbs. The top of her boot sunk into his groin. The preacher dropped to his knees, face white, mouth open and sucking air in short, hard gasps. He turned toward the Indian who stood just to the side, the baby bouncing in his arms.

"You planning . . . on doing anything . . . besides playing nurse maid to that child?"

Montega grinned. "I thought to lend her my hatchet, but she seems to be doing fine without it."

Chapter Forty

Jeremiah shifted gently, ever so carefully, in the saddle, puffed short breaths through an open mouth. To his right, the mare's shadow stretched long over the sea of grass. The setting sun tinted the world the greening-pink of a leaf unfurling a tight bud. Or, it could be the throbbing pain in his groin affected his vision. He gritted his teeth, focused on his bum leg. Preferred the ache of a healing bone break over the nauseating bounce of the saddle against his bruised manhood.

Ducking his head, protecting his face from flying fists, he'd looked up into her eyes the moment her boot connected with his privates. Adeline. Soft, gentle child. At that moment the woman would happily have killed him dead as any gut-shot Yankee. Hell, he felt gut shot. It wasn't so much the kick as her rage that had stunned him. Well, the shock was some the result of the kick. That woman had taken lessons from that damn mule of hers. He was going to be walking spraddle-legged for a month.

A whooping Indian rode in sweeping circles just out of pistol range to the west. Montega held one arm tight around the laughing, shrieking boy, the other hand slapped at the rump of the roan. Jeremiah's mare tossed her head, required correction every few steps to keep her on track, slow and steady, instead of joining the stallion in his wild gallop. Each time Jeremiah reined in the animal, a jolt of light shot from the saddle, through his crotch and up into his gut.

From behind him Adeline's voice lifted with the words of a hymn. Like the whisper of an angel, like a soul not one bit repentant for the attack she'd made on his person.

"Come then you souls by sin oppressed.

Ye weary wanderer after rest.

Ye poor and maimed, halt and blind,

In Christ a hearty welcome find."

He slapped the reins on the mare's neck, gritted his teeth against the white heat that knifed upward making him gasp and dribble saliva onto his shirt front. The mare jolted forward, parted the grass and plunged away from that angel's voice behind him. Jeremiah rode out the pain, did not slow the horse until he was confident he'd outrun the hymn's last verse.

From out of his own shadow, like mist rising on a new day, the sergeant appeared, strode easily beside Jeremiah's horse. The apparition waggled his blue tongue, a grin grotesque in that war-ruined face.

"Lucky for you, I know this one, Preacher. Goes sumptin' like this he-ah, don't it?"

Jeremiah's groan startled the mare and she skittered, jerked her head. He swallowed the jolting pain, gave himself up to the inevitable, the sergeant's voice wet and cloying in his ears.

"This is the time, no more delay;

This is the glorious gospel day.

Come in this moment at his call,

And live to him who died for all."

The words of the hymn did not so much convict as annoy Jeremiah. He ground his teeth until the bad molar reminded him of the futility of fleeing God, cut his eyes to the ghost. The sergeant had gone. It was Maggie who walked easily beside him, her long skirt swishing against the swaying grass, her green eyes steady on his. He pulled the mare to a stop.

Maggie laid a gentle hand on his bad leg. "This woman. This Adeline?"

Like the scent of some long-forgotten flower, her voice came to him as a reminder of the simple clear joy of childhood.

"This woman is different." Maggie did not turn those clear eyes from him. "You will not kill this one." She laughed. "Though if you do not quickly change your ways, Adeline's angry face may be the last thing *you* ever see."

"Maggie?" He stretched his hand to her cheek, touched empty air. "No!"

He clung to the saddle horn, slumped on the horse, bowed his head.

"I am hollowed out, Lord. An empty drum awaiting your hand. Or death. I've no more strength to fight."

He opened his eyes to the empty flow of warm wind over prairie grass. No answer came, no touch of the divine. He sat the horse as an empty vessel, resting on life's waves, devoid of faith, no current to carry him onward. The boy's shrieking laughter washed over—but did not touch—him. Afternoon sun, golden in its westward descent, bathed but did not warm. A soft breeze rippled the waves of grass. Pain ebbed and flowed in a predictable tide, but he floated above it, looked down at his life and understood he was done.

He heard the mule's plodding steps, the swish of grass against the animal's belly, a woman's soft humming. Jeremiah neither anticipated nor dreaded Adeline's approach. Her presence or absence meant nothing. Behind him, the humming stopped, saddle leather creaked. She came to his side, both hands gripping the tight reins. The mule stretched his neck, curled his upper lip toward the mare. Each tug of the big animal's head lifted Adeline to her toes in the stirrups.

"It's time to stop now, Jeremiah." She spoke sharply to the mule, then laid her left hand on Jeremiah's leg, between boot and aching knee. "We need to eat, rest, and make a plan."

He studied the freckles splashed across her cheeks, wondered at the way, even now, they drew his touch.

"Would you have killed me back there, Adeline? If given a chance? Would you have seen me dead?"

She did not flinch. "If I'd a wanted to kill you, we wouldn't be having this conversation."

High overhead a hawk or a buzzard soared effortlessly in a sky washed of color.

"I'm sorry I left you alone in the woods after we came together. I was afraid. I ran."

He did not have the strength to dismount the horse. Perhaps, at the end of this conversation, he would simply lean to the side and fall dead into the prairie grass.

Adeline turned her gaze from his long enough to slip from the mule's spade back, force the animal's stumpy face to hers. She spoke firmly, twisted a soft ear and led Hector a few yards away. The mule's eyes rolled white and then the animal snorted, dropped its head and tore off a chunk of grass. She strode back to Jeremiah.

"Turn loose the reins. It's time to rest."

"I don't believe I can do that."

"You can't do anything else."

The reins slid from his hands, the mare moved under him. Warm tears wet his face and, for just a moment, he wondered who was crying. Hooves pounded toward him. Voices whispered secrets. Cool hands and strong arms pulled him to the ground. He stood in thigh-high waves of yellow-green pressed against a woman's softness and gave himself up.

He knew nothing more until he woke in a purple twilight to the smell of meat cooking over an open fire. Flat on his back, hidden in tallgrass, his bad leg throbbed, anchored him to the earth. He lay still and listened to horses tearing at the prairie, the grinding of blunt teeth. The boy, Billy Boy, slept in the crook of his arm. The child smelled of dirt and youth and new piss. Jeremiah turned his head to the left and the gloaming light caught the orange of Indian blanket and a fist-sized offering of larkspur. He shifted on the ground and searing pain shot from leg to chest. His groin ached. He readjusted his knee. No lightning bolt shot from crotch to belly.

He sat up carefully. His head below the grass line, he felt himself invisible. No. Not invisible. Non-existent. The child beside him whimpered in sleep, found his thumb and sucked greedily. Jeremiah massaged his bad leg, listened to a duet of voices coming from a few yards away. Through a swaying veil of tallgrass, a small fire in a blackened clearing licked at whatever slow and infirm animal that damn Indian had ridden down and killed.

The child stirred in his sleep, released a loud fart that smelled of spoiled meat.

Jeremiah wrinkled his nose, strained to hear the conversation at the campfire over a rustling breeze.

"Osage do battle in honor."

"That ain't true." Adeline's voice sliced the air, quick and sharp. "I've heard tell how you peel the skin from your captives, cook them alive over campfires just like this one."

Jeremiah smiled at her reply to Montega.

"It is best not to believe half of what you are told about an enemy. Osage battle for hunting territory, and for horses and women, and for honor. Never, until the arrival of the bluecoats, has it been our purpose to destroy the enemy, wipe them from the face of the earth. That kind of battle kills body and spirit. In a war such as that, there are no winners. Only dead men."

"I'm the one went to Jeremiah every night while his leg festered and then, finally, healed. I'm the one been living with the man for near a year." Adeline's words popped in the air like the crack of a whip. "You think I don't know Jeremiah lives with haints? Think I don't understand the man is half-dead his own self?"

Jeremiah lifted the sleeping child, cradled the boy's warmth to his chest. He rocked slowly from side-to-side, felt himself alone and empty, the soft weight in his arms neither burden nor possibility. A whisper swayed the grass and he imagined himself at the bottom of a deep sea. The words of Jonah came to him, as though the prophet slipped beneath his skin.

Out of Sheol I cried and You heard my voice. You cast me into the deep, into the heart of the seas, and the floods surrounded me. Your billows and waves passed over me.

Jeremiah clung to the sleeping child, lifted empty eyes to a night sky scattered with the cold, dead light of stars.

I have been cast out of your sight. The waters closed around me even to my soul. The deep claimed me. Weeds wrapped my head. I sunk down to the moorings of the mountains.

The child woke in his arms, struggled to sit, patted Jeremiah's wet cheeks with tiny hands.

"Da, da, da."

From the campfire Montega's low voice carried to Jeremiah.

"The time may come, woman, when you will be forced to decide between the living child and a man wounded onto death."

Jeremiah hung suspended, invisible, did not draw breath. The swish of tallgrass against a swaying skirt raised his eyes. The prairie sea parted and Adeline stood over him, bent and lifted the child from his arms, held the boy easily against one hip.

"Come." She offered her hand. "The meal is ready. You need to eat."

Chapter Forty-One

H eat rose to Adeline's face and the blackened rabbit haunch burned her fingers. At the first lip-burning bite her mouth filled with saliva and her stomach growled. Jeremiah sat silent beside her and Montega, legs tucked under him, pulled meat from the hare's back bone, his teeth catching the light of the fire between them. William bounced in the folds of her skirt, his mouth open in a delicate O, waiting for her to chew tiny bits of meat and place them on his tongue. At each taste the boy clapped his hands, his head bumping against her breasts.

Adeline turned to Jeremiah, his face no more than a shadow in the dark. "We need to talk some." She tore off a hunk of meat, the charred rabbit so good she nearly swooned. "Who's chasing us this time?"

The men exchanged looks across the blue flames of the campfire. Jeremiah washed down a mouthful of meat with a long drink from a flat-sided canteen. The outline of his Adam's apple rose and fell with each swallow. Adeline turned away to keep from laying a finger against the rough flat of his cheek to convince herself he was flesh and blood and not some cold haint come to tease and aggravate. She shifted the boy against her, looked up into a moonless dome of velvety black. Stars nested in a night sky so close she felt she could reach up and capture their brilliance in her palm.

Beside her Jeremiah cleared his throat.

"We need to get you on a train west before they show up." The vibration of his voice like waking on a windless night to the rustle of a window curtain. "The boy complicates the matter. Here to Kansas City's two weeks hard traveling."

211

She didn't like the flatness, the emptiness of his voice, the way he stared into the flames and spoke as though by rote. Maybe Montega was right. Jeremiah was never going to come home, not truly home, from that bloody war. Still, it made her angry the way he sat there like a dead man, talked like it was William who had caused their troubles.

"It's not the boy what shot seven men 'tween my front porch and barn. It's not the boy what killed the sheriff in Rampage."

Jeremiah turned the profile of his face away, stared off into the night. She shivered with the knowledge that he had left her again, that while his physical body sat beside her, his thigh touching distance from her hand, he was lost in the dark night.

"The men lying dead in your yard rode in with intent to kill, Adeline." His voice aimed away. Her throat closed with the knowledge that he spoke not to her but to the waves of tallgrass, to the emptiness around them. "Perhaps you'd have preferred being raped and killed. Perhaps you do not care enough for that child on your lap to be concerned that his brains would have been left to stain some rock or fence post. Maybe you think that Indian across from you would have been better left to hang."

Jeremiah turned to her and flames danced grotesque shadows over his face.

"I do not kill for pleasure, Adeline."

A stifled laugh burst from the other side of the fire and the backbone of the rabbit, stripped of meat, flew from Montega's fingers, scattered ashes and made a small, gray hollow in the fire's edge. Sparks rose into the night.

"You got something to say, Indian?"

For the first time that night, anger flared in Jeremiah's voice.

"Da? Da, da, da." William reached his pudgy arms to the man beside her.

Adeline raised her voice over the child's. "You've not answered my question, neither of you." Darned men anyways, just what she needed right now. An old fashioned pissing contest.

"Will the town of Rampage put together a posse now you killed their fat sheriff? Or is it Rangers you fear?" She reached across the coldness between them, shook Jeremiahs' arm. "I've a right to know who's chasing us."

William slipped from her lap, crawled a wide circle around the fire. Half-way around the dancing flames, the boy sat flat on his butt, stretched his hands to the heat.

"Hat!"

Adeline laughed. "Very good, William. That's right. Hot!"

The boy threw himself onto his hands and knees again, crawled to Montega who lifted the child over his head. William screamed in joy, threw his arms straight out to his sides.

"Hat! Hat! Hat!"

Montega rose effortlessly, without a word carried the boy into the tallgrass.

Adeline waited until William's squeals were no louder than the buzz of night insects. A log shifted in the fire, and flames flared orange, sparks rose, bright for a moment and then gone. She stared at the side of Jeremiah's face, wondered why she ached for this cold and complicated man. Her skin tingled with the memory of him rising above her, moonlight striping his skin, the air filled with the sharp smell of the wild spearmint they crushed beneath their bodies.

"My guess is Rampage has, by now, dug a hole big enough to bury their sheriff." Jeremiah stared into the fire, did not look at her. "I do not believe they will pursue us. It's a town of farmers, not gunmen, and the sheriff was neither well-liked nor much respected. At least, not according to his wife."

"How is it you know the man's wife?"

He shifted his gaze from the fire, looked her full in the face. "The woman has hair the color of a polished hickory nut. I always looked forward to a brief stop in Rampage on my saddle-preaching circuit."

Adeline did not drop her eyes, anger flared like the sparks that flew from the fire to sew orange stitches in the black night. "Are you so frightened of me, Jeremiah, that you cannot abide even a moment's peace between us? Must you push and stab and hurt to chase me away and protect yourself from your own heart's desire?"

He licked his lips. The air between them warped and quivered with heat waves and she could not decide whether to strike him with hard fists or taste his skin with the tip of her tongue. From a distance she heard

William's joyous squeals. Jeremiah cleared his throat, pushed himself awkwardly to his feet and laid another gnarled oak branch on the fire.

"I am not concerned with a posse of farmers. You are safe enough for now." He turned and faced the night. His back to her, his voice came as if from a deep, dry well. "My worry is the renegade Texas Rangers."

"You think Rangers will come for us?" She rose, brushed blackened grass from her skirt, frowned at the soot that powdered her hands.

"They will come." He stared away from her, out into the darkness. "No matter what happens, you must take the boy and get to Kansas City. There will be no problem boarding the train with the boy. The fat bankers who own the Kansas Pacific care nothing for the color of a ticket holder's skin. They think only of gold." He nodded his head sideways. "Cross their palms with enough filthy lucre and they'll even let your buck Indian over there on board."

She took two steps, laid both hands against his back, his shoulder blades like wings under her palms.

"We'll go together." She dropped her hands to the small of his back, slipped them around his waist, pretended she believed in this dream. "You and me and William. San Francisco's a good place for a new start."

He captured her wrists, unwrapped her arms from his waist, and stepped away from her touch. "You and the boy can make a new start."

The fire flared, showed her the silhouette of a man walking away. She followed a few steps.

His voice brought to mind cold wind through the dead branches of winter-killed tree. "I am tired, Adeline. Tired unto death. Montega spoke rightly. Killing is all I know. I cannot remember the last time I felt joy when I wasn't taking the life of another human being."

She caught up to him again, laid her hand on his arm and forced him to look at her, meant to lead him away from the fire and into the tallgrass. He pulled loose from her grip, turned his back and strode away, his shape melting into the darkness.

She stood, arms wrapped across her breasts, stared into the night that ringed the small fire surrounded by an unending sea of swaying grass.

"Tell the Indian I'll ride drag." His words came to her from out of the black depths. "Keep your fires small or, better yet, do without."

"Jeremiah?" She ran toward his voice. Stood in the blackness outside the light. "Jeremiah. Please. Stay with us."

She stood there in the dark until the fire was nothing but embers. The night's breeze carried the sweetness of the honeysuckle vine mixed with the odor of rot from a nearby hawthorn tree. The smell reminded her of how Pa always said there weren't no all good or all bad folks.

Each one of us, Adeline, carry the seeds for the honeysuckle same as for the thorny, smelly hawthorn. We got to decide our ownselves which a them seeds we plant.

She had felt so alone when Pa and then Ma died. Abandoned. Lost. Like a downy fledgling pushed too soon from the nest by a spring storm.

Well, this bird had grown feathers. With or without Jeremiah, she would make a good life for herself and for William. And, by God, no bully or mealy-mouthed man better ever again get between her and her dreams! This time next year, if she had to fight her way along every mile between this prairie and San Francisco, she'd get there. Just keep putting one foot in front of the other until she and William were gazing out at the Pacific Ocean.

Adeline turned her face to the stars, lifted her arms and extended her fingers upward as far as she could stretch. She swirled in a circle, grass catching at the cotton of her skirt in a rustling like wings parting the air. She shouted praise to the sky, did her best to sing the words out into the darkness, surround the man who walked away.

"Weeping may endure for the night but joy cometh in the morning."

The shouted words still hung in the night when a small streak of light marked the path of a shooting star, no grand gesture, but a momentary trace of a promise she grasped, claimed as her own. There came then, a whisper on the wind, a small, still voice that spoke of love carried on the night's thick black air. Adeline smiled, turned from the dark and walked resolutely to the fire's light.

Chapter Forty-Two

Jeremiah rested a few hours in the heat of each day. His need to stop dictated more by the mare's requirement for rest and water and nourishment, than by any desire of his for respite. The movement of the horse between his thighs or the prairie hard against his back or hips as he lay on the ground, it did not matter. He lived in a gray stupor where the pain of his leg bled into the desperation of his soul. The preacher dwelled somewhere between sleep and waking, his only thought to protect the woman and child a few day's journey to the north of him.

He believed the Rangers had followed his path to Rampage, the rumors of the dead sheriff drawing them like flies. From Rampage, the trail would be easy to follow. What he did when they came, their horses parting the grass around them, would depend on how many they were. How Rangers had gotten mixed up with the detritus of the James gang was a question Jeremiah did not care to ponder. He did not care if they be good men or bad, consecrated to God or to Satan's legion. That was a question for the theologians. His duty was to protect Adeline until she and the boy boarded a train to Kansas City. Nothing else mattered.

He did not pray. When memories of Adeline rose in his mind—her face in the firelight, the delicate curve of her neck or sway of her hip—he pushed the visions away roughly before hope could capture and distract him. Gil and the sergeant, even Maggie, abandoned him. He lived in a misty, colorless world where cannons erased birdsong and men bled and died and begged for death as the smoke of battle raged around them.

None of it mattered. He rode the mare or stretched himself on the ground. The horse ripped clumps of grass from the prairie or drank noisily from a shallow stream. Jeremiah stared up into a sky washed of color where buzzards soared on the promise of death. Life did not touch him. Without fear or hope, he rode forward, seeking one last battle.

Each afternoon clouds built in the west, a thin dark line of promise above the parched yellow grassland. At nightfall, like the sleep of an insomniac, the rain lost interest in the tease, blew away in dry-eyed emptiness. The sky pressed its weight upon him, sun burned his skin, stars shone cold and distant. He ignored it all, searched for a dust cloud that meant riders. Hungered in the night for the sight of a small fire, the faces of gold-seeking Rangers and outlaws lit by orange flames. Saw nothing but coyotes and lone riders and farmers. He struggled to remember how many days he had trailed behind the shoeless tracks of the stallion and the wide U-shaped marks of the plodding, gold-laden mule. He traced and retraced their steps, each day allowing more and more distance between him and Adeline.

A glimmer of fear settled upon him at odd intervals. What if the rangers did not come, if life were no more than a trudging illusion of progress through this colorless void? What would he do if, for all his backtracking, he arrived in Rampage without encountering the enemy? What if he were given the opportunity to ride north, board a west-bound train, find and join Adeline and the child? Was it possible he could start a new life in a far distant city beside an ocean he had never seen?

But these thoughts were rare and stirred only a thin glimmer of panic in his chest, easily pushed aside to be smothered by the thick gray world through which he rode.

He had endless time to make his plan. In daylight his mind swirled with details. A trail of black powder. The Enfield, cocked and ready to fire a dry charge. A thin leather line between his hand and the trigger of the war-smoothed rifle that would light an inferno. Again and again he saw a wall of flames. Heard the crackle of burning death, the whoop of wind in a tallgrass fire. Each night he tossed in a land of missed opportunity and poor decisions. Reached for the hand of Maggie. Saw his mother's face, tears flowing through a smile as she kneaded bread for his last dinner home before leaving for war. Woven through each vision, each night-time image, was the soft voice of Adeline. Jeremiah squeezed his eyes shut until bright flashes of light lit his eyelids, pushed hands tight over his ears. Days were long. Nights were longer.

On a morning that dawned crisp and clear, the sky cloudless and the air so dry a lit match flared and crackled like a cannon fuse, Jeremiah sat the mare and studied a dust cloud sweeping destiny directly into his path. His heart beat quickened. His face ached with the unfamiliar movement of a smile. He swung his bad leg over the mare's head, felt alive again, eager for battle.

The sergeant squatted in the tallgrass, his faded blue hat cocked at an angle, his ruined face both leer and challenge.

"I come to tell ya we got your back. Be waitin' over yonder." The dead man motioned with his missing chin, indicated a shallow dent in the prairie, no more than a thumbprint in the land's flatness pressed from the hand of laughing God.

"Long time no see." Jeremiah glared.

"I come and go," the sergeant grinned, flapped his tongue, waggled his eyebrows, and disappeared into tallgrass that flashed with the sun on bayonet tips.

Jeremiah chopped at the prairie with a short pick. Bent at the waist, he could see nothing but swaying stalks of prairie grass, smell only the dry dust he stirred at his feet, the sharp tang of his own tickling sweat. He did not look up, paid no mind to the ghosts whose murmurs stirred the tallgrass all around him. He dug a long, shallow trough across the tracks left by a mule and a stallion.

There was plenty of time to accomplish his tasks. The Rangers and the riffraff riding with the disbanded lawmen were still several hours out. If the cloudless sky hadn't been white and dry as a bone, he'd have had less warning. Maybe God had not abandoned him altogether. He removed the bridle and saddle from the mare, would not leave her trailing reins. If God owed him any favors at all, he prayed the bay horse would reach the safety of the stallion once her job was done.

The horn was warm and smooth under his hand, the job of sprinkling black powder from the narrow mouth made easy by the suffocating stillness of the air. Jeremiah smiled at the thought that the world held its breath, awaiting the outcome of his last battle. He looked into the drought-bleached sky. A half-dozen buzzards circled. Jeremiah chuckled, studied the spread wings of the dull-black omens. He grinned with the confirmation that his life was, after all, of no more importance to the world than as a meal for carrion.

The mare grazed easily, pushed her long face through tall, yellow grass and ripped purple clover from the prairie soil. She lifted her head and Jeremiah fancied the horse watched as he readied his position behind the only cover in the area, a dead oak, the tree fire-hollowed and black as the clouds that raced toward him from out of the west. Good sense dictated that he stay astride the mare. But common knowledge often led a person astray. Besides, he was a foot soldier, not a cavalryman. He fought best with his boots on the ground.

He cocked the Enfield and gently laid it at the edge of his newly-made trough, making sure there was an abundance of black powder in the rifle's pan. No need for a ball. Surprise was his most potent weapon. His trick would either work and he would kill, maim and turn back the enemy, or his tactic would fizzle to nothing and he would die having failed again to protect the woman he loved. Either way, this was his last hour on earth. He smiled down at his work. Dry grass disguised the gun nicely and there was naught to do but wait.

The blackened interior of the oak seemed a fitting hiding place. He leaned against the fire-softened wood, fingered the leather thong and studied the western horizon where a line of dark clouds thickened and built and pushed as if to meet the red cloud of dust that grew larger in the east. A red-tailed hawk shrieked. The mare lifted her nose and nickered.

God's voice came to Jeremiah from out of the wind-rustled grass.

Return to me and I will return also to you.

"Go away you old fool." Jeremiah's voice rough from long silence.

The horizon darkened with rain's promise, lightning forked in the clouds and Jeremiah saw horses rear, fill the sky with terror. God's voice shook the earth.

"Will you leave me no peace? Even now?"

Prairie grass rippled, the long-dry air tight with ozone and coming rain. A voice came to him then, soft as the bleat of a lamb and strong as the roar of a lion.

Does a loving father turn from his son when the child has lost his way?

Jeremiah swiped his eyes, slipped from the hollow of the tree, knew the time had come.

Thunder rumbled. Horses pounded the earth. Lightning lit the sky in a pulsating flash from horizon to horizon.

Six men.

Only six.

Two Rangers riding point. Careless fools, they rode side-by-side, close enough for talking. Close enough for killing both with one bullet. The rest of the enemy strung out behind in a lopsided V. These were men who did not hesitate for those few seconds it took a civilian to overcome the societal prohibition to kill. The Ranger on the right slowed and pointed toward Jeremiah's mare. A quarter mile away from the trap, the bay ran in wide circles below a booming sky lit from within.

Jeremiah's heart slowed, his breath deepened. Thunder shook in the same instant that an undulating, rippling flash of light lit the world. He caressed the thin leather between his thumb and finger, smiled, waited until the back hooves of the rangers' horses cleared the narrow trough he had dug. He jerked the line, felt a tug on the Enfield's trigger, a give in the tension.

A long moment passed, a split second when he knew he had failed and would die without saving Adeline and the boy. Die a miserable failure to every person he had ever loved. Then there came a sound like the feathered wings of some celestial creature whooshing, parting the air. The tether had pulled the Enfield's trigger, the rifle's charge igniting the line of black powder.

From behind the blackened tree, the Henry tight against his shoulder, Jeremiah sighted down the gun's long barrel. A ragged line of fire crackled along the trough, hesitated and then red flames swept into the sky. Black smoke veiled the air between the front-riding Rangers and the remaining men and horses. Men in ragged butternut and faded blue rose from out of the smoke, parted the sea of grass and waded into battle.

The preacher's first shot toppled the man riding drag on an Appaloosa gelding. The man fell backward across the spotted rump of his horse. The gelding reared. The man lay invisible in the tall grass. Muskets roared and a man whose face was stained in black powder smoke swept past, the tip of his bayonet flashing in the sun. Jeremiah sighted, fired again. A second enemy slipped in the saddle.

Wind whipped the red flames to a crackling, roaring frenzy. Horses screamed in terror and panic. The preacher stepped from behind the dead tree, the repeater at his shoulder, fired into the panicked cluster of men. He strode into the devil's own hot breath. Fire licked his face. He saw a pale horse, ringed in sparks, fire trailing from its mane. He swung the rifle toward the Rangers and fired into the rearing horses like shooting in a dream. The rifle snugged into his shoulder, a part of him, poured death into the black smoke and leaping flames and screaming men and horses.

Jeremiah pressed the curve of the trigger sixteen times. Did not stop until the rifle was empty. He stood then, alone among the dead, facing a wall of fire. He felt the touch of his mother's hand on his arm, begging him not to ride north. Heard cannon fire and the screams of those long departed. He saw Maggie rise up from the planks of an old porch, a flash of blue safe and unopened in her tight fist.

The sergeant ran from out of the fire, his torn face lit with flames that streamed from around his head like a halo. Gil appeared within the wall of fire and smoke. He grinned at Jeremiah, winked. The fire's growl deafened, the roar an open mouth that swallowed everything in its path. Soldiers, horses, loved ones and ghosts, all burned to ash in the mouth of God.

Heat blistered his face. Jeremiah dropped to his knees. The earth shook with thunder and fire that rained down from the sky to join with that wall of all-consuming heat blasting toward his kneeling form. He saw Adeline's freckled face framed in the window of a moving train, hair pulled tight at the base of her neck, the child, William, pressed to her breasts. He wept at the hope in her eyes as she searched the Kansas City station for a man on a bay mare. The preacher curled in a ball, tucked his face to the earth, and welcomed the roaring breath of God that finally, blessedly cleansed him of his sins.

About the Author

 Pamela Foster grew up in the redwoods of northern California where her family has raised all manner of mischief for eight generations. She's lived on the banks of the Mauna Loa on the Big Island of Hawaii, on the edge of the Mexican Caribbean, in the prickly sticklies of the Arizona high desert, and on the tropical coast of Panama. She now lives in the Ozark Mountains of Arkansas with her husband and his retired PTSD (Post-traumatic Stress Disorder) service dog.

When she's not writing—or teaching writing workshops—Foster volunteers her time to raise public awareness of PTSD and its effects, speaking at Veteran's Centers and civic groups and facilitating the Northwest Arkansas chapter of INTERACT, a support group for families of veterans.

Find Pamela at:

http://pamelafosterspeakerwriter.wordpress.com/

http://woundedwarriorwife.wordpress.com/

https://www.facebook.com/PamelaFosterAuthorSpeaker

https://twitter.com/FosterPamela

Dear Readers,
If you enjoyed this
book enough to review
it for Amazon.com
or Pen-L.com, I would
appreciate it!
Thanks, Pamela

MORE GREAT READS AT
Pen-L.com

11008021R00140

Made in the USA
San Bernardino, CA
03 May 2014